ALL *The* REST

CHRISTINA BERRY

Published by PVR Publishing

Edited by Christina Consolino

Cover design by KiWi Cover Design Co.

To old Austin
It was fun while it lasted
But change is like shit
It happens

NOTE FROM THE AUTHOR

Hello Readers!

I hope you enjoy the book. Some content within may be triggering or upsetting to some readers. This book contains details about mental illness, bipolar disorder, cutting, suicidal ideations, psychiatric confinement, childbirth, pregnancy, alcohol use, and a brief mention of animal cruelty.

Christina

1

The house looks like the *Addams Family* mansion, all creepy and kooky with its sweeping gables and gothic corbels. I half expect a cloud to pop up out of the clear blue sky and flicker lightning all around, like this is a dinner party at a haunted mansion rather than Thanksgiving with the family at Jake and Nicole's new place.

My street skates clatter over the road, and I grimace at the other houses that dot the wide expanses of manicured lawn. This neighborhood, with its beige bougie opulence, seems very much *not* a good fit for Jake and Nicole—Jakole for short. But now, as my eyes take in their weirdly wonderful gothic gem, I love it.

And I'll bet the president of their home owners association is shitting actual bricks. Seriously, I'd pay cash money to see these neighbors challenge Nicole over her design choices. That would be a fight worthy of pay-per-view prices.

My skates squeal as I come to a halt in front of an eight-foot-tall wrought iron gate, an ornate design featuring bats and spiders and a bull's skull adorning the top. I try to push it open, but it won't budge.

Glancing around, I spot two cameras trained on my position and a security keypad beside the driveway. With all this security and walls as tall as Jericho, I have to wonder if any of Jake's obsessed fans have tried to get a little too close to Mr. Big Shot Rockstar.

"Hello! Let me in!" I shout at the keypad as I push all the buttons at once. Then I blow a kiss at the cameras and do The Macarena until someone buzzes the gate open, and I slip through.

The driveway winds up toward a bluff overlooking the lake, and I put some muscle into my ascension. I aim for the chimney stacks of Jakole's gothic mansion, which peak above the bows of the mesquite trees.

When I've reached the apex of the driveway, clotted with cars, I see the wee ones playing in the yard. Blowing kisses at my adoring fans—all two of them—I execute a pretty impressive arabesque before spinning to a stop. Tommy and Mia erupt in delighted squeals. Cute little fuckers, those two.

Tommy—Jakole's son—is five and adorable. He looks like his daddy—complete with long black hair parted in the middle and braided to his waist—but he has his mom's gorgeous green eyes.

Wiggling beside him is Mia, Greg and Violet's feisty three-year-old daughter, in the cotton-candy cloud of a powder-pink princess dress. Don't let the dainty outfit fool you, though—Mia is a tornado of energy with a black belt in badassery just like her mama.

"Shaywall." Mia butchers my name adorably as I skate right into her and lift her up in a spin, like she's a Disney princess on ice. She squeals with glee, at a frequency so high only dogs can hear it. When I set her down, I tickle Tommy until he dissolves into a puddle of giggles. Once I'm sure the kids have adequately trumpeted my arrival to the adults in the house, I let each of them take a hand and tug me inside.

"Take your skates off in my house. What, were you raised in a barn?" Nicole hollers at the precise instant I cross the threshold. I stick out my tongue at Momzilla. She might be retired from roller derby these days, but it was awfully naive of her to install floors you can't skate on.

"I was raised in Florida, so…kind of." I shrug as I bend over and unlace my skates. I'm sporting my Ryan Gosling socks. Each foot is a different half of his face, and I can make him waggle his chin with my toes. Big hit with the TSA agents whenever I fly.

Tommy runs to his momma and tangles his arms around her leg while she watches me take off my skates like a good girl. When I straighten up, I ogle Nicole's belly. "Dang, woman, you're as big as a house."

Nicole smirks and settles her hands on her big ole preggers belly. Jake knocked her up again, this time with twins. She's fixin' to pop and complains all the time about it, but she's over the moon. I never would have pegged Nicole for the mom type, but damn does she love making babies with her rockstar.

I can't help it—I touch her belly. Even though it's considered rude, and with Nicole I could lose a finger, I do it anyway because I love baby-on-board bellies, and I think Nicole and I have achieved the I-can-touch-her-without-permission stage of friendship.

She smacks my hands away. "No touching the merchandise."

Or not.

Feeling some weird need to carry a baby myself, I pick up Mia and hold her on my hip. She plays with my hot-pink hair, delighted with how it matches her dress.

Tommy points at his mom's belly and informs me for about the eighty bajillionth time, "That's my bwothers in there."

"What? No way!" I gasp. "Your brothers? How do they fit in there?"

"They're little."

"Not that little," I say to ruffle Nicole's feathers.

She mouths the word "bitch" so her precious first born can't hear, and I wink.

Then Nicole gasps and grabs my hand, holding it to her belly so I can feel one of the little nippers bend it like Beckham. Gotta hand it to Nicole, she breeds fighters. Tommy, as sweet as he can be, came out screeching like a banshee and yanking on his daddy's hair within half an hour of touchdown. He hasn't stopped moving or talking since.

I turn to Tommy, who has also set his hand on his mom's belly. "So, T-Man, when do you get to meet your brothers?"

"In five days." He holds up his little fingers with their cute little fingernails that his dad helps him paint black. "Daddy says if they don't get here soon, Mommy is going to reach in and pull them out herself."

"Well that's…graphic." I grimace at Nicole.

I lace my fingers with Tommy's, swinging our arms together, and change the subject. "What are you going to call them?" It's a prompt more than a question. Everyone within earshot for the last eight-and-a-half months knows the answer, but I never deny the proud big brother his fifteen minutes. Soon, those twins will steal the show, so I make it a point to shower Tommy with attention, like he's his daddy on stage at Madison Square Garden.

"One is named Gregory, like my uncle, and the other one is Hezekiah, like my grandpa," Tommy declares with glee.

"Daddy," Mia squeals as her papa—aka Tommy's Uncle Greg—turns a corner and joins us in the entry, apparently summoned by the call of his name.

"Mia Monster, tell your daddy you want to join the roller derby rec league in the Big Easy," I say as Greg kisses my cheek and unwraps his daughter from my neck.

"Daddy, I wanna join the whoa er derby weckley in da bickeezy."

"Close enough." I shrug.

"We'll look into it." Greg kisses his daughter's cheek, then smirks at me. I only smile. His daughter is a future derby diva whether he likes it or not. Violet tells me she can't get the girl into normal shoes since I mailed her a pair of tiny toddler skates for her birthday.

When Violet comes out of the kitchen, I see she has a baby bump now too.

"Damn, what's in the water around here, and where do I get a glass? Y'all are popping out babies like it's the new fashion or something."

"Good to see you too, Sher." Violet hugs me.

I swallow the lump in my throat and try to ignore my jealousy. I've been baby crazy pretty much my entire life, but these sharp pricks of bitterness and resentment are new. I love seeing my breeder friends happy. Really, I do. But why can't I be a happy breeder too?

"Sher Bear!" Ari comes out of the kitchen to hug me, saving me from my downward spiral.

"You're not preggers too, are you?" I ask, just to be sure.

"Oh, God no." Ari laughs as Alex, that gorgeous man she calls a husband, comes out and hugs her around the waist. I've never understood why these two don't want kids. I mean, I get it: everyone has their reasons and can make their own choices in life. But, damn, they'd make beautiful babies, like, seriously, top-shelf, premium-quality babies.

Jake comes out of some room down the hall. I think it's a recording studio or practice space or something. He told me once, but I wasn't listening, too focused on staring out their picture window overlooking the pool and displaying a ridiculously expensive view of Town Lake. Tommy goes running into his dad's arms, and the big ole warrior man comes padding across the black marble floors barefoot, carrying his son.

"Did you work out the details on that last song?" Nicole asks when Jake slides his free arm around her, resting his hand on her big belly and kissing her neck.

Jake answers, "Yep. It's brilliant, going to be our next big hit."

Since joining Mammoth, Jake and the singer, Aidan, have become a transatlantic songwriting duo, penning more than a few chart-topping songs over web-cam. One even earned a Grammy last year. All while their wives pop out adorable little spawn. Must be nice to have it all.

Dang, there's that green jelly monster again. Today is Thanksgiving. A time for feeling thankful for what I *do* have. Not envy and covet what I *don't*.

Sheryl Ann Novak, do better, girl!

"Now that our late little lassy is here, we can start Family Dinner Night. Everyone grab a drink and a seat." Nicole directs, and the whole house springs into action.

Taking one of Alex's beers from the fridge, I grab my usual spot at the table. Everyone settles into their little family pods around me. I have no pod. I'm the seventh wheel—ninth and soon to be eleventh wheel when you count the kids. I'm the last orphan of this weird family of ours, and it's been this way for over five years.

Perpetually single—that's my curse. Not because there's anything wrong with me; I'm awesome. It's all the lame dudes. I may be small in size, but I've got a personality as big as Texas. Some might say it's *too* big. I've yet to meet the man who can handle this much woman. So I remain single…and childless…and I'll be thirty-five next month! Growing up, I always assumed I'd be a mom by now. But here I am with no baby and no prospects, my biological clock banging like a gong.

"It's that Sixkiller sperm. It's unstoppable," Jake says. He's been bragging about his sperm since they found out they were having twins.

"Please don't talk about your sperm at the dinner table," Nicole grumbles as she pats her belly.

I could use some of that Sixkiller sperm right about now.

"Uh…what?" Jake frowns at me. "I suddenly feel very uncomfortable."

Whoops. "Did I say that out loud? Ignore me."

"Gladly."

But, seriously, why didn't I think of this before? I don't need a man to have a baby. I only need his sperm. How hard could it be to find some sperm? Not from Jake, obviously, since he's eyeing me like I'm an evil witch trying to steal his seed. But surely there is some guy out there willing to give me the baby batter I need to bake a bun in my oven.

My body is ready. Let's do this.

I make the decision at the same time I make the announcement. Standing, I clink my knife against my glass so loudly everyone turns to me, looking worried, like maybe I've broken something. I clear my throat, raise my arms, and proclaim, "I'm having a baby!"

They look stunned and a bit confused with their mouths hanging open, food frozen on forks in midair. Their shock lasts only a brief moment before everyone speaks at once.

"What?" they say in such harmony you'd think it was choir practice.

"You're pregnant?" Ari asks.

"Not yet, but I will be."

"Huh?" Jake frowns.

"I'm going on a sperm hunt."

"A hunt?" Greg asks. "Like, with a gun?"

What? "No! Duh. With my feminine wiles. Or I might pay them. I haven't decided."

"Wait. Wait. Wait. You're going to hire a guy to"—Jake stops himself, takes a deep breath, then spells his question—"f-u-c-k you?"

"Um! Mommy, Daddy spelled a bad word," Tommy says.

"How do you know it's a bad word?" I ask Tommy.

"Because you only spell words when they're bad."

"Oh yeah? Well, what does I-L-O-V-E-Y-O-U mean?"

Tommy blinks at me, so I help. Using the sign language I've been teaching him, I say and sign, "I love you."

Tommy giggles, and it's the sweetest sound in the world. My smile reaches all the way down to the tips of my toes.

Meanwhile, the adults are still fixated on the details of my plan, as if I somehow magically know the details. We're in the infancy phase here, people. Well, the pre-infancy phase, really.

"I mean, maybe, if the guy's super smart and good looking and worth the money, then I'd pay for some seed." I shrug. "I'm also open to the idea of a one-night stand."

"What's a one-night stand?" Tommy asks.

Jake leans back in his chair to dole out some fatherly wisdom to his son. "You know how you have two nightstands in your bedroom, one on each side of your bed?"

Tommy nods.

"Well, some people only have one nightstand."

Nicole laughs at Jake's explanation and chokes on a sip of water.

"No! No. No. No. No. No!" Ari looks legitimately upset as she sets down her fork and scowls at me. "I one hundred percent veto this idea, Sherrie."

"It's called Operation Insemination, and you're not the president of me. You don't get a veto."

"I will be damned if I let you f-u-c-k a bunch of dudes *raw* so you can get pregnant."

"Oh, that's rich coming from you, Little Miss Hedonistic Self-Discovery Girl."

"Excuse me? Are you s-l-u-t shaming me right now, because—"

"Ari, you know I love you and I love s-l-u-t-s, but you've literally slept with every man at this table—"

"Not me!" Jake declares.

Greg and Alex remain silent, smirking at each other. I laugh out loud at their comfort with one another these days. It wasn't always so easy going. When I first met Ari, she was married to Greg, but they'd agreed to open their marriage. Ari was footloose and fancy-free, fucking her way through the men of Austin. That's how she met Alex. I'd called it from the start—she was so in love with him—but it took her a minute to come to the same conclusion.

"Fine," I amend, "you've slept with two-thirds of the men at this table. Plus, like, half of Austin. Now you want to turn around and tell me I can't?"

"Sher, it's not the same thing at all."

"How is it different?"

"Well, for starters, every one of my, uh, nightstands wore a condom."

"Daddy, what's a condom?"

Jake chuckles. "A piece of latex."

"What's latex?"

"Rubber."

"What's rubber?"

"You're the one who wanted to teach him English," Jake says to Nicole.

Ari continues, "You can't just *do* a bunch of random dudes without protection unless you want to get knocked up with a whole lot of STDs along the way."

"Mommy, what does S-T-D spell?"

"Nothing, honey. Aunt Ari doesn't know how to spell. Ignore her."

"Okay, fine," I huff. "I'll ask them to get tested first or something. I don't know. I'll figure it out. Stop raining on my parade."

Ari softens. "Sorry. You're right—I'm being a needless pain. You're a smart woman. I have faith in you. So… Congrats, babe, you're going to have a baby!"

"Oh God!" Nicole shouts, and the tone of her voice is pained. Every other conversation in the room stops. We stare at her, concerned and confused. Her posture changes, curls forward a little as she looks down at her big baby belly then over at Jake, her eyes wide as her complexion pales. "It's happening."

2

It's funny how a vague announcement like, "It's happening," can change everything. But everything changed in that instant. What had been a jovial Thanksgiving meal with our found family became a chaotic rush to get the "t's dotted and the I's crossed" or whatever, and then get everyone to the hospital.

Greg and Jakole left first, with Greg driving while Jake sat with Nicole in the back. Getting Nicole into the car turned into an ordeal when a contraction hit. She looked miserable. I fought the tears in my eyes as her fingers went white with her death grip on the door frame of the car.

Once they were off, the rest of us took charge of organizing the children, collecting Jakole's go bags, and putting away leftovers. Then we left for the hospital in a couple of cars.

Now, we wait. It's so much like the day we all sat here waiting for Tommy to be born. The only difference now is there are children waiting with us. The couples, though, remain the same. Five years later and Jakole are growing their family again. Ari and Alex—Arex never stuck—are still gleefully footloose and childfree. And Greg and Violet —I like the name Violet too much to use anything else—are making googly eyes at each other, like they can't wait for their upcoming appointment with this labor of love.

And I'm still alone.

What is it about me that I'm always alone? I'm so fucking cool, and yet… If I'm so fucking cool, why doesn't anyone want to be with me or make babies with me? Why has every boyfriend I've ever had left? And on their way out, they always informed me that something about me was the problem. "Listen Sher, you're cool and hot and shit, but you're too—*fill in the blank*. To some I'm *too loud*. Others called me *too talkative*. One insisted I was *too demanding*. The worst is the myriad of men who didn't even bother to get specific and left because I'm just *too much*. What does that even mean? Too much *what*?

Always the same. You're too, too, too, too, too. The problem is you, you, you, you, you. No man has ever given me the so-called classic "It's not you, it's me" line. I guess I should appreciate their honesty, but it doesn't hurt any less to be told, over and over again, that I'm the problem.

I've always been the problem. When I was a kid, my teachers complained I didn't pay attention in class; I was too fidgety and talkative. But did anyone stop to wonder if I was bored and should be given something more challenging to learn? No, instead they flunked me and moved me to the "remedial" class. My mom said I was too unruly and energetic. But did she think to consider it was my effervescent personality bubbling to the surface? No, she punished me with "time outs"—endless, boring hours alone in my room. The doctors labeled me hyperactive. And did anyone question prescribing amphetamines—a stimulant—to calm me down? No. They didn't.

Greg frowns at me, and I realize I've been staring at him and Violet, probably with covetous desire in my eyes, likely freaking him out. Time for a mindful moment. I take a deep breath and look around the room, listing in my head five things I can see: mauve chairs, a green Ficus, dated magazines fanned across a side table, a window with a view of the parking lot, and Mia in her little princess dress pulling on one of her daddy's fingers. With another deep breath, I list four things I can hear: Tommy chattering as he plays with one of the kids' games in the corner of the waiting room, a

Stroke Alert announcement on the loud speaker, Mia reminding her mom that Daddy promised her ice cream on the way home, and some robotic beeping from somewhere down the hall. Another deep breath and I focus on three things I can feel: the hard vinyl of the mauve seats, the cool breeze from the air-conditioning vent, and the soft cotton of my T-shirt. This time when I breathe deep, I scent the air for two things I can smell: antiseptic cleanser and some sort of institutional air freshener. And lastly, a taste: I suck a little harder on the cherry lollipop I've pacified myself with.

"Auntie Sher, did you know I'll be a big bwover soon?" Tommy announces as he rises from the floor by the games and hops across the room to me.

"I did!" I love this kid. He reminds me of me at that age, so excited and curious and filled with pure energy that pours out of his smile. I squeeze him and he laughs, but I don't let go until he's wiggling and giggling and slithering out of my arms to run around the room in high-energy circles. Mia is pretty much oblivious to what's happening around her, but she joins her cousin in movement, twirling in her fluffy pink dress.

In one of Tommy's squeaky squealy drive-bys, he grabs my hand and pulls me out of my chair. I follow him over to the kid's corner of the waiting area, where colorful puzzles and toys keep the kids' attention. Mia cheers when she sees an adult has come down to their level and flops into my lap so she's a part of whatever game we're playing. Pushing colorful beads around on their loopy tracks and trying to get a marble through a maze, I go along with it.

"Hey, Tommy, come here buddy. Let's talk for a minute," Jake says, and everyone turns to the doorway where he stands.

He looks pale, terrified, though he's trying to hide it behind a stoic facade for his son's sake. Still, we can all sense his fear. Even little Tommy's face grows serious with worry. Kids are smart; they sense when something's wrong. He hesitates a moment before he goes over and sits on his dad's lap.

"Hey, my man, so listen. Remember when we talked about the possibility that Mommy would have to have surgery so we can bring your brothers into the world?"

Tommy nods, but he won't look at any of us, just stares at the floor.

Jake continues, "Well, the doctors have decided that's what's best, but it will make Mommy tired and sore, and it might make it hard for her to hug you for a few days. But everything is okay, and we're going to get to meet your brothers very soon, okay?"

"Is Mommy scared?" Tommy asks. His little voice is so sweet, so precious and innocent, and so worried. Clearly, Jakole have prepared Tommy for the possibility of having to deliver the twins by C-section. Still, surgery is a scary topic for kids.

Hell, it's scary for me too. Tears reach the corners of my eyes, and I have to look away, over to where Mia watches the exchange with her own childish apprehension as her mom rubs her little shoulder.

Jake's voice breaks a little bit as he says, "You know your mom— nothing scares her. But *I'm* a little scared. Are you?"

Tommy gives another tiny nod.

"It's okay to be scared. But she's going to be all right. Can I have a hug?"

Tommy nods and turns around, flopping his arms around his dad's neck. Jake holds his son a little longer than usual, petting his hand over his little boy's braids. "I'm going to go in there now and hold Mommy's hand, okay?"

"Okay."

"Will you be really good for your aunts and uncles while you wait?"

"Yes, I'm always really good."

That's the first time Jake smiles, and it's the sweetest thing. That man loves his family so much, and I can see how badly he wants to be back with Nicole while she goes through this part, but he's taken the time to include his son and soothe Tommy's nerves.

Jake demands four hugs and four kisses from Tommy—one set for himself and three extra to share with Nicole and the twins—then he holds onto his little boy a little longer as he looks around at all of us, the grownups. He knows that by informing Tommy in a calm manner, he's also informed us, and it's on us now to keep Tommy feeling light and excited and active, while the rest of his family works hard to stay safe and healthy.

We all nod at him, and he kisses the top of Tommy's head before he goes down the hall again. Once he's gone, Violet and Greg and Alex and Ari join me and the kids on the floor, and we all play games and fiddle with the toys.

I don't know how long we sit there, playing like preschoolers. Normally, this sort of thing would be fun for me, but my stomach is in knots after what seems like hours of faking my jolly cheer.

Finally, Jake comes in, and he's smiling so much. "Tommy, guess what?"

"Daddy, why are you wearing a hat and a dress?"

Jake reaches up and pulls the pale blue bonnet off his head as he shifts out of the apron.

Watching his dad strip out of the OR gear, Tommy's face lights up as realization hits him. "Am I a big bwover now?"

"You are!" Jake hugs his son and stands tall, holding onto the little boy with all his body, heart, and soul. "They're with Mommy right now. Are you ready to meet them?"

We pretty much levitate off the floor. Greg carries his daughter and squeezes Violet's hand as they follow his best friend to meet his name-sake. Ari and Alex follow right behind them. I come in as the caboose of this party train, rolling down the corridor in my skates, because I didn't think to bring normal shoes with me to Family Dinner Night.

Jake takes us into a room, and there in the center of an adjustable bed, with pillows and blankets all around her, Nicole rests queenly atop her throne, smiling wider than I've ever seen. Her hospital gown is tugged down, and on her chest, the tiny twins lay skin-to-skin on their momma.

The beauty of this sight, the beauty of *them*, overwhelms me. They shine with bright, pure light, precious little bundles of love and happiness. The world hasn't gotten to them yet; it hasn't beaten down their spirit or flattened their joy. I envy that purity, that simplicity.

I sop up my tears with the sleeve of my shirt. At least I'm not the only one crying. Greg is a total mess as he stares at the child his best friend honored with his name. And even Ari looks a little misty-eyed.

We whisper in this sacred space, congratulating Nicole on a job well-done while we touch the twins, stroking their soft black hair and tickling their tiny feet. Jake strips off his shirt, then takes one of the babies against his own bare chest. He sits in a chair and hoists Tommy onto his thigh so the little man can meet his new brother Kiah up close and personal.

It's family time now. While we're all extended family in a sense, this space is for Jake, Nicole, and Tommy to bond with the two newest Sixkillers. So, we leave.

It's hard to believe only a few hours have passed since we arrived at the hospital. It's late, though, after midnight. My little pal Mia is asleep on her daddy's shoulder, but I'm wide awake. I catch a ride with Ari and Alex back to my house, where I find my version of "kids" waiting for me with lolling tongues and slobbery kisses. Dallas, Darryl, Sodapop, and Mr. Wigglebottom—my precious pit bulls—love me unconditionally. Well, okay, they love me on the condition I keep feeding them, but right now, I will take it. I need hugs and cuddles and face licks and all that pittie magic. But soon after eating, they spread out on the floor to snore like the wheezy old men they are, so I put on my skates and go downtown.

3

THURSDAY, NOVEMBER 25, 2010

"Dude, aren't you that guy who used to tour as a sideshow freak at that big music festival, and you'd, like, actually lay on a bed of nails, and you pierced your scrotum on stage and shit?"

"No," Manic answers flatly as he serves the man his frosty beverage with an even frostier attitude.

"Ah, come on. I know it was you. I saw you, like, eight times in 1999."

Manic stares at the dude, not even bothering to respond. Fact is, Manic was a sideshow performer with a traveling circus. It wasn't one of those lions-and-tigers-and-bears circuses. This featured contortionists and sword swallowers. Manic was known to lie on a bed of nails while people walked on him, and he'd hang things from his piercings. I've seen him perform. This is how I know he has a generously proportioned dick with a Prince Albert piercing.

The dude who can't take a hint opens his mouth to argue again, but Manic cuts him off. "You have your beer, and I have your money. We're done talking. Move along."

"Fucking asshole," the guy mutters under his breath as he takes his beer, sloshing a little onto the bar top and walking out to the back patio.

"Way to earn that one-star Yelp review," I try to joke.

Manic shrugs. "Like I give a fuck."

"Jeez, what crawled up your ass and died, Grumpelstiltskin?"

"First of all, I never pierced my scrotum on stage. Second of all, why would I want to chat with some random tourist about shit I did ten years ago when you're here, and I'd much rather talk to you?"

Aww. "Well, aren't you sweet. Happy Thanksgiving, Manic. What are you thankful for this year?"

He makes a strange face and shakes his head, like there's nothing on his list. "I don't celebrate Thanksgiving."

That makes me sad, which compounds this low I'm already feeling. It's strange to be down. Usually, I'm floating high like an escaped balloon, and everyone is trying to catch my string before I hit the ceiling. Today, my helium is thinning, and I'm half deflated. And why am I fixated on balloons?

"What's the matter, Sonny Sher?" I grimace at his nickname for me. I love Cher, sure, but the Sonny & Cher era of her oeuvre was never my favorite. Still, I like that I've earned a special name in his book, and it's a diva name no less. Well, it's fifty percent diva, I guess.

I stare at Manic because I don't know how to answer his question. Also, I can't help it. Manic is one of those people who's weirdly hand-some. Not pretty like a supermodel, more like rugged, tough-guy handsome. Plus, he has this scowl that can either freeze you to your core or light your panties on fire, depending on the day. I'm still not sure which version I'm looking at today.

His expression grows concerned with my silence, and I like that he truly cares. That's something I've always loved about Manic: What you see is what you get. If he looks concerned, it's because he is.

Finally, I say, "Nicole had her babies."

Manic frowns. "Are they okay?"

"Yeah, everyone's fine. They had to do a C-section, but that's some-what common in the case of twins, and the little ones are cute as buttons, which is an expression I've never understood. Buttons aren't particularly cute, you know?"

"I don't understand. If everything is okay, why do you look like someone pissed in your beer?"

I look at my beer, sniff it suspiciously.

"I didn't piss in your beer."

I shrug and take a sip, admitting, "I think I'm depressed."

"Why?"

"Because…" I'm lonely and unloved, possibly unlovable. And what the hell? I'm fucking awesome. I've got personality coming out of my ass. I'm smokin' hot and a hellcat in the sack. Yet, no one wants to be with me for the long haul. And fine. Fuck 'em. I don't want to be with those sorry-ass dudes either. I'm done hoping for my happily ever after with some milquetoast man when all I really want is a baby. Why not admit that? Say the words. "I want a baby."

Manic's frown deepens. It's like his frown sinks beneath his skin, and he frowns at me from the depths of his soul. "You want a baby?"

I try to frown at him from my soul too. But I have no idea how to do that, so I just nod. "Yep."

"Why?"

"Well, I used to want it all. I wanted the happy ending with the perfect man to fall head over heels in love with me and sweep me off my feet and shower me with affection and give me orgasms for days and all the rest, you know? But I've waited and waited. Everyone says, love comes when you least expect it, so I tried hard not to expect it. But it never came, and I'm turning thirty-five next month, and I'm giving up on all the rest. I just want a baby."

Manic gives me a pitying look, which I hate, and pours me a shot.

"What's this?"

"An early birthday shot."

I drink it. Manic pours the glass full again.

"What's that?"

"A birthday shot for the twins."

"Aren't you going to drink with me?"

"Not drinking tonight."

Oh. I drink my shot alone. "Pour another one for the other twin."

Manic does.

I drink the third shot. He doesn't pour me another. In fact, he puts the bottle away, far away.

"Manic, do you want kids?"

"Nope."

"Why not?"

"Cuz I don't."

"Okay, but…why?"

"Why are you so curious about me and my interest in kids?"

I shrug. "I'm a curious person."

Manic glances around the bar, everyone jabbering about everything and nothing at the same time. He leans a little closer as he says in a muted voice, "Well, I'm a private person, and my reasons are private."

"But, I mean, what if you never had to take care of the kid or meet them or anything, just be the sperm donor?"

Manic leans onto the bar directly across from me. He braces his arms on either side of mine, his fingers tracing delicate lines over my elbows.

His closeness feels new, which is odd. We've hugged before. We hug all the time. He even kisses me on the cheek sometimes. This is different.

I ogle the man, who's looking pretty fine in jeans and a dark Henley. He has his sleeves pushed up to his elbows, giving me a show of the tattoos that mark him from his knuckles to his neck. He's also started letting his winter beard grow in, and the dark scruff on his jaw makes my fingers itch.

His signature black cowboy hat gives him a punk rock cowboy vibe, and the shadow it casts across his face makes it difficult to see his pretty blue eyes, but I definitely feel them. The way he stares at me right now makes me feel scrutinized, like a cute little specimen on a microscope slide.

"What are you asking me, Sher?"

Well, shit. It's the most valid question asked tonight. What *am* I asking him?

I take a deep breath to clear my mind and fill my lungs with Manic, his own brand of scent that's some combination of detergent, whiskey, and leather. That heady aroma, mixed with the warm booze in my belly, sends my attention in new directions. I've always found Manic attractive, but I've never been attracted to him. There is something off-limits about him, and I've always respected that silent Keep Out warning. But today, staring into the oceanic depths of his eyes, I see a lure. I want to dive deep and drown in him.

I look down at his hands, touching me so softly with calloused fingers, and I can imagine how his rough grip would turn gentle for me, for a baby. I watch the way his fingers stroke my arms, his sexy knuckle tattoos that read "FUCK" on one hand and "OFF!" on the other.

Heed the warning, girl.

Manic is not interested in you like that. He's a friend. A weird and enigmatic friend who's prickly on the outside and prickly on the inside too. Plus, we've remained friends this long *because* I never dove in and went for his lure. The idea of Manic being just another guy who doesn't want to be with me for more than a weekend is unbearable.

I move my gaze away from where he's touching me to where he's staring at me, where he looks ready to drown me in his deep blue depths, and then I look past him to the television over his head. *Alien,* Manic's favorite movie is playing again. It's the part when they're all eating, and the alien pops out of John Hurt's stomach. "Eck! Talk about a c-section."

Manic's body language completely changes. He straightens, his posture rigid, his fingers no longer touching my elbows, and he's no longer looking deep into my eyes. He pours me a water and sets it next to my beer, then he wanders over to a different corner of the bar to serve someone else. I watch him go, then I watch the rest of the movie and drink the water, ready to sober back up and skate home.

4

SUNDAY, NOVEMBER 28, 2010

"Come on, Trevor, these anal glands aren't going to express themselves," I say in my most professional tone. Then I ruin the illusion by adding, "Though, oh my God, wouldn't it be funny if they did express themselves? Like, Anal Gland One says to Anal Gland Two, 'I'm having a shitty day. You got any liquor?' And Anal Gland Two is all, 'Lick her? I hardly know her.' "

I laugh at my own joke and look up to find Trevor staring at me in horror. Note to self: Trevor doesn't have a sense of humor. Note to the person who makes the shelter shift schedule: stop pairing me with the humorless vet techs.

"Well, go ahead there, Trevor. Harvey is ready for some relief." I brace the adorable little beagle with the itchy booty, holding him still for our safety and his, while Trevor does the dirty work. I always like to start my trainees off with a good old-fashioned anal gland expression before lunch, a test of their mettle.

Trevor does a thorough job, and as soon as his finger is out of Harvey's bum, I loosen my hold on the dog.

"I'll bet your booty feels better now, doesn't it, H-Bomb?"

Harvey is a happy boy, wagging his little tail and trying to lick my face as I weave and dodge his big pink tongue.

"Save the kisses for your butt, buddy."

Trevor tosses his gloves, then gives the dog a couple of pets as Harvey goes into self-cleaning mode. I'll give Trevor high marks for his efficient treatment and friendly bedside manner, even if he can't take an anal gland joke.

"Sheryl, call for you on line two," Dawneese hollers from the hall.

I give Harvey several more pets then leave him in Trevor's capable hands.

It's Ari on the phone. "Hey girl, just checking in."

"Checking in?"

"Yeah, you were kind of weird on Thanksgiving."

Weird? Isn't that pretty much my normal state of being? Still, Ari's timing is perfect. "Wanna meet for happy hour and talk about Operation Insemination?"

Manic is working the happy hour shift. Once upon a time, I thought he was a vampire, but the older he gets the less he can tolerate the drunks at last call and opts for tolerating the sun instead as he opens the bar rather than closing it. Can I blame him? I'm a nightmare when I'm drunk, all handsy and emotional. I can't imagine having to wrangle, like, forty of me out the door at closing time.

"Sonny Sher, what brings you in again so soon?"

"Your handsome face and attentive service, of course."

Manic smiles a little. A little smile is all you can ever hope to get out of Manic, so I give him a big, broad grin in return. Then Ari comes fluttering into the room with her pretty doe eyes and accidental hotness, landing her ass on the stool beside me, and Manic's attention shifts. I think he's always had a crush on her, but then he went and introduced her to wonderboy Alex, and any shot he had was shot down.

"Liar." Manic smirks at me. "I see you're two-timing me with Ari yet again."

Ari plays the little game we always play with him. "You know we love you most, Manic."

"Uh-huh." He looks dubious and shakes his head while he pours our drinks as well as a set of three shots, one for each of us. Interesting how *now* Manic will drink with me when Ari's around. I try to ignore the little pinch of jealousy that causes. I try, and I fail.

When we've had our shots, Manic moves on to other customers, giving Ari and me a chance to talk privately. Ari immediately dives into the deep end of conversation. "Spill it—what's with all the baby crazy stuff?"

"I want a baby," I answer simply.

"Why?"

"Because I do. Why don't you want one?"

"Because I don't."

We nod. Then Ari says, "It's a bit sudden is all."

"It's not sudden. I've always wanted a baby. And now everyone else is having them, and I'm stuck here like a mosquito in amber, with all this DNA in me, wasted."

"A mosquito? What?"

"But I'm running out of time. That fucking clock is tick-tick-ticking in my head so loud I can't think about anything else."

"What clock?"

"Jesus, you really don't want kids, do you? The *biological* clock, the clock that says, 'Oh, Sheryl Ann, don't forget you turn thirty-five in twenty-seven days, and you've got no man and no prospects, *and* you're ovulating soon.' "

"So? You're only thirty-five. You have at least a decade before menopause. Plenty of time."

"Bitch, I'm thirty-four...for twenty-seven more days."

"And then you turn thirty-five. So?"

"So? *So?* I'll be geriatric!"

"Thirty-five is *not* geriatric."

"Actually, technically, it is. The name for a pregnancy when the mother is thirty-five or over is a 'geriatric pregnancy.' Look it up." Ari actually takes out her phone to look it up. When she sees I'm right, I point at the screen. "See? I'll be geri-fucking-atric, and I don't have the one thing I want. Everyone around me has what they want. You have the Kinkmaster 5000. Jakole are swimming in dirty diapers. Greg and

Violet are all mushy eyed and kissy face as Violet bakes a sibling for Mia in her oven. And I'm sitting here, a lonely little spinster spinning my wheels."

"Kinkmaster 5000?" Ari barks out a laugh.

"Out of everything I said, that's what you heard?"

"I can't wait to tell Alex what you called him."

"Woman, don't make me spank you."

"That's not actually a threat." Ari winks at me, but she turns serious. "And I hear you. I'm sorry you feel lonely. I never knew you felt that way."

"Don't believe everything you see on my hard candy shell. Here in the ooey-gooey center, there are feelings and deep thoughts and shit."

"Well, thank you for letting me see your gooey thoughts. And I understand about loneliness. I do."

"How could you? You've never been alone. You went from married to Greg to poly to monogamous with Alex in a microsecond."

"You can be surrounded by people and still be lonely. But stop making this about me. Let's talk about you." Ari crosses her legs and folds her hands in her lap like a shrink. "So, you're going on a baby daddy hunt?"

"I guess. I mean…the logistics you mentioned about STDs and stuff sort of took the wind out of my sails. It all sounds complicated and messy."

"Well, yeah, making a baby *is* messy. But it doesn't have to be complicated. Just ask your prospective donors to get tested."

"But that takes the spontaneity out of it, don't you think?"

"Spontaneity? You're talking about making a baby—that shouldn't be spontaneous. Unless…wait…Are you planning to keep the baby a secret from the father?"

"Well, yeah."

Ari frowns. "Why?"

"Because it's not any of his business. I just need some sperm in my hoohaw, not a daddy in my life."

"Okay, don't take this the wrong way, but that seems kind of… rapey to me."

"What's the right way to take that?"

"It's like you're stealing a man's seed to create a child, which is a lot more than just hooking up for a one-night stand. If you're going to partner with someone for copulation, that's one thing. But if you're goal is procreation, your partner should be fully informed and consenting."

"Some wing woman you are, making me feel like a rapey, seed-stealing witch on day one."

"You know I'm right."

"Yeah, I know." Of course she's right. Still, I huff out an exhausted sigh.

"Seriously, the conversation doesn't have to be too complicated. Just approach a guy, explain that you want to have unprotected sex with him because you want a baby. Tell him you don't expect anything from him, you don't even need to know his name, and he can walk away without any obligation to you or the child. But you need proof he's STD negative and consenting to the possibility you might become pregnant. And in exchange, he gets to do all sorts of nasty, dirty things with your tight little hard body as long as he comes inside. I'll bet you get more than a few takers."

She makes it sound so easy. But for me, it's very complicated. When it comes to communication, I can never stay on topic. I'd probably start that conversation fine and end it with a detailed explanation of the fertilization process. The guys will be running in the other direction.

"Do you need your wingwoman to help with this part?" Ari offers, and I could kiss her.

"Yes, please."

"Okay." She claps her hands and looks around the bar. It's early still and not crowded. Slim pickings. "What about that guy?"

"The one in the corner?" I take a long look, then turn back to my friend. "No."

"What's wrong with him?" Ari asks as she sips her drink.

"His ears are too big. They're all out of proportion to his face."

"So close your eyes while he inseminates you."

"No, big ears are genetic. I don't want my poor little baby getting picked on for her Dumbo ears."

Ari smirks, looks again, and nods to a different man. "What about him?"

He looks nice enough, but when he glances our way and sees two hot women staring at him, he gets this creepy look in his eyes that completely turns me off. Ari and I say in unison, "No."

"The guy in the red shirt?"

Manic swings by to refill our drinks and says, "The guy in the red shirt always dies first."

I laugh at his dorky Trekkie joke, and he winks as he turns and walks away.

I stare at the guy in the red shirt for a moment, but he looks boring. "Is being boring a genetic trait?"

When Ari doesn't answer, I glance her way to find her attention drawn in a different direction. Then she asks, "Do I have to point out the elephant in the room?"

I point at the guy in the corner. "You mean Dumbo ears over there?"

"What? No. And I didn't mean to literally point. Sherrie, please stop pointing at that guy. I'm talking about figurative pointing at the figurative elephant."

"Huh?"

"How can you be so insightful about my love life and yet so blind about your own?"

"What love life?" I grumble.

"Exactly! Sher, what would you say if I told you there is a man in this room who has been in love with you for years?"

She makes zero sense. I look around the room. The only man in here I've known for years is Manic, and he doesn't love me. He can barely tolerate me. It's Ari he ogles.

"Sher! Open your eyes. He's literally standing right in front of you." Ari is the one pointing now, and she's pointing right at Manic. To be clear, though, he's not *literally* standing right in front of me. He's standing several feet away, behind the bar, helping a customer and frowning at us as Ari continues to point at him.

"Are you talking about Manic?" I finally hazard a guess.

"Yes!" Ari says, and we both turn to look at him.

I notice—not for the first time this week—that he's a good-looking man. Tall, with a strong build. His muscles aren't bulky like those you get from lifting weights; they're the long, sinewy kind that come with endurance. I shiver at the mere thought of Manic's *endurance*. But let's face it—when a guy carries himself with that much cocky confidence, you know he's gotta be a marathon man in the sack. Plus, I've seen him perform his circus act. So it's easy to imagine he's a giver when he puts that big dick to work, with his piercing rubbing in all the right places.

Manic is without his cowboy hat at the moment, his hair thick and messy, begging for a finger comb. And his ears, well, I never noticed how well proportioned they are, even despite the thick gauges in his distended lobes.

He looks annoyed that we're staring at him and takes the towel out of his back pocket to clean the bar. Now I'm imagining being manhandled by those rough, calloused hands with the FUCK OFF! knuckle tattoos. *Hot.*

Yeah. I would absolutely let Manic do dirty, nasty things to my tight little hard body even if he insisted on wearing a condom, but…

"*But* what?" Ari asks.

Did I say all of that out loud?

"*But* he's not in love with me." I let out a big belly laugh that turns into a whiskey burp. "I mean, of course we're friends and shit, and I love him to bits, but, like a brother. You know, like you and Jake."

"I can guarantee you, Manic does not love you like a sister."

As if on cue, Manic comes over and pours more whiskey shots for us, plus one for himself. "Why are you ladies pointing at me and giggling?"

Please don't answer that, Ari. I'm not ready for this conversation—

"I'm helping Sheryl hunt for a baby daddy," Ari announces.

"Seriously?" Manic frowns at me. I mean he *really* frowns. He looks downright angry. I'm frozen like a deer on the train tracks, with a steamy locomotive bearing down on me. His eyes, normally a deep oceanic blue, are steely gray. "You're trolling the bar looking for some random asshole to knock you up?"

When he puts it like that, it sounds awful. But basically, yeah. Slowly, I nod.

Manic's frown deepens. "Have fun with that," he says and walks away. Whipping his towel out again, he gets busy cleaning the bar.

I look down at the three shots of Bushmills he poured and left untouched before us. Ari lifts one of the drinks to her lips and winks at me over the rim, then tosses it down the hatch. What the hell is she grinning about?

I protest. "See, if he was in love with me, wouldn't he have volunteered to be the random asshole to knock me up?"

"Oh my God, Sheryl! His huffy response is even more proof he's into you. He's probably calculating how to murder whichever guy you leave with tonight."

"Why?"

"Because he's besotted with you."

"Nuh-uh."

"Yeah-huh."

"Nuh-uh."

"Yeah-huh. And if you're so convinced I'm wrong, why not ask him?"

"Ask him what? If he loves me, or if he'll knock me up?"

"Either." Ari shrugs. "Or both."

I huff, frustrated. Ari doesn't understand the situation I have with Manic. I've known the man for years—almost a decade, I'd reckon—and yet I hardly know him at all. I consider him a dear friend, but he's a mystery to me. I've never trusted anyone as opaque as him, so that's new, but I like to see through people, and Manic is as clear as mud. My granny used to say I could see auras, and I guess she's right. People tend to have a shine to them, or there's a darkness. Manic has neither or maybe a little bit of both.

"If I ask him if he loves me and he doesn't, then what does that do to our friendship? And if I ask him if he loves me and he does, well, what does *that* do to our friendship? And if I skip all that emo shit and just ask him to impregnate me, there's that pesky friendship question again."

"First of all, please do not use the phrase 'impregnate me' when approaching your baby daddy candidates. It makes you sound like an alien queen from outer space sent to planet earth to crossbreed with humanity."

I lift my arms and in my best Dalek voice, say, "Inseminate!"

Manic—who is the geekiest *Doctor Who* geek I know and has a Dalek tattooed on his left arm—glances up from where he's fixated on cleaning the same spot on the bar, rubbing it with his towel so vigorously he's going to sand the finish off the wood.

Okay. Yeah. Maybe I should go ahead and ask him. I mean, I piss off Manic all the time, and he still seems to consider me a friend. So what harm would an honest question cause?

Mentally, I pull my big-girl panties up and holler, "Hey James."

"Don't call me that," Manic says as he comes over.

"Why you so mad?"

"I'm not mad."

"Coulda fooled me."

"What do you want, Sher?"

Here goes nothing, "So listen, James, I was wondering if you'd be willing to get me pregnant."

"No." Manic walks away again.

What the fuck?

I look to Ari, and her eyes go wide with astonishment as she mouths, "Wow." Then she shrugs and starts typing into her phone. Really? In this, my moment of greatest rejection, she's on her—

She pushes her phone in front of my nose, and I see she's done a search for… Wait what? I pull the phone out of her hand and look more closely at it. In the search bar are the words *sperm banks in Austin* and below are a few matches on a map. "They open tomorrow at eight. Want to make an appointment?"

5

MONDAY, NOVEMBER 29, 2010

"How about Seth?" Ari asks and slides a binder over, showing me her favorite of the sperm donor profiles. "Says here 'He has gorgeous green eyes and a muscular build. He's a perfect Southern gentleman with a love for football and fishing.' Southern charm *and* muscles, what's not to love?"

I stare at the photo of Seth and sigh. "This reminds me of when families come to the shelter to adopt a dog, and we give them our staff assessment of the dog's temperament. I half expect this to finish with, 'Seth is house-trained, and, when tempted with a treat, will follow basic commands like *sit* and *roll over*.' "

Ari points at the photo. "Whatever, he's adorable. Look at his bow tie and those pudgy cheeks."

I mean, she's right. Seth was a cutie patootie when he was a little boy. "I wasn't expecting them to use childhood photos of the donors." I flip past Seth to the next page in the book. "I guess it makes sense though. I'm shopping for a cute baby, not a cute random dude who squirted into a jar."

"So romantic." Ari chuckles.

"Hey, this was your idea!" I point out for the millionth time. "I wanted to get preggers the old-fashioned way with a rooster all up in my hen house, but you had to kill the vibe with your preaching about diseases and communication."

"Yeah, you're welcome." Ari sounds indignant when she asks, "Why'd you flip past Seth? What's wrong with Seth?"

"What sort of name is Seth anyway? Is it biblical?"

"Yes," Ari answers. "Seth was the third son of Adam and Eve. After Cain murdered Abel, God gave them Seth."

I smirk as I turn the page on Collin and Brandon after that. "So God was like, 'Sorry that fifty percent of your kids are fratricidal lunatics and the other fifty percent are dead. Here's Seth. Third time's a charm!' " I flip past a few more donor profiles, feeling none of the joy I thought this would bring. I usually like shopping, but my mood is all wrong today. Slamming the donor binder shut, I pronounce: "You know what? I hate this. I don't want to do this."

"Okay. But why not?" Ari asks.

"Because… I don't know. Just because!"

Gah. Must I have a reason? I don't want to have a kid this way, not if I can help it. The memory of how I make a baby should be a fun one, with lube and toys and fornication. Also, I can't stop thinking about Manic.

Since Ari planted the Manic seed in the soil of my brain, I can't dig it out. I look at these photos of cute little boys and wonder what he looked like when he was little. And then my mind goes on this whole sojourn to a place where I imagine what his babies would look like, what *our* babies would look like. With his eyes and my smile, his quiet stoicism and my brash panache, we'd make the *best* babies.

But he said no.

I sigh heavily and hand my binder over to the nice woman at the clinic. Ari rubs my back as we leave, asking, "Ready to go play with some newborns?"

"Yes please." I sound as sad as I feel. And why do I feel so sad? I honestly don't know. Manic's rejection? Seriously, just add it to the pile. Rejection is my middle name: Sheryl Reject Novak. Being rejected is nothing new for me, and the icky feelings those rejections stir up are nothing new either. So why does Manic's one-word rejection still sting?

Maybe precisely because it *was* just one word. No equivocating. No explanation. Just no.

Damnit, I'm fixating on it again. That one syllable kept me up all night: counting the letters, taking its measure, weighing its worth. That little word is like a .22 caliber bullet, a tiny little thing that can tear you to shreds. And that's what I feel—shredded.

"How you doin', sexy mama?" I ask Nicole as I sit beside her at the table. She looks as great as ever. It's Jake who looks like a mess, an adorably frazzled father of three.

"Like someone cut open my abdomen and pulled two tiny humans out," Nicole answers between bites of food.

"Metal!" I throw my hands up in devil horns.

Nicole adds, "Actually, I'm pretty okay. Having Greg and Violet here has been a lifesaver. They've taken care of so much. I don't think we could do this without them."

I try to control my jealousy. I'd offered to help, but Greg and Violet are the godparents, and they've got it covered. I'm not needed—Sheryl Superfluous Novak.

But it's hard to stay bitter. Violet and Greg are awesome, and they're parents too. They get it. They know better than me what needs doing. I glance across the table at Violet, who grins at me while her husband holds his tiny namesake, ignoring his food while the rest of us eat. Over his shoulder, Jake paces around the living room, swaying Kiah in his arms as he sings quietly in Cherokee.

My heart squeezes at the sight of the two dads in the room doing dad-like things. I mean, let's face it—dads are sexy when they gentle those manly hands to hold little babies. It's hot when they care about something other than themselves. There's a special kind of romance in fatherhood.

My eyes tear up, and I force them away as I come to the irritating realization that I'm full of shit when I try to tell myself I don't want all the rest, just the baby. I want it *all*. More than just the sperm, I want the donor too. I want someone to bring me ice cream and pickles when I'm pregnant and craving. Someone to lovingly dick me down with pregnancy sex and naptime sex and get up every other time there's a cry in the night. I want the baby, yes, and I want the baby daddy too.

And that's all completely unattainable to me if I can't even get a guy to stick with me for more than three weeks and five days. That's how long Stephen Lowe was in the picture before he "went on tour" and never returned. He left Austin and me without a word. At least he didn't waste my time with a speech about everything he found intolerable in me. I appreciate that very much. Regardless, he's the last "relationship" I had. And that was five years ago. Everyone since then has lasted two weeks or less.

Ugh. All this selfish jealousy is messing with my appetite. I barely touch the brisket Ari and I brought on our way here from the sperm bank. While everyone else digs in, I push the meat around with my fork, feeling sorry for myself. I wonder what my aura looks like today because I certainly don't feel shiny.

Like some of my tainted emotions will rub off on him, I wash my hands before I sit down on the floor with Tommy, who's playing with a couple of little cars.

"T-Man, what have you got here?"

"The cars *Eduda* sent me." I grin at his name for Jake's Uncle Eli. It's the Cherokee word for grandfather. Since Jake's family was killed in a car accident when he was a kid and Nicole isn't close with her family, Jake's Uncle Eli has become Tommy's ad hoc grandpa.

"Oh, that's nice." I point at the El Camino. "I like this one the best. Wanna know why?"

Tommy nods. "Why?"

"Because it's neon green, plus it's a car with a truck bed. Which is, like, the coolest thing ever. Don't ya think?"

Tommy shrugs and hands me the El Camino like it means nothing to him. Silly boy. I work on mastering three-point turns with my little green car while he races a couple hot rods. He's being very quiet. The quietest I've ever seen him, so I have to ask. "How are you doing, buddy?"

"Um," he considers. "I'm okay."

"Well good." I nod resolutely. "How are your little brothers doing?"

"They sleep a lot, and we have to be quiet so we don't wake them up." I love how he uses the royal "we" here, and I can perfectly picture his parents using that approach with him so he feels like part of the quiet team. But five-year-olds are loud. This kid is being so good for his family, but he needs a break.

"Ah." I slide behind him so I can scratch his back. "If you ever feel the need to get loud, let your momma know you want to come hang out at Auntie Sheryl's house, okay? We can scream and holler and play with the dogs and—"

Tommy turns, and his eyes light up, trying to keep a lid on his volume as he asks, "Can I jump on the trampoline?"

Hmm. Technically, Nicole doesn't want him on my trampoline until he's six, but he's five and a half, and I've put safety pads over the springs in anticipation for the day when Mama Rollins-Sixkiller relents.

"Let's ask your mom, but I think it'd be okay." *Please don't kill me, Nicole.*

"Mommy!" Tommy jumps up and immediately modulates his voice when his dad's head snaps up from where he's managed to get Kiah to sleep. "Auntie Sheryl says I can go to her house whenever I want and jump on the trampoline."

"Oh she did, did she?"

Tommy nods excitedly, and I roll my eyes. *Way to throw me under the bus, T-Man.* Still, I will advocate the fuck for this kid to get to jump on the trampoline. I hold my hands in prayer and give Nicole my best puppy-dog eyes. She smirks at me and turns to her son, stroking her hand on his braids. "Well then, I guess you can, but only if you're really careful, and you're not allowed to jump when Auntie Sheryl isn't there to watch you, okay?" She says that to both of us, and we both nod big.

"Cool. Kiddo, it's a date."

"When?" He blinks dark lashes over those big green eyes and he's so freakin' irresistible.

"How about tomorrow? Lunch time?"

Greg pipes up, "I need to run errands anyway. I can drop him by."

I whisper over Tommy's head, "Mia?"

Violet shakes her head. Mia—who is already down for the night—is afraid of dogs. They're working on it, but my house would be too much for the little girl's anxiety to handle. I hate it and wish I could help her come to love dogs for the amazing love bugs they usually are, but I'm just happy I get to hang out with my favorite little man for a while.

As that thought goes through my head, Ari hands me a new little man to fall in love with. This is baby Greg. It's my turn to hold him. I cradle the little cutie and rock him as I mostly just sniff his head. God, I love that new baby smell.

Alex watches me for a moment, then asks, "How's the hunt going?"

Ari shakes her head and nudges him in the side like she's trying to stop his line of questioning. He doesn't get the message. Anything short of that decapitation hand gesture across the throat won't work with this crowd. We ask awkward questions. It's what we do.

I try to keep my tone light as I answer. "Not great. There's this guy named Seth who's a contender."

"Is he drug and disease free?" Nicole asks as she adjusts herself to breastfeed Kiah, using a nursing pillow to hold him without hurting her incision.

"Well, he's a sperm donor, so I assume his jizz has passed all the requisite tests."

"Oh, a sperm bank," Violet says and Greg nods. "Smart."

"Why do you think they call it a bank, anyway?" I ponder, then answer my own question. "I guess because it's where you go to make deposits and withdrawals. So anyways, anyone up for karaoke tonight?"

Every single person shakes their head. Not a damn one wants to join me downtown to sing it out, which—once upon a time—was our post Family Dinner Night tradition. They're all busy now with family and relationships and shit. And my skate sisters Tynisha and Rachel moved to Portland and Boston years ago. I'm on my own, again.

"What's the name of that band that sings the song about the woman who wants another baby? You should sing that one," Nicole offers.

Jake pipes up for the first time tonight, finally eating now that

Nicole is feeding Kiah. "Ace of Base. And that song isn't actually about a baby. She's cruising to get laid."

"Yeah, well, either meaning applies tonight. Right, Sher?" Nicole smirks at me.

"Right." I sigh.

6

MONDAY, NOVEMBER 29, 2010

I slosh my beer a little as I belt out the lyrics to Ace of Base's "All That She Wants." Nicole's right; this is my theme song in every possible way. I'll take any form of "baby" I can get my hands on right now.

I can still hear Ari lecturing me about trolling for hookups, but she can go clutch her pearls elsewhere. I'm not in the mood to listen to reason or logic or common sense. I want an orgasm—the good kind that curls your toes and makes you shiver. And if it results in a baby, all the better.

I've come downtown loaded for bear in a sexy, blood-red corset and leather skirt. I'm wearing the harlot lipstick to match, and I ditched my car at the house in exchange for my street skates. I'm a roller bitch in heat, and I need some relief.

From the look of a few of the men in the crowd, they want to scratch my itch. Which is great. Except, that guy in the back. I've heard him sing. He couldn't find the key in a bag full of keys. Automatic disqualification. And the one eyeing me from up front has the dance moves of a sea lion. I am not ready to see his sex moves.

I finish my song and return to the table I share with a few of the other karaoke-night regulars, accepting compliments and exchanging small talk. But no one here interests me. This outfit, this attitude are wasted here. My thoughts are a block and a half away, with the man slinging drinks at a different bar.

"Why no?" I shout as I barrel through the door and roll my way to the first empty seat at Manic's bar.

"Hello to you too, Sonny Sher," Manic says without looking up from the beer taps. He knows it's me making all the racket. Apparently, I'm the only chick in town who roller-skates to the bar.

"Why did you say no?"

"To what?"

"Don't play games. Why did you say no to getting me pregnant?"

"Jesus, Sher, this again?"

"Yes, this again. I need to understand. It's all I could think about as I was flipping through the pages of donors at the sperm bank today—"

"You went to a sperm bank?"

"—because I kept wanting to know what is so wrong with me that literally no one wants me."

"Don't be ridiculous—"

"Don't tell me I'm being ridiculous when the thought of being a baby daddy for me has you running away like I have a pot of boiling water in one hand and your favorite bunny in the other."

"What?"

"Be honest with me, Manic. What is wrong with me?"

Apparently, that was my beer he was pouring because Manic sets it in front of me as he looks around at the other drinkers, all watching me like I'm the main event for tonight's show. After a moment, he nods toward an empty corner of the bar, and I take my beer when I follow him over there.

As quietly as he can, Manic says, "There is nothing wrong with you, Sher. You're...amazing."

Aww. That's a sweet thing to say. Still, I frown at him. "Then why won't you give me what I need? Why do you deny me?"

"Deny you?" The expression on Manic's face is something I've never seen before. He looks like he's in physical pain, like my questions are some great torture. "Are you seriously asking me to get you pregnant?"

"Yes."

"You want to have sex with me?"

"Sure."

"Sure?" He raises a brow, and I can't tell if it's because he's surprised, excited, or disappointed to learn I'm game for bumping uglies with him.

We're getting off track, though, so I bring us back to the point. "So will you?"

"Have sex with you?"

"No." Wrong track. "Get me pregnant."

"No." There it is again, that one-word declaration with not an ounce of emotion in his eyes as he says it.

"Why?"

He rolls his eyes at me, looking exhausted now. "I don't want kids. Okay?"

"But you wouldn't even have to meet the kid. I wouldn't expect anything—"

"I said no."

"Why?"

"Personal reasons."

"What personal reasons?"

"Personal *fucking* reasons!" He pretty much shouts at me.

A wise woman wouldn't poke. I'm not a wise woman. "Wait, when you say 'fucking reasons,' do you mean, like, erectile dysfunction, or were you using the word 'fucking' for emphasis?"

"For *fucking* emphasis!" Manic is definitely shouting now. Then he hisses the rest of his words through clenched teeth, trying not to literally bite my face off or keep our conversation private, I guess. "There is nothing *fucking* wrong with my *fucking* dick. I simply do not want children, and my reasons are *fucking* personal and none of your goddamn *fucking* business, Sher, so stop *fucking* asking me."

He's right. Oh my God, of course he's right. It's incredibly awful that I won't take his no as the answer. No means no, always. He said no. He was clear and succinct. Yet here I am trying to coerce him to change his mind and demanding he explain himself. It's disgusting.

I nod, realizing how terrible I've been to him these last few days, and all at once my emotions go haywire, and I burst into tears. Which makes me feel even worse, like I'm using the tears as emotional black-mail on him. I'm not. Swear! I don't even know where these tears are coming from. If I could put them back in my eyes, I would. But they're splashing against the bar and watering down my beer.

Manic walks away, and I cry harder, feeling so alone in this room full of people. But then a pair of arms wraps around me. I look down at those tattooed knuckles I know so well and burst into a fresh round of tears. Manic has come around to the patron side of the bar to comfort me. It's so damn sweet.

I resist his affection at first, feeling guilty for laying all this shit on him and then having him comfort me on top of that. But he squeezes me a little tighter, and I melt into his arms. Spinning around on my barstool, I bury my face against his chest, breathing deep, filling my senses with him. He smells so good.

"I'm sorry, Sher. I really am. I wish I could be that guy for you, but I can't."

Can't. "Can't" is such a weird word to me because while it's usually used to indicate an absolute, it rarely is. Is "can't" actually a "won't" in this case, and isn't "won't" negotiable? No. Stop. Coercion is not okay. He said no. Respect that.

"Please don't apologize. You don't owe me an apology. You don't owe me anything. I tackled you with this, and it is totally within your right to say no. I'm the one who should be sorry, and I am. I over-stepped—I do that a lot. I hug people without asking, and sometimes people don't want to be hugged, and you should ask first, but I forget. And now this…"

Manic lays a kiss on the top of my head. It's the sweetest gesture, and it brings tears to my eyes again. Manic is rarely sweet or soft about anything he does, so when he shows you that side of himself, it feels especially special.

After another gentle squeeze, he returns to the well side of the bar and starts serving drinks again. This place is mostly empty, a quiet

Monday night, but a few of his patrons have been waiting patiently for service while I fell apart. I grimace at them in apology and sip my beer. Once they're tended to, Manic comes over to me, asking, "Why do you want a kid so bad?"

No one has ever asked me that before. It's a good question. I scrunch up my face as I consider my answer. "I have a lot of love to give, and no one to give it to."

Manic's expression changes to something so terribly sad I nearly burst into tears again. He clears his throat, and the expression is gone in an instant, like it never happened. "Any kid will be lucky to have you for a mom."

My heart flutters a little. What a nice thing to say. "Yeah?"

He nods.

"Thanks."

He still looks sad. It's not that depths-of-despair level of sadness I caught a glimpse of before, but it's still heartbreaking to look into his deep soulful eyes peering into mine and feel such a cold loneliness coming from him.

I want to understand it, but before I can ask, Manic lets out a heavy breath and walks away. He cleans the bar like it's the first spring above ground after a nuclear winter. He's dusting behind bottles and shit.

Occasionally, he'll come over to me and refill my beer. But mostly he leaves me to my thoughts, which is awful because all I can think about is him. I can still feel the soft caress of his kiss on the crown of my head. My hair is parted down the center into braids—a lot like Tommy and Jake's hair—and it was right there on the part where his lips brushed my skin. I want to feel that again. I want to have the weight and warmth of his arms around me again too.

Fucking Ari, putting all these stupid ideas in my head. And now I can't get them out. I'm fixating on Manic. Watching his every move, noting the way he treats other female customers, sometimes a little flirty, other times completely transactional. Does he have a nickname for any of them? I don't know since I don't know the women's actual names. I guess I could ask, take a poll. For science.

Instead, I set a coaster over my beer—the customary way to kindly ask strangers not to roofie me—and roll over to the bathroom to check my makeup after my impromptu crying jag. My mascara is a little smudged, but there's no serious damage.

When I come back out, a guy in a biker cut with sparrows tattooed on his neck sits beside my beer. I slide in, and I'm about to sip my drink when Manic comes and pulls it out of my hand. "Let me pour you a fresh one," he says eyeing the guy beside me.

I eye the guy, too, wondering if he did something to my drink, but if he had I know Manic would have called the cops and tossed him out on the street. I've seen him do it before. Guess he's being safe rather than sorry in this case.

When I have my new brew, I take a long sip while the guy beside me tries to put my beer on his tab. Manic stares daggers at him. When my guard dog steps away to serve other customers, the man beside me slides a little closer, too close, and asks, "Is that guy your boyfriend?"

"No," I watch Manic work, his attention divided between me and everyone else here.

My answer seems to please the stranger, who gives me a devilish grin. He's an attractive guy, with jade green eyes and good bone structure, a stubbled jaw and long blond hair that looks tussled by the wind. Between the tattoos on his neck and arms and the colors patched on his leather cut, it's not hard to guess he's a biker, and I wonder what he rides. It's been too long since I had the purr of an engine between my thighs.

I lean a little closer to him now too. Maybe this would be an opportunity to work on the honest dialogue Ari insists I need to have with potential sperm donor dudes.

"What's your name?" I ask.

"Sean."

"What do you ride?"

"A Triumph Bonneville," he answers.

Hot. I love motorcycles, and Triumphs are among my favorites. This guy just scored a point.

"What's with the roller skates?" he asks.

"I'm a skater."

"Ah."

"You want a shot?" I offer.

"Sure."

When Manic stops ignoring me long enough to come by and check on my beer level, I order two shots of Jameson. Bushmills is what I drink with Manic, exclusively. To drink that with Sean would be a sacrilege. Still, Manic frowns.

"Can you trawl for men somewhere else? It's distracting."

Well, that was rude. "Can we have those shots, or do you really want me to go somewhere else?"

Manic scowls the entire time he pours the shots. I take one and my beer in my other hand and stand. "Want to talk on the patio?"

Sean nods and follows.

It's a cool night in late November, but at the middle of the patio is a fire pit with a water fountain in the center. I love the sound of the fountain water trickling as the firelight moves across the walls, like the shadows are dancing.

I pull out one of the wire mesh chairs for the table closest to the fire, and Sean joins me, sitting closer than he needs to. We do our shots with a clink of our glasses, and when we've swallowed, Sean finally bothers to ask my name.

"So, Sheryl, why was that guy talking about you trawling for men?"

Here goes nothing. "I want to get pregnant. So I'm looking for a guy who'd be willing to knock me up. No strings attached."

Sean chuckles. Guess that's the first time he's heard that pickup line. I sip my beer, waiting for him to come at me with questions.

Sean seems surprisingly unfazed. "Are you asking me to fuck you?"

"Well, first I'd need proof you're disease free."

His expression shadows. "Proof?"

"Yeah. We could go to a clinic together."

"You start with 'no strings attached,' but this is starting to sound like strings." He moves one of my braids over my shoulder with his pinky finger and stares at the rise of my breasts over my corset as he talks.

"I just mean, no strings attached as far as the baby is concerned. Like no child support or—"

Sean laughs, and the sound is oddly cruel. He sets his hand on my knee, and I stare at the snake tattooed up his arm; its eyes are slits, and its fangs glisten like the snake is about to strike. "Listen, sweetheart, how about we trust each other and have a good time tonight?"

"That's not what I—"

Just then another dude in matching cut and colors claps a big hand on Sean's shoulder then flops into one of the chairs across from us. He eyes me as he asks, "Hey man, who you got here?"

This guy isn't as attractive as Sean. His hair looks dirty, and his eyes are mean.

"Sheryl. She wants our help to get pregnant."

Our help?

"Is that so?" Mr. Mean Eyes leans in, his gaze moving all over me like groping hands. He laughs, and I flinch at the stale scent of his breath.

In an instant, I'm on my skates, certain I want nothing to do with these two, but Sean catches my wrist in his grip.

"Where you going, gorgeous?"

"I need another drink."

"Well, Travis can help you with that, can't you, Travis?"

"Sure can." Mean-eyed Travis stands like he's going to head back in just as two more bikers in matching cuts join us on the patio, slapping Sean and Travis on the shoulders in greeting. *Fuck. I am so screwed right now.* How did I manage to land myself in the center of a biker gang bang? And not the *good* kind of biker gang bang.

I twist my wrist, but Sean tightens his grip and watches me with cold cruelty in his eyes. Gross. I can't believe I was prepared to have sex, willingly, with this guy. And that bored him. He's far more excited by my resistance now. *Well, fuck him…not literally.*

With my free hand, I slap Sean across the face. The assault stuns him enough to let go of my arm. It surprises all the rest of them, too, giving me a window of opportunity. I seize it, turning and pushing off the chair to skate back inside the bar. The group's surprise only lasts a moment.

"You think you can hit me and get away with it, you little bitch?" The once-handsome asshole shouts, spit flying from his lips, fire burning in the empty depths of his eyes as he stomps forward, leading the chase like they can catch me.

Fools. Don't they know who I am? I'm Sher Nobyl, the all-time winningest jammer in flat track roller derby history and five-time MVP. I'm Sher the shadow, a ghost on wheels. I've hit speeds of up to twenty miles per hour on these beauties—though I doubt I could top out tonight in this clingy little skirt. Still, I'm faster than these assholes could even imagine.

The two newest additions to the group are big burly guys who throw blocks to try and stop me. With a dodge and a weave, I duck beneath their grabby hands and thread the needle as I skate right between them.

I breathe a little easier when I reach the inside of the bar. From here I can skate right out the door, book it up the sidewalk, and be out of sight and out of mind in a blink. Except, there are people in the way. *Too many people.* The dinner theater next door must have let out because all the retirees who enjoy slumming at a dive bar after a night of comedy are lined up to order margaritas. There's no way I can navigate the crowd without hurting someone.

Fuck. In a split-second decision, I change course and crouch so I can limbo under the bar top and scoot right into the safe refuge of the service well with Manic. Too late, I notice the floor of the service well is covered in squishy, perforated rubber mats. My skates hit the lip of one, and I go sprawling across the floor, skinning my knees and elbows until the far wall stops my momentum with a bruising bang.

The elders in the room gasp and gawk, excitedly peeking over the bar to stare at me there on the ground. It's Manic's reaction, though, that has my attention.

"What the fuck?" He frowns at me, then his gaze turns to my pursuers, and his expression transforms. In general, Manic never looks particularly happy, but he never looks particularly angry either…until now. His expression is terrifying, a rising rage boiling in his eyes and hardening the lines of his face. When he speaks, it's like a dragon blowing fire across the bar. "Get the fuck out of here, now."

I can't see much from my vantage point here on the floor, but I can hear plenty, or rather, I can hear the absolute silence that falls over the room, except for the haunting chords of Elvis Costello's toxic ballad "I Want You" on the jukebox. It's like everyone is holding their breath, waiting. Manic's posture remains rigid as his fingers reach below the bar and wrap around the grip of a solid wood baseball bat. Slowly, he lifts it to his shoulder. It's a scary escalation. What if he's brought a bat to a knife fight, or a gun fight?

Manic repeats his words with a calmness so taut with tension my teeth clench. "Get the fuck out of here. Now."

I recognize Sean's voice when he finally speaks. "Best watch yourself with that pussy, my man. Bitch's got claws." *Asshole.*

Manic doesn't react, doesn't flinch, doesn't move a muscle. The sounds of commotion, a couple strings of choice cuss words, and the bang of the door slamming open and shut suggest my biker gang has left the building. But I don't exhale the breath I've been holding until Manic's posture loosens, and he slips the baseball bat back under the bar.

Apparently, everyone in the room was holding the same deep breath, and as soon as we let it out, excited chatter fills the space. The dinner theater crowd loved our little performance.

Show's over, folks.

I work to straighten from my gangly sprawl across the floor. Everything hurts. Manic helps me up, his mask of rage slipping away as he asks me, "Are you okay?"

I try to nod, but pain shoots up my neck, so I groan out, "Yeah."

I can't get steady on my feet. Even when Manic helps me out from behind the bar to a stool on the customer side, my knees wobble and my feet slip and slide like I'm trying to roller skate on ice.

"Everyone, I'm sorry for the delay. If you'll bear with me, I'll get your drinks served in a moment," Manic announces to the room as he goes back behind the bar and picks up the phone, pinching it between his ear and shoulder as he pours a glass of water.

Everyone watches me curiously while I check the condition of my knees and elbows. They're ugly, sure, skinned and bloody, but I've hurt myself far worse in derby practice. It's why I normally wear pads when I street skate. Not tonight though. They would have messed up the aesthetic of my sexy-pixie ensemble. Mistake #1.

When I'm a little steadier, I try to stand. Manic pulls his mouth away from the phone to shout at me, "Sit down."

"I just—"

"Sit the fuck down, Sheryl. Now."

I pout at him. "Don't talk to me like I'm a five-year-old."

"Then don't act like a fucking five-year-old. And while we're at it, don't start a bar fight with bikers ever again. We clear?"

"I didn't start a fight, I—"

"Sher, this isn't a game. Those weren't weekend warriors you were playing with. Those were one percenters. And I aimed a bat at them. So do me a big fucking favor and sit down while I take care of this. Okay?"

Take care of this? What is he talking about?

As irritated as I am, I comply. When Manic returns with a glass of ice water, I guzzle it and eye the first-aid kit he opens. With gentle fingers, he inspects the injuries to my knees and elbows and pokes through my hair like a momma monkey grooming her young.

It's sweet, the way he nurses my wounds, dabbing peroxide on the scrapes and gently blowing the sting away before applying bandages. For some reason I picture him doing that as a father, blowing on his daughter's boo-boos. My eyes tear up, and I bite back the sob lodged in my throat. Jesus, what is with my emotions tonight?

The door swings wide, and Manic jumps to his feet in a defensive posture. But the man who enters is another employee here. The guy is as big as a tank, so everyone just calls him Tank. He nods to a few friendly faces and smiles at the clutch of waiting customers as he comes over to Manic and me.

"How you feeling, sunshine?" Tank asks.

"I've been better. But I've also been worse."

Tank grins and turns his attention to Manic. Manic nods to his colleague. "Thanks for coming in so quick. I can come back to help you close—"

"No need. I got this. You take care of your girl."

Your girl? Who's Manic's girl? Wait... Is he talking about me?

"What's going on?" I ask.

"Tank's finishing my shift so I can take you home."

"Manic, I'll be fine. I've hurt myself way worse than this before."

"It's not because of your injuries."

I frown, confused.

"Do you think those guys actually went away? They're out there waiting for you. I'm not letting you skate home alone. Got it?"

He's mad at me again, which irks me. But he's probably right, which irks me even more. When Manic sees I'm not going to argue, he softens his tone and takes my hand in his. The contact sends a wave of warmth through me. And when he helps me balance on my feet, urging me toward the door with, "Come on, let's go," I follow without hesitation.

7

TUESDAY, NOVEMBER 30, 2010

What is happening right now? Where am I? How did I get here? And why am I wrapped up like meat in a burrito?

I blink my eyes open and try to understand the situation. It's bright enough I can recognize my bedroom, but when I try to turn over, I'm tucked in so tightly I can't budge. Twisting my neck for a better view, I wince as pain lances through my head and shoulders, reminding me of the biker-fight slash skater-wipeout last night.

Wiggling my arms loose from the comforter cocoon, I manage to pull part of the sheets up to check what I'm wearing. Everything. The corset and leather miniskirt are not the most comfy PJs, but they beat waking up naked with holes in my memory. Only my skates and socks have been stripped off. All around me are the sweet sounds of dog snores, indicating my boys have piled onto the bed with me, as per usual. What's new is the man asleep in their midst.

Manic.

He looks so peaceful when he sleeps. The curl of his eyelashes cast soft shadows over his cheeks, and his hair is smushed and messy. He's on his back, his hands spread out from his sides, one of them so close to me it's like he fell asleep holding my hand. The dogs have decided he's their favorite pillow, each of them draped across some part of him, with Mr. Wigglebottom's bottom pressed against me like he'll boot me out of bed if I move too much. Traitor.

I stroke my fingers through Manic's hair, liking the soft texture of the strands that tickle my hand. Manic wakes with a gasp, blinking at the brightness of daylight as he looks over at me. Then he smiles, and it's more smile than I've ever seen on him before, which is a stroke to the ole ego.

"Good morning," I say with a soft sigh.

"How are you feeling?" he asks.

"Sore." Understatement of the year. I really didn't think I was that hurt last night, but I can barely move this morning.

"Do you remember much? You seemed out of it when I got you home."

"I don't remember getting home or being home. Why don't I remember? I didn't drink *that* much."

"I think your adrenaline was in overdrive. When you crashed, you crashed hard. You wanted to lie on the floor with the dogs, but I carried you in here. I was afraid to leave you alone. Wanted to make sure you kept breathing." He looks a bit bashful, and isn't that the cutest thing ever.

"You watched me breathe?"

He nods. "Well, until I fell asleep. Sorry about that."

"Sorry? Whatever. I'm cooking you breakfast as a thank you for watching over me."

Manic gives me his small smile this time, like now that he's awake and fully functioning he's got a governor on his expressions, keeping them within carefully regulated limits. "It's after breakfast. It's past noon."

"Irrelevant. It's always breakfast time in my kitchen." I try to hop out of bed and stumble, my injured knees screaming at me along with every muscle in my body. It's a whole Hallelujah Chorus of screams.

I straighten my little leather skirt and tuck my wayward boob back into my corset—apparently sleeping in corsets is like sleeping in tank tops; the girls find a way out—then stretch as I walk to the kitchen. The dogs follow, their nails clicking on the floor in a rhythm I like to call the hungry hustle. I do an injury-modified version of the actual hustle to the rhythm in my head as I introduce Manic to the mutts, slip on my apron, and start pulling items out of the fridge.

"Where do you get your energy? It's impressive," Manic asks from the doorway.

I glance over the fridge door and grin at him. "Thanks. It's my disorder."

"What?" He yawns and glances around at the décor in my kitchen, taking in the bits of tile and broken glass I glued to the ceiling and jingling the little bells that hang from a vest on Clarice, the bald mannequin who sits atop my fridge. Then he moves to my coffee maker, setting it to brew. He's still in all his clothes, too, except his boots and socks. It's not every day you see a man like Manic padding around your kitchen barefoot. It's endearing.

"Attention deficit hyperactivity disorder," I clarify.

"Oh." He scratches his neck. I've noticed he does that when he's uncomfortable. "Do you take anything for it?"

I lay strips of bacon into a skillet, then start cracking eggs into a bowl. "Yeah, I basically take amphetamines, which is weird, right? Why would you give uppers to someone with hyperactivity? But they help. I mean, I still have a lot of energy and a skosh of executive disfunction, but at least I can hold onto a job now. I've been seeing a therapist for a few years, too, trying meditation and mindfulness. You know, shit like that." A cold frisson of anxiety rolls through me. "Why? Do you think I need more drugs? Am I too energetic?"

"No. No." Another little crack of that smile as he finds mugs in my cabinet and serves up coffee for us both. "I like it."

He likes it? My energy? Most people don't. I've been told, quite a few times, that it's "exhausting just watching me."

My cheeks flush with heat because I think maybe he's flirting. When a man takes you to bed and compliments your mental disorder the next morning, that's flirting, right? But probably not. I'm getting ahead of myself again. I turn my attention back to the eggs. Whoops. I've cracked a dozen. Sure hope he's hungry.

There's a knock at the door, and the dogs go bonkers in their usual way, everyone running to sniff excitedly at whoever is out there. My hands are coated with egg whites, and bacon grease sizzles in the skillet, so I turn to Manic, pleading, "Can you get the door?"

He raises a brow, like it's an odd request, but he does it anyway. I set my cast-iron skillet on a burner and get it going with a little pad of butter while I whisk the yolks and whites together, nearly spilling everything onto the floor when a tiny person lassos my legs together with his arms and hollers up at me, "Auntie Sher!"

Oh crap! I completely forgot I had a trampoline date with Tommy today. Well, perfect. I'll fill him up with eggs, and then he'll puke them all up while jumping.

"T-Man!" I holler back, set the food aside and wash my hands as quickly as I can before lifting the little dude up for a proper hug. Everything hurts when I do, and I consider painkillers, but instead turn to where Manic and Greg stand awkwardly side by side at the doorway, watching Tommy and me hug it out.

They're about the same height, but that's where the similarities end. Greg has always been pretty straitlaced, at least on the outside, while Manic looks like a menace. I like the disparity. I like that I have a whole spectrum of strangeness in my friend circle.

"Greg, you hungry?"

"No, I already ate, thank you. Just here to drop off Tommy. I can be back in a few hours. Sound good?"

I nod. "Works for me."

With that, Manic and Greg shake hands, and Greg leaves. Manic lingers by the door. "Maybe I should head out—"

"No. I'm cooking you breakfast, remember?"

Manic tries to smile, but it seems forced. Shit. What if all those times he told me he doesn't *want* kids, he was really telling me he doesn't *like* kids. Personally, I can't understand how that's even possible. Kids are the best! But that's just me and my opinion. Manic is very different from me and probably has very different opinions. And now I'm forcing him to stay here and hang out with a kid, his breakfast reward morphed into a punishment. God, I have got to stop being so pushy. If Manic wants to leave, I should let him.

I open my mouth to give Manic an out, but he steps into the room, indicating he's going to stay. So I make introductions.

With T-Man still perched on my hip, I say, "Little Mister Tommy Rollins-Sixkiller, I'd like you to meet my friend Manic Monroe."

Tommy giggles. "Manic is a weird name."

I smirk at the kid before agreeing with him. "It is a weird name for a weird guy. Guess it's a good thing 'weird' is so *cool*, because that makes Manic extra super-duper cool. Amiright?"

I nod, and Tommy mimics me. Manic's expression softens a little. Tommy wiggles for me to put him down, and when I do, he walks over to Manic and extends his hand in formal introduction, saying, "Hello."

After a brief hesitation, Manic shakes Tommy's hand, and my heart squeezes at the sight of the cutest thing I've ever witnessed in my whole damn life.

Then Tommy hollers at the dogs and darts off to chase them around the sofa in the living room. Manic's rigid posture melts into a relaxed pose as he leans against the wall.

"So that's Jake and Nicole's kid?" he asks.

"Yep, the first of three."

"And that dude who was here, Greg, is Ari's ex-husband, right?"

"Also yep."

Manic nods to himself and sips his coffee, watching me work. When the food is almost ready, he moves to the cabinets and pulls down a few plates without me having to ask. I start dishing up bacon and eggs on each, and he dutifully sets the table. Jeez, when I said he was cool, I didn't know he was *that* cool. The dude is, like, legit considerate.

"Tommy," I holler. "Time for second breakfast."

"Second bweakfast!" Tommy sings in response. The little hobbit is obsessed with the *Lord of the Rings* movies. When he goes to pull out one of the chairs, Manic helps, and my heart squeezes again. I should schedule an appointment with my doctor to have that checked out.

Manic takes the seat across from me, with Tommy between us, and I try not to notice how blissfully domestic this all feels.

After breakfast, I invent a new house rule: no jumping on the trampoline for an hour after eating, hoping it will reduce the likelihood of an upchuck incident. Tommy is so used to a similar rule for swimming that he doesn't question it, instead chasing the dogs in endless circles around the yard.

Manic settles onto a shady patch of my lawn, agreeing to watch the dogs and child for a moment. Not ready to put the "tramp" in trampoline while there are children present, I change into a sports bra and cutoffs. Rejoining the party in the yard, I program House of Pain's "Jump Around" on my playlist and crank the volume, then shimmy up onto the nylon of the trampoline.

Tommy comes racing over to me, and I pull him up. His first few steps on the bouncy mesh are like Neil Armstrong, so I narrate, "That's one small step for Tommy, one giant leap for...also Tommy."

I take his little hands in mine as we start to jump together. I keep it pretty tame for him and his short legs, none of the tricks or flips I usually perform when I'm on my own. Wouldn't want to ricochet the kid into the neighbor's yard.

Tommy is having the time of his life. His eyes sparkle with merriment, and he squeals with glee. We jump until every muscle in my body aches, my injuries from last night throbbing with pain.

I have to take a break and insist we both sit down on the trampoline for a moment. But Tommy isn't ready for a break. He leans into me to whisper in my ear, "Do you think Manic wants to jump?"

I glance over at the man, who's stretched on my lawn, sunning himself with the dogs. His fingers lazily stroke up and down Mr. Wigglebottom's back, and the dog grins with pure, unadulterated love. It's the cutest thing, but frankly, I'm surprised Manic is still here. After breakfast, I was expecting him to make his excuses and leave—especially after I tamed the titties into this bounce-proof bra. I'm not even putting on a good show for him. But there he is, watching us.

"I don't know," I answer. "Do you want to ask him?"

Tommy's hopeful gaze meets mine and he nods. I shimmy off the edge of the trampoline and heft Tommy down to the ground. He walks over to Sodapop and pets the big pooch's speckled head as he bashfully asks Manic, "Will you jump with me now?"

Manic's eyes widen like he's surprised—or maybe panicked—by the request.

Holding my breath, I wait for the rejection. Prepared to push through my aches and pains so the kid can keep jumping, but Manic says yes.

Wait. Did Manic just say yes?

I stare in awe as Manic pretends like he needs Tommy's help to get himself up off the ground. When Tommy tugs on his arm, Manic uses his legs to propel him up, then makes a big show of overcorrecting, like Tommy doesn't know his own strength.

Oh, my heart. This is the cutest thing I've ever witnessed.

Tommy belts out peels of adorable laughter. I could absolutely kiss Manic right now. Who knew he could be this…sweet? It's like there is this whole hidden person inside him, and damn do I want to see more.

I settle onto the sunny spot Manic vacated and watch the two of them, focused on the way Tommy's little fingers disappear inside Manic's big, tattooed hands and how they both smile. With each bounce, they soar higher. Tommy squeals with glee, and Manic's smile spreads beautifully across his face. It's like the sun breaks through his cloudy demeanor, filling us all with such warmth.

"Manic, huh?"

I jump out of my skin when Greg settles beside me on the grass. Admonishing the dogs, I complain bitterly, "Some guard dogs you lot are, letting any old Tom, Dick, and Greg wander in."

Greg chuckles at my side, loving on the lazy pooches. I watch Manic and Tommy jump for a while longer before answering Greg's question. "He's nice."

Greg squints from the sun, watching the same thing I am. "Yeah, he seems like a good guy."

Eventually, Manic and Tommy stop jumping and sit on the trampoline to catch their breaths. Tommy teaches Manic some elaborate hand shake, and they share some words, laughing at jokes I can't hear. I like that they have this private exchange while Greg and I look on. It seems extra special that way.

When Manic comes down and helps Tommy to the ground, the kid runs straight to his uncle. Breathless and excited, he proclaims, "Uncle Greg, I jumped on the trampoline."

"I saw. You went pretty high."

I tickle the kid. "You sure did. I'll bet you're tired now."

"I'm pooped," Tommy admits with a deep sigh.

His brow is sweaty, his hair sticking to the sides of his face, and he's rubbing his tired eyes. Indeed, he's pretty pooped. *His mom is going to love me!*

I give Tommy a long hug until I have to let him go. With one final farewell kiss on the cheek from me, his uncle carries him to the car, and I watch them leave. Manic comes up beside me, watching them leave too.

When Manic and I are alone again, I say, "You're still here."

"You're observant," he responds.

I'm glad you're still here. I keep that part to myself, instead asking, "Do you have to work tonight?"

He shakes his head. "Tuesdays and Wednesdays are my weekend."

"Oh! Me too. Well, not normally, but I had to work at the shelter during the holiday weekend, so I get the next two days off."

Manic nods.

Feeling self-conscious all of a sudden, I look down at my feet and kick the grass with my toes as I ask, "Wanna stay for dinner?"

Manic doesn't take long to consider before he answers, "Yeah."

8

It's too nice for walls and a roof. Tonight is one of those perfect Austin evenings, when it's not so hot it melts the skin off your face. And it's not cold yet either.

I grab a package of sausages from the fridge, and we take them back to the yard to cook. I'm the grill master, while Manic makes his signature margaritas from what I have in my liquor collection.

We sit at my patio table, eating Kielbasa, drinking margaritas, and watching the sun set. The dogs beg for food, and I toss them each little sausage treats until my plate is empty and everyone is happy. That's when the restlessness kicks in. I'm nervous.

I've known Manic for many years, but it was always in the context of the bar, a patron and server relationship with a hunk of tiled bar top between us. I've never been truly alone with him, in the quiet without a jukebox soundtrack, just spending time together, until tonight.

It's nice. He has a calming effect on me. Still, my legs twitch, and my fingers drum against the table until I think I'll go mad. Springing to my feet, I bounce a couple of times and ask, "Want to jump on the trampoline some more?"

"What about the one-hour rule?"

"Oh. I made that up so Tommy wouldn't puke all over the place."

Manic smiles out of half his mouth. "You go. I'll watch."

"Okay." I hustle over to the jumper and climb up onto my feet, bouncing away the excess energy. This thing is part of my therapy. It helps me focus, gives me a way to rest my racing mind, and it wears me out so I can sleep more easily.

I push myself higher and higher, pulling tricks each time I fly up into the air—a herkie one time, the splits the next, a backflip. Manic applauds from his chair as he watches.

Eventually, I burn myself out and come down to sit on the nylon, enjoying the way it sways under my weight. Manic comes over, and I move to let him have the trampoline for himself, but he stops me.

"I don't want to jump. I just want to sit with you."

Oh. Okay. Manic shifts his weight onto the fabric, and I can't help it when I slide down toward him. We meet in the middle, laughing awkwardly because we're practically on top of each other. My breath halts in my lungs as his lips come close to mine. His eyes shine with the last rays of the sun as he moves his gaze from my eyes to my mouth then back again.

Is he going to kiss me? I don't know. Do I want him to kiss me? I think so. With bated breath, I wait, but it doesn't happen. Instead, Manic lies on his back, spreading his weight out so it doesn't drag us both to the middle anymore.

Oh. Okay. I lie down too. It's a beautiful night, and as the sky darkens, I can see more and more stars sparkling above.

"Did you see that?" Manic asks in a whisper. I don't know why he's whispering, except something about the weightlessness of our bodies and the celestial beauty overhead makes this space special, a peaceful place, a place where you whisper.

"See what?" I whisper too.

"The falling star."

"I missed it." I sigh with sadness. "Did you make a wish?"

Manic doesn't answer, and I don't pry. Maybe he's not a star-wishing kind of guy, and that's okay. Next one that falls, I'll make wishes for us both.

"Do you see Leo?"

Huh? "Leo?"

"The constellation."

"Oh. No. I never learned those. Except for the two dippers that look like frying pans."

"Here." Manic shimmies a little and presses his cheek against mine. His stubble feels prickly. I like it and press my face to his a little harder. Then he lifts his hand and starts tracing a pattern overhead. Oh, he's pointing out the constellation.

Squinting one eye shut, I try to pay attention to what he's showing me. There are so many distractions: Manic's warmth against me; his heady, masculine scent; the sound of his breath going in and out; the way the shadows of night play in the pattern of the tattoos on his arm…

Then he fritzes my brain completely when he reaches for my hand, clasping it in his, and uses my finger to trace imaginary lines between the stars. His grip is rough, calloused, and strong, but somehow incredibly gentle. *Girl, focus.* I concentrate on paying attention again, fixating on the tip of my finger and the stars beyond. Angling my head, I grin when I finally make out the shape. "It really does look like a lion."

Manic nods, and that prickly stubble moves over my tender skin, sending a shiver through me. I half expect Manic to drop my hand, but he doesn't. Instead, he laces our fingers together and rests our joined hands between us.

Is this… Are we… What's happening here?

"So you went to a sperm bank, huh?" As far as random questions go, that's one of them.

"Yep."

"Did you find the donor you're looking for?"

"No, Obi Wan, they were not the donors I was looking for."

Manic chuckles at my lame joke, but he says nothing, like he's waiting for me to tell him more.

But what more is there to say? How much does he want to know? How much do I want to tell him? I was enjoying whatever this was we were sharing. But now we're back on *that* topic again.

Silence stretches between us, as far and wide as the starry night above, and it feels big and empty and depressing. I hate silence, so I fill it, "I don't think I'm going to go that route if I can help it."

"Why not?"

"Because," I huff with frustration, "I don't know. I guess I'm a traditional gal who wants to make a baby the old-fashioned way, with hot sweaty bodies and toe-curling orgasms, you know?"

"There's no guarantee some random dude is going to give you a toe-curling orgasm."

I smirk because he's right. The chances are low, actually. It'd be just my luck to get pregnant from bad sex and have to carry a mediocre memory of faking an orgasm every time I looked into my child's eyes.

With a dramatic huff, I complain, "I know. Don't you think I know that? God, why is this so hard? Everyone else has what they want with their perfect lives and perfect loves and perfect babies. I just want a third of that—I mean I want all of it, but I will settle for a third—and I spend all my energy hoping and praying and begging and compromising, and still I can't have any of it."

Shit. That was a really whiny, passive-aggressive rant, wasn't it? I shut up, not sure how to save us from the bottomless pit I'm digging into this conversation.

Silence falls between us again, and Manic squeezes my hand a little tighter, which I like. But then he lets it go, which I don't like. He props himself on his elbow so he can look me in the eyes when he says, "I'm sorry."

I'm not sure what he's sorry about. I would ask, but his shift in position has brought us closer together again. With his weight up on his elbow now, I slip and slide until I'm more or less under him. I grin up and he smiles down at me. It would be the perfect moment for him to kiss me, but instead, he repeats himself. "I'm sorry."

"Why?"

He considers for a moment, not moving, still balancing his weight so he's right over me, so close. When he speaks, he's whispering again, and it feels so intimate. "I wish I could be that guy for you."

"But you can't?"

He shakes his head, no. It's the same answer he's given me all along, but this time, I see something in his eyes as he rejects me.

Sadness, regret, longing… I'm not sure, and he quickly looks away as he settles on his back beside me.

I don't think I've ever felt as alone as I do right now. I'm right here beside him and still shut out of whatever turmoil brews inside.

I'm a little mad, actually. We were having a good time until he brought this subject up. Now we're disconnected again, for reasons he won't share.

"Manic, are we friends?"

"I don't have friends."

Oh.

"But I do have people I care about. Not many. I can count those people on my fingers."

Oh?

"And you're one of them."

Oh! I almost shimmy with excitement at his admission. It's the closest thing to emotional affection I think he's ever shown me. I consider the best response, something meaningful and special to show him that he counts for me too. "Which finger am I?"

Manic holds up his hand between us and wiggles his pinky. "This is you, my little pinky Sher."

My little pinky Sher. Well if that isn't weirdly romantic, I don't know what is.

"You're one of my finger people too. This is you." I hold up my middle finger.

Manic laughs, like truly laughs, and I think it's the first time I've ever heard that sound. It's lovely the way his laughter shakes his whole body and quakes through mine and sends little waves of motion undulating across the trampoline.

We've settled into another shared silence, just us and the stars, when Manic speaks again. Slightly more than a whisper this time, he says, "Ten years ago, I had a vasectomy. So even if I gave you a toe-curling orgasm, it wouldn't give you what you want."

Oh. Wow. Okay. My mind races with questions, thoughts, ideas, too many to count or even consider. Just one word surfaces, one question to rule them all: Why?

"I know you're probably wondering why I had the vasectomy. But I'm not ready to talk about that yet."

I blink up at the stars, lost. There is so much he's saying to me right now, even though he's saying very little. I am desperate to learn more, to *understand* more, but the why can wait. I'm glad he trusted me to share that truth. So I let it go. "Okay."

And there's something I need to share with him too. "You know, a baby is just one of the things I want."

He glances over at me, his gaze hot against my skin, but he doesn't make a move or ask me to explain. Not that I need to; I think he understands perfectly. I slide my hand to his and lace our fingers, then let myself drift away with my thoughts, with the night, with exhaustion, holding onto him like we're a pair of river otters floating under the stars, relaxing together, linked.

9

WEDNESDAY, DECEMBER 1, 2010

I wake with the sun, the heat of its rays on the side of my face as it peeks above the horizon of my fence. Bleary-eyed, I squint against the brightness and jigsaw the pieces of last night's memories back together.

Shaken awake by my movement, Manic makes a low grumbly noise in the back of his throat. It's far too sexy to be an effective deterrent from engagement. On the contrary, it makes me want to cuddle up with the grumpy grizzly bear.

Instead, I get a brilliant idea. "Let's go swimming."

Manic emits more grumbles as he flops onto his back and covers his eyes with an arm. He does manage to speak a little though, asking, "What? Why? Where?"

He's clearly not a morning person. Unlike me. "Swimming. Because. The lake."

"I don't have my swim trunks."

"We won't need them where we're going."

Manic peeks one eye at me over his arm. "You want to go to Hippie Hollow, really?"

"Really!"

"It's November."

"That statement is both accurate and irrelevant."

"The water will be cold."

"Are you telling me that Manic Monroe, the guy who hangs shit from his dick piercing, can't handle a little cold water?"

Manic grins. "Hanging shit from my dick elongates it. Cold water has the opposite effect."

I laugh. "Who are you trying to impress with that thing?"

"You, of course."

What? I flop onto my side so I can see him better and poke him in the stomach. "Oh! You confusing boy, why can't you make some sense for once? Why are you flirting with me after you stone-cold rejected me a couple days ago?"

"I rejected getting you pregnant. I didn't reject *you*."

"What's the difference?"

"Everything."

"Whatever." It's way too early for deep thoughts. I want float-on-the-surface thoughts right now. And speaking of floating on the surface... I hop up onto my feet, being extra bouncy. My movements send Manic rolling toward the middle, so he has to get up too. On our feet, we face off. "As I was saying, let's go swimming."

Manic stares at me for a moment, mulling it over. I realize too late that my simple plan of inviting Manic to join me for a swim is actually pretty complex and layered with meaning. I'm inviting him to spend time with me...naked. And he's flirting with me. Hmm.

Before I can think through the intricacies of my invite, though, Manic looks me dead in the eyes. "Okay. But we're taking Sally."

Who the hell is Sally?

Apparently, Sally is a motorcycle. Or, as Manic puts it, "She's a fully restored 1986 FXRS Low Rider."

"Oh, a vintage Harley—be still my heart." I purr my words and flutter my lashes, acting like a cat in heat for the sexy black and chrome beast parked beside my green dragon—aka my Subaru—in the driveway. I must have been really out of it the other night not to remember taking a ride on this beauty. When he smirks, I ask, "Why do you call her Sally?"

"As in Sally MacLennane." When I stare blankly, he adds, "The Pogues song," then sings a few verses. He can't hold a tune. It's adorable.

Seeming embarrassed, he changes the subject by shoving the only helmet at me and commanding, "Put this on."

While I strap it on, he straddles the bike, then helps me adjust the chin strap to cinch it tight. I hop awkwardly and manage to swing my leg over the bike and snuggle up to him, wrapping my arms around his middle when he starts the engine with a rumbly roar.

I love motorcycles, always have. There's an energy to them that you don't get when you're driving a car, even a fast car. It's the wind, the sunshine, the loud sounds. Plus, everything—as in *everything*—vibrates. It feels feral and wild, and I squeeze my arms around his middle when he cranks the engine and we take off. That's the other thing I love about motorcycles—everything you do on them, you do together. Riding, unlike driving, is intimate. Both Manic and I move with the road and with each other as we make our way through the curves and switchbacks of the hill-country roads that take us west to the lake.

Hippie Hollow is hands down the best nude beach in Texas. Of course, it's the only nude beach in Texas, so it's an easy list to rank on. The rocky shore is nearly deserted on this chilly morning. Just a few elderly regulars bob in the water or stretch out like leathery lizards on rocks.

Manic and I find a nice flat boulder to call our own. I lay out a couple of towels and then get to stripping. He watches me. It's like he's always wondered what my hidden parts look like. I'm not shy, so I get naked and let him look his fill at this fine specimen of womanhood. He gives me the cutest little hungry-puppy look and freezes as I spin for his perusal. "Like what you see?"

"Yes, I really like what I see, Sheryl. I always have."

His tone is so serious when he says it, so matter-of-fact as he pays me a weirdly huge compliment. It catches me off guard. I open my mouth to respond but just sputter awkwardly.

He thinks I'm beautiful? I mean… Of course, I already knew I was, but hearing him say it carries a special sort of weight, affecting me on a deeper level. These are definitely not float-on-the-surface thoughts, so I ignore the muddy emotions Manic's words stir up and ogle him as he strips.

He has the perfect amount of muscles for my taste, long and lean, and his tattoos look especially colorful in the bright sun. I want to scrutinize every inch of him. Manic has always seemed sort of rough to me, like his edges are sharp enough to cut. But there's a softness to him, too, a vulnerability that I've always found super freaking sexy. Which is why, when he hesitates to drop his jeans, I nearly salivate like Pavlov's dogs. And when he finally does, I gasp a little bit. Oh. My. He's erect.

I glance around at the other swimmers and sunbathers, wondering what the proper etiquette is for a boner at the nude beach, but it's practically deserted on this cold November morning, so I stop worrying and look my fill.

I mean, I've more or less seen his dick when he performs. But he'd always wrapped it in duct tape to avoid being arrested for indecent exposure. Without the duct tape condom, Lord Almighty, it's a gorgeous dick. Veiny. I love veiny dicks, and I love the piercing that loops through the tip. Now that he's committed to the nudity, he's not shy about his body. He stands facing me, looking as delectable as hard candy. Yum.

Surface deep, I remind myself, then turn and step into the water. It's cold, sure, but so is the air, and I'd rather shiver in the water, so I step in deeper, as far as my tits, before I start to squeal from the frigid temperature. The water is in the sixties, not cold enough to kill us. But super-duper bracing.

I turn to him, noticing that his cock still stands proud as he watches me, and my teeth chatter a little as I say, "Come in the water and shrink that thing down, big boy."

With a quirk of his lip he answers, "Whatever you say, little girl." He follows me in, walking until he's balls deep, then dunks under the surface. He comes up gasping, teeth chattering, but swims to get his blood pumping.

Not one to be left behind, I dunk under and swim with him out to the buoy line that marks the edge of the swimming area. I float on my back, letting the breeze chill my damp skin as the winter sun works to warm it. Glancing over at Manic, I find him staring again, his eyes fixed on my tight nipples and the piercings through each. He's not the only one into body mod here.

Feeling a bit too exposed and vulnerable, I flip forward, do a somersault in the water to get my hair out of my face and surface to tread water beside him.

"I'm bipolar," Manic says.

I blink. It's all I can do. I'm stunned. A statement like that is not even remotely surface deep.

"That's why I got a vasectomy. I've read that the condition can be hereditary, and I don't want to curse some kid with this." He splashes his hand up from the water to thump his temple with his thumb. "My mom was fucking nuts, but she was never diagnosed, or if she was, no one told me. It wasn't until I was almost thirty when I found out the hard way I had it too."

It breaks my heart to learn he got a vasectomy for that reason. I don't understand it at all, but I want to. "What happened? How did you find out?"

"It was during a tour with the circus. I was in a deep depression. Cutting myself. A lot. I knew I needed help before I made the final cut, so I went to a clinic in one of the towns we hit, and the doctor prescribed antidepressants. They worked...too well. I shot straight up into mania and had an episode on stage, cutting myself in the show. The guy who ran the circus frowned on spilling blood in our acts, so everyone knew something was wrong when I cut the shit out of my arms."

"Why did you cut yourself?"

"Because... It felt so fucking...*good*." His face turns pensive, and he pauses a moment before saying more. "They took me to the ER, and I was put on a forty-eight-hour psychiatric hold, and then held for another forty-eight hours until they admitted me to a psychiatric facility for two weeks. The circus left without me, and I was trapped in Ohio while the doctors figured out what was wrong with me."

"That sounds very traumatic."

"It was a turning point in my life. Nothing has been the same since. And that's why I can't be your guy. I'm sorry if I've made you feel undesirable. God, if anything, you're the one thing in this world I truly desire."

What?

"But I can't give you what you want. I don't want to curse your child with my diagnosis."

A flush of anger courses through me. He thinks he's a curse? He's gone through with self-imposed eugenics to spare a child from being like him? What the hell? He's amazing, and he doesn't even realize it.

I swim over and wrap my arms and legs around him. He freezes, nearly dunking us both when he stops treading water. But he recovers quickly, wrapping his arms around me and kicking his legs to keep us afloat.

"First of all, consider this—you're not bipolar."

"I am—"

"Hey! Don't interrupt me. Just listen."

Manic smirks, but he zips his lips and listens.

"It's like that old saying, Is she wearing the dress, or is the dress wearing her? "

He frowns. "I have no idea what you're talking about."

"Consider for a moment the possibility that *you're* not bipolar but rather you *have* bipolar disorder."

"What's the difference?"

"Well, I mean, don't get me wrong—everyone is allowed to experience their diagnosis in their own way. But the way I see it, your bipolar disorder is part of you, but it's not the whole of you. It's like, you're a delicious cake, right? And you're made up of all these yummy nummy layers. Your bipolar disorder is just one layer. It's the lemon cake layer."

Manic grins with one side of his mouth, and his arms squeeze me a little tighter against him.

I continue. "It's the same with me and my disorder. They are pieces of us, but they do not define us. We wear the dress; it doesn't wear us. Second of all, you're not a curse."

"I'm broken, Sher."

I fight him on that. "You're not broken. You're amazing. You're fascinating and funny and strange." My eyes catch on his, holding his gaze, and I soften my voice. "You're beautiful and kind and good. And every single day, you have to work your ass off to overcome shit that other people don't even have to imagine. So don't ever think that your disorder makes you less than them. It makes you *more*. Trust me, I should know. I've had to work hard to be this awesome."

I wink with that last part, and he looks at me like I've lost all my marbles. Like the marbles have trickled right out of my ears and splashed into the water. Maybe he didn't understand. I'll say it again. "Manic, you're amazing, not despite your disorder but because of it. Anyone who thinks otherwise is wrong."

There is a moment when I can see him, like, really see him, his eyes showing me the way in, and I can see all his strengths and vulnerabilities, all his heart and soul. It's so beautiful. *He's* so beautiful. But he shuts those clear blue eyes, closing himself off to me again.

"Have you ever had suicidal ideations?" he asks.

"No."

"Well, it's scary. It's like there's this parasite in your brain, and it's trying to kill you. It wiggles into your thoughts, and it sounds logical as it tries to convince you to make the final cut. And the rest of you knows it's dangerous, knows it's trying to hurt you, but you're paralyzed, unable to shut it up."

Jesus.

"I don't want to bring a kid into this world to have to deal with that. Kids are pure, filled with joy and happiness, and this, it…taints me. I was afraid to even touch Tommy yesterday for fear I'd rub off on him."

I know that feeling well.

Manic brings a hand out of the water like he wants to touch my face, but he doesn't. His palm hovers so close, but not close enough. "I'm afraid to touch you too. You're so bright. I don't want to dim your light."

Goddamnit. I wish he didn't feel this way about himself. And I truly don't know how to fix it, so I take his hand and kiss the palm. If he thinks he's tainted, it's time to dispel that myth right now. I move his palm to touch my cheek, and he flexes his fingers, caressing them over my skin, curling them around the back of my neck, tangling them in my wet hair.

Hovering my mouth so close to his I can practically taste the sweetness of his breath, I whisper, "You're not tainted." I lean in a little more and brush my lips against his as I add, "You're not cursed. You're wonderful."

Manic freezes, his hand on my face trembles, and he tightens his grip around the back of my neck, holding us both there. Below the water, his other hand clutches me tight against him, his fingers spread across my ass. I wonder what he'll do next. My heart pitter-patters in my chest, and my breath comes in a jagged shiver, my nerves tingling with anticipation.

His eyes bore into mine, and in the depths of his gaze, I see he's waging some inner war. I watch and wait, growing more desperate for him by the moment. Finally, I guess he either wins or loses the battle because he hisses out a breath and smashes his mouth against mine.

God, his kiss. It consumes me. It devours me. His lips are soft even as his kiss is hard. I gasp, and his tongue probes into my mouth with sweet demand. Our tongues clash, and our tongue piercings make erotic little clinking sounds like fighters jousting.

His hand on my ass squeezes, and between us I feel the thick throb of his cock, desperate for me like I'm desperate for him.

And in the midst of all this, the revelation hits me like a bolt of lightning: Manic is the man for me. Forget about the kid—it's the man I want now. No doubt in my mind. All this time, I've looked and looked for him, and he was standing right in front of me.

Manic pulls away from my mouth and presses his forehead against mine, staring so deep into my eyes I reckon he can see straight into my soul just as I can see into his. I open my mouth like I have something insightful to say, but all that comes out is, "I really like lemon cake."

Laughter rumbles through him and in a deep, dark voice, he whispers, "So do I."

10

After our enlightening swim and epic make-out session, Manic and I haven't spoken, and it's driving me nuts. Everything that used to be relaxed and easy between us is weird and confusing now. I mean, what are we? I've been friends with Manic for a long time, but never once has he stuck his tongue down my throat while I rubbed my clit against his rock hard cock. That's all new.

Are we friends? Kissing friends? Is dry humping in water just a casual thing that friends do sometimes? I don't have friends per se, other than Ari and Nicole, and I've totally made out with Ari, so... maybe? I don't know.

It's so weird and confusing.

I haven't been that hot and bothered in eons, maybe never. Manic's mouth untangled the spaghetti of my brain and had me considering dumb things like, *It'd be so easy to slip and slide onto his beautiful cock right now.*

But Hippie Hollow has a strict No Fucking policy, and I didn't want to get banned for life, so I pushed off of him and floated with my thoughts for a while. Now we're on the shore, lounging like lizards on our rock, and not speaking. It's not one of those angry nonspeaking situations, just an awkward one.

Manic lies on his stomach looking luscious as the sun brightens his skin and the ink of his tattoos. I can't stop ogling his ass and the way it slopes so smoothly to the small of his back. My eyes inch along the muscles of his naked body, and, *God*, I want to touch him and lick him and suck his dick.

My fingers ache with the need to reach for him. My body can barely resist the urge to sit on him and massage his back, to feel every inch of his strength. Plus, I think a back rub would benefit him. He carries a lot of tension in his shoulders. I took a couple of classes on energy and healing, and I could make him feel so good…

"Can I massage your back?" I blurt out my question like it's burning my tongue.

Manic squints one eye open at me.

"I was going to crawl up onto your ass and start rubbing, but I remembered I should ask first before I touch people. So, may I please massage your back?"

"Uh, okay."

I climb on top of him and stretch my fingers before I attack. I'm really good at massage. My hands might be small, but they're mighty. Reaching into my bag, I rub a couple drops of coconut oil into my palms to smooth over his skin. He moans, just from that little bit of touch, and I smile. This is going to be fun.

Starting with some light petrissage, I move my hands in a smooth, kneading motion to awaken his muscles and stimulate circulation. Then I get into the good stuff, moving my hands up his back like lobster claws, pulling and rolling the skin over the muscle.

He moans again, long and low, and my eyes flutter shut from the deep masculine sound of it. It's sexy when he makes those noises, and his body feels so good, hard and soft in all the best ways. I run my thumbs along his spine, working the tension loose, and that's when he comes unglued. "God, Sheryl, yes. That feels fucking amazing."

Damn, he gives good praise. I purr. Literally purr.

Manic's moans are starting to hint at desperation, and some of the tension returns to his body as his hands fist the towel above his head, like there's something—someone?—he desperately wants to hold onto right now. Is he as turned on as I am? Because I'm getting so wet he can probably feel it where I'm sitting naked on his ass.

With my thumbs working the tension loose from the base of his neck, I lean forward to ask, "Do you want to go back to my place?"

"Yes." He answers before I even finish the question, and he rolls over beneath me until I'm straddling his waist and his rock-hard cock juts up between us. We both look down at it, then our gazes connect, and he repeats, "Yes."

I barely have time to greet the dogs before Manic takes the lead, and he's one of those men who leads with his tongue. He cups my face in his palms and takes my mouth in long languid strokes. It's easy to imagine his tongue on other parts of my body, the piercing teasing me with each taste.

I moan into his mouth, and he picks me up, coaxing me to wrap my legs around him as he carries me to my bedroom. With a kick, he closes the door—no dogs allowed for a while. He tosses me on the bed, then dives down onto me, pawing at my clothes.

"I want to taste you," he says against my lips.

I pull away from his kiss to nod furiously, wanting to say, "yes, please," but my stupid brain betrays me. "Do you have any venereal diseases?"

Manic stops licking my throat to raise his head up and blink down at me, then he laughs.

Shit. I think I spoiled the mood with my question. But... "It's important to discuss these matters *before* we start with the taste testing and other fuckery. Cuz, I don't have any condoms in the house, so whatever we do today, it's going to be raw."

"I have a condom and no VDs."

"You don't need the condom. I haven't had sex since the recession started. Not that the two things are related, I just mean—"

Manic kisses me. And thank God he does because I really need to stop talking about the economy and venereal diseases. His hands curl into my hair as his tongue slides into my mouth, taking me in deep, long strokes. I gasp, breathing him into my lungs, and clench my fists in his shirt, just to hold on as he takes me under his spell. His kiss is mind-altering then mind-numbing and eventually mind-blowing. By the time we come apart to catch our breath, I can't remember the English language let alone what I was talking about.

When he turns his attention back to stripping me out of my clothes, I have no concerns, commentary, or complaints. Manic does what he wants: He tastes me. My neck and shoulders, my tits and nipples, and finally he slides his tongue down my body, tracing a circle around my navel before he comes to a stop between my legs.

He slips my knees over his shoulders and clasps his tattooed hands across my waist—sexiest belt ever—holding me still as his mouth goes to town. The man clearly has an oral fixation because he doesn't just eat me, he devours me.

"You taste like happiness," he mumbles. And what a thing to say. I try to imagine what happiness tastes like but can't keep my thoughts straight as he dips his tongue inside while the calloused pad of his thumb strokes my clit.

His tongue piercing wreaks havoc on my senses. I yelp and writhe, and his fingers clinch tighter, digging into the flesh of my hips, holding me still so he can feast. God, his hands are sexy. I want him to fuck me with his FUCK fingers and get me off with the OFF! fingers.

And the Lord must hear my prayers because that's exactly what Manic does. Using what I'm pretty sure is his middle U finger to press inside me, he works with a combination of teeth, tongue, and piercing to tease my clit until I'm hardly coherent, breathless and writhing.

"Fuck yes, that's my girl. Come for me, baby," he commands, and I have no control over my own body when he says things like that to me. Following his orders, I melt into him, my body quaking as I arch off the bed and scream so loud the dogs howl and scratch at the door.

When I come down from my heavenly high, I pull Manic up and kiss him deeply. I want to taste happiness too. Then I strip his clothes off and push him onto his back to take him into my mouth.

I've wanted to do this for hours. And I want to do this for hours. I love giving head. It's weirdly relaxing, plus it makes me feel powerful, like I'm She-Ra: Princess of Power or Xena: Warrior

Princess. I'm Sheryl: Princess of Penis in control of this big strong man. I like it.

I take Manic deep, letting my piercing scrape along the underside of his cock, then revel in the sounds he makes. He's so sexy when he gasps and begs.

He grasps for me, too, pulling my hips to move me to a new position. And when I move to where he wants me, I end up straddling his face. *Oh!*

Still sucking him, I squeal a little when he sets upon me with his fingers and tongue. *This* is happiness. Happiness is sixty-nine.

Manic teases my ass and slowly presses his pinky inside as he strokes two fingers into my pussy. And ain't that a shocker. I yelp with surprise at this strange new sensation, and he pauses to check in. "Is this okay?"

"Yes," I moan, and he strokes his fingers nearly all the way out before pushing back in, a little deeper each time. His tongue juts out to tease my clit as he keeps stroking me, and I completely unravel.

Good. God. He has a wicked tongue.

I tease him, too, tickling his Prince Albert with the tip of my tongue, then swallowing him to the hilt. He groans and pumps his fingers a little harder and deeper inside me. But not so hard and deep that I come. We both take our time with this, perfectly content to suck and tickle and taste the other in languorous delight rather than the normal frenzied rush to orgasm.

I love it. For me, good sex is about the journey. And this is really good sex.

Finally, I start to suck him with gusto, ready to bring him off in my mouth, desperate to taste his happiness. Does semen without sperm taste the same? This inquiring mind wants to know. But I don't think too much about it because he's working me to another orgasm too.

I take his balls in one hand and gently scratch them with my nails as I pump my other fist and suck the head. With a huff and a groan, his orgasm slams into him and he comes in hot, delicious streams against the back of my throat. I swallow everything he gives me.

He pumps his fingers inside me with the same rhythm I use to suck his cock dry, and his tongue lashes my clit until I explode with my second orgasm, screaming and gasping, still fisting his length like I might fly away if I don't hold onto something.

My dogs are in a panic in the hallway, howling like wolves, confused and upset by the sounds I'm making. But me, I'm spent. Completely totally, one hundred percent spent. Collapsing on top of Manic, my face mashed against his thigh, my eyes drift shut with sleepiness. Manic moves me around like a little rag doll until we're realigned face to face. He wraps me in his big, strong arms, cuddling me so gently, and kisses my forehead. "I've always wanted to do that with you, Sher."

I grin as I wiggle a little tighter against him. "Really? Even the butt stuff?"

"Especially the butt stuff."

"I guess Ari was right," I sigh.

"About what?"

"She said you're in love with me."

Manic's eyebrows hit his hairline.

Shit. That was the wrong thing to say. I used the L word at the wrong time. Literally, we just finished sucking and hand fucking each other. This is no time for any L words other than "leave" or "see you later." I messed this all up.

Cringing, I glance up, almost afraid to meet Manic's gaze. I half expect him to make an excuse and a rapid exit, but he doesn't. He hugs me a little tighter as he says, "Hmm."

11

THURSDAY, DECEMBER 2, 2010

"Let me get this straight—you said the L word, and he just fell asleep?" Ari asks.

"No. I told him that *you* said he felt the L word for me, then he said, 'Hmm' and fell asleep," I explain.

Ari stands there staring at me, a giant purple dildo in one hand and a riding crop in the other. After a moment of contemplation, she says, "Hmm," and walks away.

"See? There's that 'hmm' again. What does the 'hmm' mean?"

"I can't tell you what his 'hmm' means, but my 'hmm' means that I think I'm right. He's in love with you." Ari hands the dildo to the cheerfully helpful sex-shop clerk.

"Or he wants my body, and he's willing to tolerate my use of the L word to get with it."

"Well, of course he wants your body—that's a given, but he also spent the night, twice. That's not nothing, Sher. It tells me he wants to chart new territory with you."

She might be right. Manic never once used those other dreaded L words like "leave" and "see you later" with me. This morning, when I got up for work, he got up too. After redressing in the clothes he'd been wearing for days, he kissed me and said he'd see me soon. Not "later"—"soon." That tiny little word choice felt huge.

I've been bouncing off the walls ever since, desperate to tell Ari everything. Which is why I'm here with her in a sex shop while she browses for Alex's Christmas present.

I peruse a display of nipple clamps as I change the subject. "Speaking of new territory, he stuck his finger in my ass. No one's ever done that before."

Ari turns to me slowly, her brows raised in curiosity. "You're joking! You've never tried anal?"

Everyone assumes because I'm a loud-mouthed libertine, I've done it all. I haven't, not by a long shot. I shake my head.

Ari bonks me on the forehead with the riding crop like she's a fairy godmother and it's her wand, stating, "Oh, girl, you are in for a treat."

"You like it?"

"Some of my best orgasms are anal," Ari insists and the salesclerk nods too.

Interesting. "It doesn't hurt?"

"It can. You have to approach it right. *He* has to approach it right."

"What's the right way to approach it?"

"Lots of prep, fingers first, a plug. You gotta get your sweet booty ready for his love injection."

I laugh.

"And lube, lots of lube. Then when he comes at you with his hot, veiny cock"—yeah, I told her about that—"you have to relax."

"Relax?"

She nods. "If you tighten up, it's not a fun feeling. Relax those muscles and let him in because dude, I'm telling you the orgasms are phenomenal. If Manic is starting you out with a pinky, then I'd say he knows how to do things right."

Now it's my turn to say, "Hmm."

"Oh! You know what you need?"

"What?" I ask, but Ari is already hurrying off to some corner of the store, so I follow.

I find her at a display of cute little headbands with furry animal ears on them, but that's not what Ari grabs to show me. With a giant smile, she spins on her heels and turns to reveal her find.

"A tail!" She squeals as she swings a silvery-gray foxtail from her fingers, and attached to the fluffy tail is a stainless-steel butt plug.

By gosh, I think she's right: I totally need a tail.

The ever-changing Austin skyline looms over me as I cross under the freeway, a flock of building cranes roosting for the night. I skate past the community service offices and the state lottery headquarters to the part of Sixth Street they call "Dirty" with a few dirty thoughts of my own. I'm in the mood to shake my tail feather at a certain someone.

Gotta say, butt plugs are fun. Getting it in was interesting, and there's still lube all over my bathroom counter. But now that it's in there, I like the way it feels. Strange and solid inside, soft and fluffy outside.

I'm fully clothed, perfectly presentable, but underneath my skirt I'm not wearing any underwear, and the tail swishes against my upper thighs as I power past tourists and locals toward the busy part of downtown. The tip of my tail peaks out from under the hem of my skirt, so those in the know will easily spot my naughty little secret.

I screech to a stop at the door to Manic's bar and swing it open, the sound of dozens of conversations washing over me as I roll inside. The bar is fairly crowded tonight, but it often is on Thursdays. Thursdays are basically First Friday in Austin, when everyone gets an early start on the weekend. My skates clatter over the tile floors, but no one can hear above the chatter. Still, Manic notices my entrance, his eyes fixing on me as he pours a beer. I skate past him, over to the pull-up portion of the bar and wait.

After he sets the beer aside and transacts the sale, he comes to me and lifts up the bar top that separates us. His smile is a little wider today. "Hey there, Sonny Sher, what brings you in here tonight?"

"I'm teasing you."

"Teasing me?"

"Yep!" I spin on my skates, arch my back to push my ass out, then flip my skirt up to show him the tail. I'm in my old skate uniform, the naughty Catholic schoolgirl skirt. Talk about a tease.

I can tell a few of the bar patrons catch the show by the sounds of their reaction. And my exhibitionist side likes the idea of people watching, apparently. I give my tail feather a little shake before dropping my skirt and spinning back around.

The look on Manic's face surprises me. I think he's mad. No, worse than mad—he looks furious. The bar top candlelight flickers over the lines of his deep scowl and in the depths of his cold, hard eyes.

Before I can ask him why he's upset, he turns his attention to someone else, shouting for them to keep an eye on things. Then he steps out to my side of the bar. My excitement at his proximity vanishes when he grabs my arm and drags me toward the bathrooms. Before I have the wherewithal to stop my forward roll, he swings the men's room door open and pulls me inside, locking it behind us.

Wait. I'm confused. Is his face emoting anger or lust? Has he brought me in here to fight or fuck?

"Don't ever fucking do that to me again!" Manic yells at me.

So no fucking then? "What did I do wrong?"

His eyes flash with blazing anger and he shouts, "Don't come into my work to fuck with me, Sher. I know to you this is just a shitty dive bar, but this is my job. This job is how I keep a roof over my head. Don't come in here shaking your ass in front of my coworkers and customers like it's a big fucking joke."

"No one saw." I try to defend myself.

"Everyone at the bar saw. The camera over the register saw," Manic barks back. "And now here I am, having to take the time to explain this to you instead of doing my fucking job."

Tears collect at the corners of my eyes, and I try to hold them back, but it's no use. I'm mortified, and I feel so stupid with this tail stuck in my ass. I haven't felt this much shame since I was a kid, the source of my parents' perpetual embarrassment.

Manic must see some of what I'm feeling from the look on my face because he softens his tone when he says, "Go home, Sher, please. We'll talk about this later."

He reaches forward like he wants to touch me, but something stops him. Instead, he turns and washes his hands before returning to work.

I remain there, stunned and gutted and desperate to quell the coming onslaught of tears. Sniffing and blotting the corners of my eyes, I look around at the band stickers layered over the urinal trough. My humiliation is made worse by the fact that Manic delivered this dressing down in the smelly confines of a dive bar men's room.

Being made to feel stupid makes me mad. Anger floods through my veins, washing over me in hot flashes and cold chills. I can't believe I plugged a tail into my ass for that man. And instead of appreciating the effort, the ungrateful jerk humiliated me.

Well, fuck you very much, Manic! If you can't handle me at my best, then you can't handle me at all...or whatever.

It's fury that stops the tears, and it's fury that pushes me forward. I shove the bathroom door open and skate straight for the exit. Ignoring Manic's side of the room completely, I swish my hips extra wide a couple of times. Let this stupid tail be the last he ever sees of me.

Back across the freeway, chain-link barriers surround construction sites where pinata shops and music venues used to be, replaced now by the wood and steel skeletal structures of future condominiums. Everything around here is being replaced by condos. The city is changing. Everything is changing...except me. My friends are building their families like my city is building its skyline. Even my beloved roller derby league is upgrading from her humble beginnings in a roller rink to bleacher seating at the convention center next season. And me, I'm still the same unruly child rolling around on skates, a little brat with too much energy.

I want to change, too, so I skate into the beauty supply shop beside my favorite mercado to hunt for a new hair color. The Atomic Green shade has a certain appeal, but it's too bright and cheery for the headspace I'm in so I keep browsing. Then I find it, the color to match my mood: Ultraviolet Void. That'll do.

With a bag of churros under one arm and a jar of hair dye under the other, I head home. The dogs are confused by my tail, so I rush to the bathroom to take it out and change into my dying clothes—a ratty old sports bra and boy shorts—before I feed the beasts.

When that's all done, I crank up some music, Siouxsie and the Banshees, and prepare my hair for its transformation. From bubblegum pink to the void, it's a dramatic change. The color's name is appropriate, a violet blue so dark it's like an absence of color. I love it, though it doesn't really fit me. It's far darker than I usually go. I'll probably change it again in a day or two. Maybe Atomic Green next time.

When the dye is applied and bonding with my hair, I cover my head in cling wrap and set the timer. Then I dance around the house with a bottle of wine and my bag of churros, glugging my drink and stuffing my face while I sing to the dogs. They love this game and sing along, barking and howling with delight. The doorbell rings, sending them into a frenzied chorus of "Who's at the door?"

I command them to hush, which they ignore, as I peer through the peephole. It's Manic. I stare long and hard at his face through the looking glass, considering if I'll answer or not. But maybe this is what I need. I'm just drunk enough to give him a piece of my mind.

I swing the door open and scowl at him. He's so much taller than me when I'm barefoot. It's not a fair fight, but I muster the courage of a fifty-foot woman and yell, "What are you doing here? Is it time for Make Sheryl Feel Like Shit Part Two: Electric Boogaloo?"

He seems surprised to see me. "You look different."

I touch the plastic wrap on my head and want to kick myself for opening the door. I forgot I look like a science experiment right now. Oh well. Crossing my arms over my chest, I try to look like a badass. "I needed a change."

I'm saved by the bell when my timer dings. I walk back into the house, figuring Manic will either close the door and run away after seeing me at my less than finest or come inside and close the door behind him. The choice is his.

Manic joins me in the bathroom as I go to the shower and unwrap my hair. "You left the door open."

I don't say anything, just bend over the edge of the tub, focused on trying not to get hair color all over my skin and the bathroom.

"I closed it so the dogs won't get out."

Now I answer, sounding indignant. "My dogs don't try to run

away from me. They know I'm worth staying for." Reason number 1,642 why dogs are better than humans.

"Smart dogs," Manic says.

I huff and turn on the water, blindly reaching for the handheld nozzle to rinse the excess dye out of my hair. Manic's boots appear beside me, and he grabs the nozzle, holding it for me while I run my fingers through my hair until the water runs clear again. It's sweet that he's helping, but it'll take a lot more than that for me to like him again.

I blot my hair with a towel, then blow it dry while Manic watches, seeming curious about the process. When my hair is dry, a billowy cascade of void violet waves falling over my shoulders, I turn to Manic and wait for him to talk.

"I'm sorry." Such simple words, and simply insufficient. He must recognize that because he keeps talking. "I was needlessly cruel in the way I reacted to you, and I'm sorry. Sheryl, I'm really… I'm so sorry."

I start to nod, but he's not finished.

"But I need to set a boundary. You can't fuck around at my work. You said before that medication helps you keep a job. Well, I have trouble keeping jobs too. Besides the circus, this is the only job I've been able to hold onto for any amount of time. I'd probably be homeless if it weren't for that bar. And now the owner's talking about selling the business to me when he retires. So I can't have you coming in there, starting fights with bikers that I have to finish or flashing your ass around like it's all a big joke."

Shit. He has a point. Considering his perspective, yeah, I crossed a line, a big one. "I'm sorry too. I didn't mean to make light of your work. I won't do it again."

"You can fuck with me anywhere else you want, just not there."

I can't help the hint of a smile that peeks out when I ask, "Anywhere?"

For the first time since I flashed my ass at his job, Manic grins at me. He takes a step closer and then another, only stopping when he has me pinned against the bathroom counter—what is it with us and bathrooms today?

And, God, he's big, so much taller than me. His presence envelopes me, his warm scent doing tingly things to my body and fogging the last remnants of anger and embarrassment from my mind.

In a low rumble, he says, "I should spank you for teasing me like that."

Uh.

"I've been hard for the last two hours, remembering you in that tail. You don't know how much I wanted to bend you over the men's room sink and shove my dick inside your wet, hot little pussy."

Oh. This is new. Guys have tried to talk dirty to me before, but it's never been this effective. At the mere mention of my wet, hot little pussy, she's drenched, drowning in desperation for his big, veiny cock. I shiver all over.

Manic's grin turns wicked, and he leans down to whisper in my ear, "Where's your tail, foxy lady?"

12

THURSDAY, DECEMBER 2, 2010

I moan in response because I seriously can't talk right now—he's managed a feat no one has ever accomplished—and I gesture at the drawer where I put my new toy, along with the bottle of lube Ari made me buy. Manic's arm is long enough to reach it. He lets out a delighted growly sound when he pulls the loot out and sets the lube on the counter beside us.

"You ready for this, baby?" he asks as he strokes the soft faux fur of the tail up my cheek, his words heating the little bit of air between us. "You ready for me to fuck you with your tail in?"

I nod furiously.

Manic's eyes flash with heat as he commands, "Turn around."

I do what I'm told, turning to lean against the counter, my fists clutching the edge in a tight grip. In the mirror, I stare at our reflection. My cheeks are rosy and my pupils dilated with excitement as Manic stares down at me. Gently, he slips his fingers into the waistband of my shorts and tugs them down my legs. He pulls my sports bra off over my head, too, my voided hair cascading all around my shoulders in a dramatic waterfall.

He takes a moment before touching me again, and it's an agonizing wait. Finally, his fingers caress the curve of my ass and slip along the crack. He does that again and again, teasing, making me so desperate I'm whining. My pussy is drenched, the wetness dripping down the insides of my thighs.

Manic uses a little of my own lube and some of the store-bought variety to wet his finger before he starts probing. I remember what Ari said and try my hardest to relax. Still, when he presses a finger inside, I yelp and clench and have to breathe mindfully a couple of times to relax again. He practically purrs behind me when he feels me loosening up for him, and he strokes his finger inside a couple of times.

It hurts at first, burns like fire, but soon the pain fades and what I feel is…good. Really good. Slowly, he slips a second finger in and this time, I'm more prepared for the sensation of fullness. I hold onto the counter with a white-knuckle grip as he prepares me. He's so gentle, using his free hand to stroke and tease my breasts as he finger fucks my ass.

"That's a good girl. You're so ready for me, baby." He kisses the top of my head as he slides his fingers out and reaches for the tail. With a little bit of lube on its tip, he starts to press in. It's larger than his fingers, and I know from the last insertion that I need to *really* relax for this one. Unclenching everything, even my grip on the counter, I trust him not to hurt me as he puts more pressure behind the plug. I whimper as the pressure builds and builds until it finally pushes through, and the largest part of the plug is inside me.

What a weird sense of relief. I sigh when the thing is seated, and Manic strokes my hair with one hand while he strokes my ass and the soft fur of the tail with the other. "Walk over to the bed and wag your tail for me, foxy lady."

Walking is a challenge after Manic's fingers turned me to mush, but I force some steadiness back into my legs and leave the bathroom for my bedroom, swinging my hips so my tail swishes enticingly. Manic growls as he follows, stripping out of his shirt and then the rest of his clothes by the time I reach the foot of my bed.

"Bend over," he says.

His wish is my command. Putting all my weight on my hands, I bend over onto the edge of the bed. I expect him to shove his cock right in and start fucking me then and there, but instead he drops to his knees behind me and presses his mouth to my pussy.

The delightful moaning sound he makes when he tastes me sends my knees trembling. His hands curl around my thighs, holding me steady as his fingers tease my clit. I'm so primed and ready I orgasm almost instantly, bucking and shivering and coming all over his tongue. The dogs howl in response from the hallway—interesting that Manic thought to close the door before any of this started.

"God," I gasp as my elbows shake, and I fall onto my face on the bed.

"Which do you want me to fuck first, foxy lady—your mouth or your pussy?" Manic's mouth is still between my thighs, his hot breath sending quakes of aftershock through me.

When I can't answer his question coherently, he stands behind me and surprises me with a spank on one butt cheek and then the other.

I yelp and come back onto my hands, fanning my hair up and out of my face. Manic reaches for my head, stroking his fingers up my scalp, then he clenches a fistful of my hair and pulls. I come up with another yelp, still so surprised by how much I like the sting on my ass, and now the sting on my scalp too.

"My mouth." I finally decide.

"That's my good girl." He lets go of my hair, and I fall forward onto the bed. "Get on your hands and knees and suck my cock."

I crawl up on the bed, my hips swaying, the tail swishing, and turn so I can take him in my mouth. He's so hard, his beautiful veiny cock weeping for me already. I savor the metallic taste of his piercing and the salty flavor of his pre cum, moaning. Sucking him deep, I tickle my piercing along the underside of his shaft with each stroke. He moans, a sound so sexy it sends shivers through me that settle between my thighs.

"Wag your tail for me, baby."

I arch my back and wiggle as commanded.

"So fucking sexy." Bending over me, he grabs my ass with both hands, stroking my tail, and playing with the plug. He pulls it out a little, then pushes it back in, out a little more and back in. Can a person come from this? Pretty sure I'm on the edge again. All too soon, Manic presses the plug firmly back into place, and steps away, pulling his cock out of my mouth.

Dammit, I wasn't finished playing with that.

Manic moves onto the bed on his knees and grabs a fistful of my hair, tugging until I'm right in front of him on my knees, too, like we're praying to each other. He curls his fingers around my neck and pulls me into a deep, drowning kiss.

His kisses are all consuming, and they are unique. Normally, when a man kisses me, it's a means to an end, just a step in the "How to Fuck a Woman" guidebook. But with Manic, his kisses mean something. Entirely separate from the sex we're having, his kisses are connection and communication. He lets himself be vulnerable when he kisses me, and so I do the same. I lay myself bare, let myself feel, and without uttering a word, I use my mouth to communicate with him, sharing everything I'm feeling.

And what I'm feeling is a lot. It's overwhelming. Tears wet the corners of my eyes, as if this is all too much. Maybe he feels that way, too, because he pulls away from the kiss, enough so we're pressing foreheads, our heated breath mixing.

He fixes his gaze with mine, and still holding my hair with one hand, he reaches the other down between us and strokes his cock against me. I moan, then yelp when he presses inside. I didn't even know this was a sex position. My legs aren't even spread open, but he's found a way.

His free hand clutches my ass now, holding me close as I take him in. The piercing tickles as his thick head pushes deeper. With the plug in, I'm overwhelmingly full. I gasp and he's there at my mouth again, swallowing the sound as he takes me with his cock and his tongue.

My clit gets a lot of stimulation in this position, and it feels so good I wrap my arms around his neck to rub myself even closer against him. He clasps both his palms on my ass now, clutching me with bruising force as he angles me so he can plunge even deeper. My knees start to wobble under my weight, and he shifts back to sit on his heels, bringing me with him to straddle his lap now. In this position, he goes deeper, and his steady strokes grow stronger. I move with him, rotating my hips as I take him in. We're moving so much, working so hard, a sheen of sweat coats our skin, and I have to scrape my nails on his back and neck, just to hold on.

The man is a fucking expert at fucking. Guiding me back up the side of ecstasy mountain, he drops me in a volcano at the top, and hot lava flows through me as I come, screaming.

He slows his strokes as I descend from my peak, then he shifts positions again, this time dropping us forward into the plain old, ordinary missionary position. But nothing about Manic is ordinary, and the way his weight settles over me, his arms wrapped around my neck, his hands cradling my face, he's totally enveloped me as he builds the rhythm back, and I'm climbing and falling all over again.

Suddenly, he's out, off of me. He grabs my hips and flips me over, then pulls me up onto my knees. My little tail wags for him, and he flops it up out of his way so he can shove his cock back home. With his hands on my hips, he pounds into me, his piercing rubbing against my G-spot, and I'm climbing again.

He scratches his nails up my spine, taking a fistful of my hair and yanking me back so I arch all the way up. With his lips on my forehead, a soft kiss in the midst of all this rough sex, he wraps his fingers around my throat, tightening enough that I completely explode.

Screaming in ecstasy, I clench every muscle in my body, squeezing him and the plug so tight that everything feels incredibly intense and just right. That's when he comes inside me, filling me with his heat as he groans and quakes behind me.

Goddamn. That was hands down the best sex of my life.

13

THURSDAY, DECEMBER 2, 2010

"What's your schedule this weekend."

"Working. A lot. It's Christmas season, which means extra shifts and meager tips," Manic says as he rubs my back.

He's been so sweet since we finished fucking about an hour ago. I like how he can switch so quickly from rough and ready to gentle kitty. Both sides are pretty awesome. The choking and hair pulling were so hot, then he took my butt plug out like he was a midwife guiding me through labor. And now he's giving me a massage. He's the perfect man.

"So I shouldn't come in flashing my tits at all the tourists I guess?" I wink at him over my shoulder, finally able to laugh about our earlier fight.

His chuckle rumbles between us as he covers me, his weight releasing what little tension I still had left inside me. His breath warms my cheek as he whispers, "I'd appreciate if you abstained from doing that, please."

"Well, since you said please." I turn over so we're tangled together, arms and legs entwined and my hair a messy void all around us. "What about Monday?"

"I work."

"Can you switch shifts with someone?"

"Why?"

"Every Monday my friends get together for dinner. You already know them all, so you should come."

He stares at me for a long moment, and I prepare for rejection. This is, after all, basically me inviting him to meet my family. True, they're not technically my family, but I feel closer to them than to my bio mom and missing dad. And even though Manic knows them, he'd be attending as my date, so that's new. I'm starting to reconsider. It's too fast. What was I thinking?

I open my mouth to rescind the invitation, but Manic answers first. "Okay."

And just like that, I have a date for Family Dinner Night. For the first time in five years, I won't be the only person alone at the table.

"I like this color." Manic twirls a strand of my hair between his fingers.

"Want some? I have more."

"Really?" His brows rise like he's considering it, and I'm struck with a genius idea.

"Oh, can I do your hair?"

"What do you mean by 'do my hair?' "

"Cut it, shave it, color it." I shrug. "You know, play."

He frowns, a true look of terror in his eyes.

Is he afraid of what I'll do to his hair? Can he not see how fabulous mine is? I've been playing with it for years. "What's the worst that could happen? If you hate it, you shave it off and put your cowboy hat on. It's just hair. It'll grow back."

He considers a minute more, looking thoughtful as he does, then agrees. I hoot as I jump out of bed. Swinging the door open while I'm up, the dogs come rushing in to inspect the room for signs of foul play, sniffing sex in the air and zeroing in on the culprit, the cause of all my hollering, still naked on my bed.

I grab Manic's hand and drag him into the bathroom. The dogs give chase when I hurry to the kitchen for a chair and return to push it into the back of Manic's knees so he'll sit. Grabbing a couple of black towels out of the cabinet along with all my hair toys—combs, scissors, clippers, and dye—I line up everything on the counter.

Then I stand before him and stare, trying to decide what to do with him. He has nice hair—a fine texture, medium brown color, and a little shaggy in length. I step closer, stroking my fingers through the strands. Manic closes his eyes and sighs when I touch him, then reaches for me, too, stroking my breasts and tweaking my nipples.

"How do you feel about a mohawk?"

He shrugs, way more interested in touching me than what I'm doing to his hair. While I use a rattail comb to create a perfect part and apply clips to his keeper hair, Manic strokes his fingers all over my body, squeezing his favorite places. We're both playing. I plug in the clippers, add the shortest clipper guard, and start shaving his head.

Manic takes one of my nipples into his mouth, tickling the piercing with his tongue, biting and tugging just a little. I yelp and wiggle and try not to accidentally mow down his mohawk in a shaving mishap.

When the left side of his head is trimmed to perfection, I give the same treatment to the right, and Manic switches to my other nipple. He's making it hard to focus. And speaking of hard, that thing in his lap looks ready to go again, even after the marathon session we just had.

I pull away from his attention to ready the dye, and he follows me to the counter, pressing up against my back, his cock pushing between my thighs. "Can I fuck you while you dye my hair?"

"I'll get dye everywhere."

"We'll be careful."

I laugh at the thought. I've had sex with this man, I've experienced his style: there's nothing *careful* about it.

"Sit," I command.

Manic lifts a brow, but he follows the order.

All the dogs follow the command too. "Good boys," I say to them all. Then I slip my gloves on and start to apply the color while Manic feels me up some more. Since I didn't bleach his hair first, the color won't be as vivid as mine—more of a deep, dark brown with violet blue highlights when the light hits it. It's going to be awesome.

As I work, I ask, "So what's your life story, Mr. Monroe?"

He looks up from where he's been laving my nipple with his tongue and pinches it as he answers. "Grew up on a hippy commune in northern California. Left when I was sixteen. Got married. Got divorced. Joined the circus. Did a stint in the mental ward. Joined the circus again. Landed in Austin. Been here ever since."

"Wow. That's a lot of life you've lived. I didn't know you were married."

"It was a disaster. Lasted less than a year."

Done talking, he goes for my nipple again. Though he does mumble, "What's your life story, Ms. Novak?"

"Grew up in Tampa Bay. Embarrassment to my mom and stepdad. Left right after high school. Couch surfed around the country. Threw paint on fur coats for a few years before turning my love of animals into an actual job. Saw an article about how Austin is trying to become the largest city with a no-kill animal shelter, so I moved here to help. Been here ever since."

"Nice," he says as he licks a line between my breasts. He's an oral fixator, no doubt about it.

I paint the last lock of hair with my brush and take a look, inspecting my work. All done, I comb his hair into one solid line down the middle, set the timer to let it bond, and start to wash up.

Manic is at my back again. "Thirty minutes, huh?"

"Uh huh." I shiver a little, already knowing where this is going.

"I wonder what we could do with thirty minutes." He strokes his cock between my thighs, and I arch my back, offering him what he wants. "That's my girl, always ready to play."

He slides inside, and I drop the bowl and brush I was cleaning to grasp the counter, watching in the mirror as he fucks me. He's such a beautiful fucker, straining all those sexy muscles as he moves his hips, slow and deep in a teasing rhythm. I love how he watches me too, our eyes meeting in the reflection as he starts to move faster, harder. Clasping my hips, he slams into me, leaving me gasping for breath and coming apart beneath him. He comes, too, huffing and collapsing against me. I love the weight of him, the sounds he makes, and how when he pulls out, his cum drips down my thighs. Things with Manic are messy and, God, I love that.

The timer dings.

Manic grins like he's proud of his timing.

"Shower time," I announce and step into the bathtub, and he follows.

First, he bends so we can rinse his hair with cold water, then I turn up the heat, and we get cleaned up. When we're out, I dry his hair and take him back to bed to marvel at his mohawk as it flops from one side of his head to the other. The Ultraviolet Void makes his blue eyes almost glow; he looks like a super hero, Super Manic.

Oh, that's an awful superhero name. Now that he's told me about his condition, I don't want to call him Manic. I don't want to repeatedly use a word that comes from a place of pain.

"Why do you complain when I call you James?"

He blinks like my rapid change of subject has lost him somewhere. I give him time to catch up. Finally, he answers, "I haven't been James in a long time. It's like he's a whole different person. He died in the psych ward when Manic was born."

"Do you like being called Manic?"

He shrugs, which isn't a no, but it isn't a yes either.

"Can I give you a new name?"

"What?" Manic frowns, and it's funny to see that tight expression on his face right now. It's his default expression when he's out in public, working, but in the time we've spent together, his face has loosened some of its tension.

"Well, James is the name you were born with, and then Manic was born with your diagnosis. Now, it's time you had a new name for your third chapter."

"My third chapter?"

"Yes, this is the chapter where you can accept your diagnosis and live happily ever after with it."

Manic's lips twitch like he wants to smile, but he won't allow it to happen. Then he speaks, and his words break my heart. "I don't think there's a happily ever after for me."

What a terrible thought, that lack of hope for a happy future. I can't even bear to consider it. I need to believe there is happiness ahead for me, and for Manic too.

In this moment, I vow to make it so. I'm capable of a lot of things. I can do this. I can make happiness happen…for both of us.

Starting with: "Please, may I pick a name for you? I'll pick, like, the perfect name—I promise. It will be a name that will allow you to grow into the next version of yourself."

He watches me for a long minute, maybe trying to see if I'm joking. I'm not joking. I want to call him something other than that cavalier reminder of the condition that changed his life. And I think he wants me to call him something else, too, because he slowly nods okay.

I leap up from my bed and barrel out the door. The dogs jerk up from the bed, too, and rush around me to see what's happening. Grabbing my laptop from the kitchen table, I return to join Manic in bed, all the dogs piling in with us.

I navigate to the baby names website I've spent way too much time on lately. First, I look up the name James, which is actually a translation of Jacob, and it means supplanter or substitute. Interesting. "Did you know Séamas is James in Irish?" I tell him over the top of my computer screen, but he smirks at me and keeps petting my dogs. "Not that I think you're a Séamas. You're not. Just an interesting tidbit. And Achilles means pain. Oh, Ignacio means fire." I waggle my brows. "A hot name for a hot dude."

"Sher, don't you have to work in the morning?"

I nod without taking my gaze off the screen. This is important work; can't afford any distractions.

"It's almost two a.m. Why don't you put off naming me for now and come sleep with me instead?"

I glance at him over my computer screen, his electric blue eyes promising very little sleep, and I set my laptop aside.

14

"Did Manic like the tail?" Ari asks between bites of salad during this week's Family Dinner Night.

"Manic jumped on the trampoline with me!" Tommy shouts with excitement—able to yell now that the babies are asleep upstairs. Apparently his trampoline adventure is all he's talked about all week.

"Yes, he did." I agree with Tommy, then to Ari, I answer, "No and yes?"

"No? Why no?"

"Well, my bad, I wore it to the bar and flashed him along with half the patrons and the security cameras. He was pretty mad about that. But then he came over to my house and we, uh"—I glance over at Tommy, eating his mac and cheese—"made up. At that point he seemed to enjoy it."

I take a bite of Nicole's amazing enchiladas and moan orgasmically. It's only after I've chewed, swallowed, and taken a sip of water that I realize no one is speaking. Glancing up, the adults around the table all gawk at me with their mouths hanging open.

"What?" I ask.

"Are you serious? You're freaking Manic?" Nicole uses her there-are-children-present vocabulary for her question.

"Yeah, I guess."

"What do you mean by 'I guess'?" Ari asks.

"Well, we're definitely freaking, but I don't know what it all means. Like, are we just freaking around, or are we like, seriously freaking?"

Jake scowls. "This conversation is seriously freaking with my head. What are we talking about here?"

I explain better. "Manic and I are a thing, maybe. I don't know."

Ari claps. "Awesome!"

Alex smiles with her. "I could never picture Manic with anyone. But now that I think about it, you two are a perfect fit."

"Well, don't get too excited. We did lots of, uh, freaking on Thursday, and I haven't heard from him since then. I invited him to dinner tonight, but he's not here." I check my phone again. He was supposed to be here a half hour ago. He hasn't shown, hasn't called, and he's not answering when I call. I even tried calling the bar. Apparently, he did take tonight off work, so where is he? "I guess something came up, or it was just a freaking fling. I don't know."

"Oh." Ari's excitement balloon pops, and so does mine.

Saying it out loud makes it real. Manic stood me up. After all that sharing and caring last week, he's not even answering my phone calls now. I thought he was different, but it turns out he's just another fuck-boy: willing to do and say anything for a quick roll in the mud.

Oh well. I don't need him. Who needs the headache of a man? All I wanted was a baby anyway, then Manic distracted me with all those orgasms. It was fun while it lasted, but I've got bigger shit to fry…or whatever.

Except…

What if he was in an accident on the way here, and he's in a full body cast and can't reach his phone? Or maybe he was kidnapped by a circus passing through town, and he's being forced to perform against his will! He could have fallen in the shower and has amnesia! "Alex, do you know where Manic lives?"

Alex nods, but frowns. "Why?"

"I'm worried. I want to check on him."

Alex doesn't remember the street or house number and doesn't even know if Manic still lives there—he went to a party there once many years ago—but he rattles off the driving directions. In an instant, I'm up and making the rounds with hugs and kisses before I'm out the door and jogging to my green dragon at the end of the drive.

Manic's place isn't far from Jakole's, but the Monday night traffic clogging the roads makes the journey arduous. I'm a frazzled mess by the time I find the little bungalow behind the western wear store where Alex directed me.

The yard is a patch of weedy dirt. The peach-hued bungalow is cute though, or it could be with a little tender loving care. As it is now, the paint is chipping off, and the porch is draped with thin fingers of ivy that make the place look unfriendly. I'm pretty sure Manic still lives here though. It fits him perfectly: distressed on the outside, a mystery on the inside. Plus, his motorcycle is parked in the drive.

The porch boards squeak as I approach the door and knock. Waiting is torture. I have no chill, and my mind races with more terrible scenarios for why he missed Family Dinner Night. I've settled on spontaneous human combustion, but that theory is shot to hell when I hear footsteps on the other side of the door.

In an instant, my temperament and temperature change. From the depths of chilly fear to the boiling cauldron of rage, I get really mad. If he's moving around in there, then he's not broken and bleeding on the floor, not burnt to a crisp on the couch. So he, like, blew me off tonight for no reason.

The door creaks open with the squeaky hinges of a haunted house, and Manic squints at me like a vampire at the crack of dusk. My heart flutters at the mere sight of him, despite my anger. Stupid heart.

"Hey," he says with a scratchy voice and steps away from the door, leaving it cracked open for me to follow him. I guess.

Well, I've come this far, so I step inside. It's depressingly dark. All the blinds are drawn shut, and none of the lights are on. Only the anemic halo of afternoon sunlight emanating from the corners of the windows illuminates the room.

"Hey?" I huff as I follow Manic to where he sits on the couch. He's staring at the wall, so I block his view. "That's all you have to say to me? What happened? Why are you here? Sitting in the dark?"

He flinches like I've hurt him with my voice. "Why are you mad?"

I plop down beside him and cross my arms over my chest. "I'm mad because you stood me up for dinner tonight, and you're not answering my calls. And it's fine if you're done with me, but tell me so—"

He curses. "Was that today? Shit, Sher. I didn't mean to stand you up. I'm not done with you, I'm… I'm having a bad day."

Those little shivers of worry are back, dousing my rage. "Why? What happened?"

"Nothing happened." He smacks the side of his head like he's trying to hurt himself and adds, "It's just…a bad fucking day."

"Oh." He's talking about his bipolar disorder. That hadn't even occurred to me, and I can't believe it hadn't. I should have considered that, but I wasn't paying enough attention to his signals. I missed the signs. Except, a no call, no show is hardly a signal or a sign.

"Sher, I'm sorry about dinner." Manic shifts a little, finally focusing on me instead of the wall. He clasps my hands in his, those rough fingers stroking mine as he says, "I will make it up to you, as best I can, I swear. But today isn't a good day for me. I'm bad company when I'm like this." His eyes are so sad they could crack my heart right in half. He shifts his head slightly, and a slash of violet hair falls across his eyes, a void over the ocean.

"I don't need you to be good company. You don't have to entertain me. I just…" I just *what?* What am I trying to say? In the end, I say the truth. "I like being around you."

Manic flips his hair out of his face so he can see me better.

Please don't ask me to leave, Manic. I don't say the words—don't want to sound desperate to stay—but I beg and plead with my eyes, with a squeeze of his hand in mine. I've never wanted to do anything more than I want to stay with him tonight. The thought of leaving him alone in this dark hole hurts my heart.

After a moment of consideration, Manic acquiesces. I nearly smile, but it doesn't feel appropriate. Slowly, he leans toward me, placing a soft kiss on my lips, then he curls onto his side, resting his head in my lap.

If his sad eyes cracked my heart in half, then his posture cracks it into quarters. He's like a lost little boy, vulnerable and seeking comfort.

And I will stop at nothing to give it. I want to hug him and love him and take care of him forever and ever. Hugging an arm around his middle, I kiss his cheek, then stroke my fingers through his hair. It's relaxing, being able to care for him, touch him, feel his fine hair flutter and fall from my fingers.

I don't know how long we sit like this. Manic doesn't sleep, doesn't even close his eyes. He stares ahead at nothing, saying nothing, doing nothing. This headspace he's in is foreign to me. I'm always saying *something*, doing *something*.

Here, the silence is total, and once the sun sets, the darkness is total too. And I sit in it, experiencing all the emotions that well up inside and flow through me.

Strangely, it all makes me feel content. Something about this shared quietness soothes me.

With my free hand, I dig my phone out to text Ari, asking her to run over and feed the dogs so I can stay the night. When she agrees, I settle in a little deeper on the couch and kick off my shoes to prop my feet up on the coffee table, getting comfortable.

I think back to my massage and healing classwork, learning about energy, how it ebbs and flows in and around us, an exchange between people. Trying to apply those lessons now, I send good energy through my fingertips as I stroke Manic's hair and gently scratch his back, trying to soothe the part of him that hurts.

I read once that depression can be so strong it presents with flu-like symptoms, actual physical aches and pains. And when Manic shivers like he's cold, I imagine that's what's happening here. The mind can be such a bitch sometimes. I pull a blanket down from the back of his couch and stretch it over him, then continue to stroke and scratch his back through the fabric.

The morning alarm on my phone sounds. Manic and I jolt upright on the couch, suddenly very awake. I guess we fell asleep at some point.

Fumbling with my phone, I manage to silence it and text Ari to request another dog sit. Then I text work.

"You stayed the night," Manic says as he rubs the sleep from his eyes.

I nod, accustomed to not speaking now.

"Why?"

"I didn't want you to be alone while you had a bad day."

He stares at me so intently, like he's looking all the way inside me. And his eyes shine like he sees something magical there. "Thank you," he says as he strokes my cheek.

"Do you feel better?"

He shrugs, which I interpret as no.

Taking his hand, I stroke his palm. "I'm taking today off work. Can we go lie down together? No funny business. I promise I won't try to seduce you."

He grins and pulls me off the couch to follow him into his bedroom. This room is dark too. Wood floors creak as we walk to his bed. He pulls the sheets back and beckons me to slide in. I do and make room for him, then encourage him to lie on his side.

I hug him from behind. "I'll be the big spoon today. You can be the big spoon tomorrow."

He lets out a deep breath and whispers as he strokes my arm. "Sounds like a good plan."

15

TUESDAY, DECEMBER 7, 2010

I wake to the sensation of someone touching my hair. It takes me a moment to remember where I am, who I'm with, and why he'd be touching my hair. Fluttering my eyes open, I find Manic sort of smiling at me as he strokes his fingers over my braids. They must look a mess after sleeping on them twice, but he doesn't seem bothered.

"How are you feeling?" I ask in my rocky first-words-of-the-day voice.

"Better."

Pushing myself higher up onto the pillow, I try to tamp down the rat's nest on my head, but it's out of control. I slip the elastics off the ends of my mangled braids and finger comb the mess into submission.

Manic sits up higher, too, leaning against the headboard beside me. Together, we stare at the opposite wall. Even with the sun up, it's too dark in here to see much, so I turn my attention to him. The expression on his face suggests the inner workings of his mind are fairly dark too. And while his scowl might intimidate a less brave soul, I have questions. "What's it like when you get low like that?"

Manic lets out a heavy sigh, still staring into the darkness. After a long moment, he answers me. "I'm generally always low—that's my baseline—but when it dips lower, I get paranoid, I guess. And when I get paranoid, I imagine the worst in people. Kindness always comes with an agenda. It can't be trusted. That's what my fucked-up brain tells me, anyway, and when I'm low, I believe it. Friendship, compassion, caring—it all feels like lies told by people who want something from me. I'm the one person I know I can trust. So I guess it feels lonely and exhausting."

"And you do this often, the distrustful thing?"

"I do this every minute of every day, to varying degrees. But when I get low, it's worse."

I curl onto my side, wanting to see his eyes when I ask, "Do you think I have an agenda?"

"Yes."

I'm aghast. "What?"

He furrows his brow with a deep frown. "Sheryl, you told me point-blank you want a baby."

Oh, right, *that* agenda. "And you told me, point-blank, you can't get me preggers. So why would I still come around if that's all I wanted from you?"

"I don't know. I'm still trying to figure that out. Maybe you want to change my mind and convince me to reverse my vasectomy." His frown deepens even more as he continues. "But then I think, you're amazing and gorgeous and this city is overflowing with dickheads who'd pay good money to fuck you without a condom. So why are you wasting your time with a useless asshole like me?"

Wow. I huff. "Paranoia sounds exhausting. I see what you mean about that."

Manic surprises me when he curls half his lip up and reaches for my hand, lacing our fingers together. "That's why last night was so strange."

"Strange?"

"Last night, being around you didn't exhaust me. Normally, I'd be second-guessing everything. I mean, there wasn't any reason for you to stay with me. There wasn't anything in it for you. But you stayed anyway. And… Lying with you, feeling your fingers in my hair, closing my eyes and breathing in your scent… You smell so good, like oranges and the ocean… And you…soothed me."

I move until I'm straddling Manic's lap. "You are literally the only person who has ever said that in my entire life. Most people think I'm exhausting. *Me*, if you can believe that." I twirl a strand of his hair around my finger as I share a little secret. "You soothe me too."

"How? Why?"

"You…" How do I put this? "Slow me down."

He scowls. Wrong choice of words. I try to do better. "I'm like a hummingbird, you know?" I flap my hands really fast to demonstrate. "Always fluttering around, and you're nectar. You give me a reason to land and stay awhile."

His scowl softens into the sweetest smile, and his arms link around my waist, hugging me a little closer to him. He leans into me, kissing my neck as he whispers, "Yeah. I'd like you to land and stay awhile."

I moan at the sensation of his mouth on me, then squeal with excitement when I'm struck with a brilliant idea, blurting it out too loud. "Let's do Tantra!"

"What?" Manic's easy smile sinks back into that deep frown. "Why?"

"Because I think it might help us."

"Help us do what? Isn't Tantra the sex that lasts for hours? Not that I'm opposed to that…"

"We could definitely go that route if you're up for it. Or we can remain clothed."

We both glance down at his erection tenting the sheets between my thighs. He's an easy riser; and he's obviously *up* for it. Changing the subject, I say, "To be clear, I'm talking westernized Tantra, not the original form. We're not going to worship Vishnu or anything, just do some deep breathing and shared meditation."

"And sex."

I nod. "Tantra is about connecting—connecting with yourself, connecting with the universe, and, in the case of Tantric sex, connecting with your partner. It can help us engage our minds and bodies, within ourselves and with each other. It's an exchange of energy. Plus, I hear the orgasms are amazing."

At this point, most guys would have dismissed what I'm saying as "hippy shit" and insist we rush toward the orgasms. But not Manic; he looks worried as he asks, "What about you?"

"What about me?"

"You said it's an exchange of energy. I'd be taking your light when all I can give you is my darkness?"

Well, isn't he just the sweetest thing. "First of all, this isn't about give and take. It's about sharing. Second of all, I have the energy of ten men. Sharing some of that with you isn't going to hurt me."

Manic takes his gaze away from mine, watching his fingers as he strokes my hair. In a quiet voice, he admits, "Sher, don't take this the wrong way, but I think I could easily hurt you, and you'd let me."

Now I'm the one frowning.

He goes on. "You're a giver. You're like the sun. You shine so bright and share your light so freely. I don't want to take any of that away from you."

"Solar power doesn't hurt the sun."

A small smile quirks one corner of his lip. "Just be careful. Because, if you let me, I will take everything. Don't let me take more than you can give."

"Okay. But we're still doing Tantra."

He twists his face and furrows his brow with more worry. It's super sweet but incredibly sad that he thinks he needs to spare me from himself. Like he's some incubus, sucking the light out of me. The thing is, he's wrong. Like totally, completely, one hundred and ten percent opposite of correct.

I meant what I said before. He soothes me. Being with him last night didn't drain me, not even an ounce. It restored me. It brought me to a place of calmness, where I could pause, catch my thoughts one-handed, sit with them. I was more relaxed than I've felt in as long as I can remember. Today I feel unstoppable, and it was Manic who charged the battery in this little engine that could.

Manic has a point, though. Codependency is my jam. Sheryl Code-pendent Novak. When I'm not careful, I tend to give too much of myself to the sorts of people who only ever take. I have done it before, too many times to count. But in the last few years, with my therapist's help, I've become mindful of that tendency. It's nice to learn Manic is mindful of it too.

Gah! I really like this guy.

I slide to the middle of his bed and sit cross-legged. Without any more prompting, Manic does the same, facing me.

"Wait, I need to pee!" I shout and spring up out of his bed, aiming for what I assume is his bathroom. Once I've done my morning business and rinsed with mouthwash, I go back to his bedroom. He's cracked the blinds open, enough to let in a soft glow of daylight, and for the first time I can actually see his room. I blink, a little surprised. There's a wall of shelves to one side of his bed, and it's full of collectibles. Half of them contain Star Trek action figurines, books, themed lunch boxes, a miniature USS Enterprise, and even one of those handheld communicator devices. The other half of the shelves are devoted to Doctor Who, with miniature versions of the TARDIS and Daleks in every color under the sun.

"Like the collection?" Manic asks when he exits the bathroom naked. He doesn't wait for me to answer, leaving the room to return a few seconds later with a couple bottles of water he sets on the nightstand.

"You are adorably dorky."

"Thanks, I think."

I strip naked, too, and sit cross-legged in the center of his bed again. Manic joins me. I shimmy closer until our knees touch and tell him, "I want to show you, with my body, how we can share intimacy and love for ourselves and each other."

That furrow in his brow is back.

"No pressure—I'm not talking big-L *love*. There's lots of little-L ways to love yourself and others, and I know we share some of them. Today, I want to touch those parts of ourselves and each other."

He nods.

"Do you trust me?"

"Yes," he answers unequivocally.

"Can I trust you?"

Now he hesitates.

"I do, you know, trust you."

"I'm not sure you should."

"Do you want a safe word, in case this gets too intense?"

He nods and says, "Dayton."

Curious choice for a safe word. Is it related to his hospitalization in Ohio all those years ago? I don't ask; that's a conversation for a different morning. I nod and instruct, "Look into my eyes."

"You going to hypnotize me?"

"No, I'm just going to stare at your soul through your windows."

"That's creepy."

"Give me your gaze, big boy."

"Whatever you say, little girl." With that, he gives me a wink and his gaze.

"Cool, so, look into my eyes as I look into yours. Try to open yourself to me, and I will do the same for you. If you need to close your eyes or look away, that's okay, but try to stay focused on me, open to me."

Manic looks panicked, so I take his hands in mine, running my fingers across his knuckles as we stare at each other. He closes his eyes for a moment, and I wonder if it's because he's uncomfortable letting me see inside him, or if he's uncomfortable with what he sees inside me. I half expect him to sever our connection and come up with a reason for me to leave.

Instead, he opens his eyes again. There's a sheen of wetness, as if he could cry. It's like I'm seeing something no one has ever seen before. And it's a privilege to meet the vulnerable person hidden under all that armor.

I soften my gaze, let him see the warmth I feel for him, as I dive into his oceanic depths. There is so much inside him, a whole school of beautiful beasts and curious creatures swimming beneath his surface. There is so much turmoil, a mix of emotions that ties him in knots. Inside him is a longing to be loved and a fear of it at the same time. To me, knowing his standoffishness comes from that needy place is one more thing to like about him.

After a few minutes, I let go of his hands so I can touch his chest, right over his heart; its steady thumps feel like tickles against my fingertips. Manic touches my heart, too, and—like he's connected some circuit between us—suddenly I feel *everything*.

Sensations and emotions circulate through us like the blood in our veins. Our heartbeats, our breathing seem to sync, combine, align. Vibrations of energy tingle off him, into my fingers, and across my flesh, like an orgasm of awakening traveling through every cell of my body and his.

It feels so good. I want more. I want to be closer. He's too far away.

Shifting up onto my knees, I crawl onto his lap. We don't need to touch each other's hearts anymore to feel the rhythm, so he wraps his arms around my waist, and I hug his shoulders as we sit like this for a long time, our foreheads pressed together, staring deep into each other, breathing together, touching all over.

I shiver, despite the heat. Manic and I both feel feverish, and his hands, like hot brands, burn everywhere he touches me.

Between us his cock stands proud. I want to connect with him in this final way, too, dying to have his heat inside me. Moving my hips, just a little, just enough, I rub my clit against his shaft. Manic groans, and his eyes grow hungry, like a ravenous wolf ready to pounce.

When he starts to move his hips in rhythm with mine, it's like we're becoming one. More than connected, we're one being in two bodies. I work my way higher up the length of him, swaying my hips in rhythm with his.

When we finally come into true alignment, he presses up and I slide down. The sensation of his hot cock and cool metal ring moving inch by inch deeper inside me is overwhelming. I hug my arms tighter around his neck and huff out the air in my lungs as Manic's hot, jagged breath mixes with mine. Finally, we are together, totally fucking together—two missing puzzle pieces that form this perfect fit.

When you're so thoroughly joined like this, small movements have a big impact. Every slight shift gives me waves of toe-curling satisfaction. His hands burn everywhere he touches, and his hot breath against my lips sends shivers through me.

We haven't kissed yet. And there is something strangely exciting about that. We're so connected, our breath and pulse and rhythm combined so completely, yet we remain disconnected in that one way. It feels taboo, but everything with Manic feels taboo…and I like that.

Our small movements become larger, our shared rhythm growing faster. I rise up to reveal him nearly to the tip then come back down to his hilt, panting and moaning as unbelievable sensation washes over me.

Damp strands of his hair fall into his eyes, but I don't need to share his gaze to know the man inside those eyes anymore. I can see him completely now, inside and out. And after today, I will always be able to see him. What is it he sees inside me? I'll have to ask him, but not now. Right now, we're climbing, climbing, climbing together.

Totally in sync, we're both close to orgasm. And Manic knows exactly when to pull back, coming right to the edge for both of us, but it's not time to go over yet. We slow, breathing together as his cock twitches with tiny movements, and I grip him tighter with a Kegel. When we're ready, we build our excitement once more.

Hours, it must be, hours of this. When we hit the edge a second time and come down, I lean over to grab the bottles of water he set aside for us. We hydrate before going again, building and building, coming so close and then absolute stillness, breaths mingling between us as we wait for our hearts to calm and our orgasms to ebb.

Finally, on the fifth wave, we share a look between us, wordlessly agreeing—this time we go over. We press our foreheads together, our eyes so close all I can see are the deep black depths of his dilated pupils. We hug one another tightly, only our hips moving now, and his breath is so hot against my mouth. I want to kiss him, but I want to wait; I'll kiss him when we come.

Huffing now, groaning and moaning and moving with such strength together, I feel that tipping point right there, right there, right *there*. I come with a gasp and cry out as the most perfect orgasm overtakes me. Like our ocean of waves, this undulates through me, too, a current that ebbs and flows and pulls me under.

It feels like I come for hours, days, weeks. And Manic, he comes with me. He grunts and huffs as he fills me with his hot cum. We don't stop. We keep moving together, extending the pleasure. Our strokes become chaotic and messy and his cum drips out all over our laps. Still, we don't stop moving, that hot wetness too good, too perfect.

Finally, our breath jagged, our hearts pounding against our breasts, we collapse into each other. And now, after all that, we kiss. But it's so much more than an ordinary kiss. It's a new connection on a new plane of existence. There is nothing ordinary for us now, no normal kissing or fucking or walking around like humans. We're angels floating together up in the clouds. We're mermaid and merman swimming together in the deep blue sea. We're unicorns frolicking—

"What, why are you looking at me like that?" I frown at him, a little concerned by the intensity of his stare.

"It's just," he presses my hair back behind my ear and gently kisses my lips, then whispers against them, "your orgasm is the most beautiful thing I've ever seen."

I lose my breath and slowly catch it again as my mind races, my mouth floundering open, at a loss for words.

He chuckles to himself. "Sorry, that was cheesy. I only meant—"

I frown from the top of my head to the tips of my toes, terrified he'll ruin this moment if he keeps talking, like he'll take away the words he's given to me. I press my fingers against his lips, silencing him to say, "That was the most beautiful thing anyone's ever said to me."

"You're joking."

I think about it for a moment, but it's the truth. Nobody ever says beautiful things to me. Except for him.

Now it's Manic who frowns all over. Then he really takes my breath away when he holds my chin between his fingers and holds my gaze with his own. "You amaze me in every way. You're bright and beautiful, and you shine like the sun. Every day I get to see you is a good day for me, and when you orgasm and your light spills out of you and touches me, those are the best days."

Oh. My. Heart. I'm speechless, stunned, and my eyes sting like I might cry. But before I can say or do anything in reaction, Manic kisses me. It's a new sort of kiss, soft and soothing, drugging me with some sweet narcotic promise shared between us.

When he pulls his lips away from mine, the calm he's given me has seeped so deep I can barely keep my eyes open. Gently, he settles us onto our sides on the bed and turns me over so I'm wrapped up in him, cocooned in his arms and scent and warmth. I struggle to keep my eyes open but let them drift shut when Manic whispers in my ear, "I'll be the big spoon this time, Sonny Sher."

16

TUESDAY, DECEMBER 7, 2010

"My babies!" I shout as I jerk up in the bed, blinking my eyes into focus.

"Your babies?" Manic wakes with a start, looking panicked. He scans the room with wide eyes, like he expects a whole army of toddlers to come at us from the shadows.

Bless his heart.

"My fur babies," I clarify, trying to corral my wild hair...again. Jesus, how many times have I fallen asleep and woken up at Manic's house in the last twenty-four hours? "I need to go home and feed my dogs and love on them before they freak out and destroy everything."

"Oh." He sounds bummed, and that disappointment in his tone makes my heart sing.

Does he actually want me to stay? More than I've already stayed today? Only one way to find out: "Want to move this post-coital bliss session to my place?"

He grins. "Yes."

"Awesome! I'll go home, love on my dogs, and get cleaned up. You can do what you need to do, then come join me. And bring tacos! It'll be Taco Tuesday...Tantric Taco Tuesday!"

"I like this plan." Manic leans in to lick my neck.

"Do you work tonight?" I ask him.

"No," he mumbles against my skin.

"Awesome!" I start to sing "Just the Two of Us" as I climb out of his bed. He swats my ass, and I shimmy my hips enticingly as I slip back into my clothes.

Behind me, he says, "I want you naked when I arrive. I like to eat my tacos naked."

"The fuck are you doing, woman?" Manic asks as he comes through my front gate and walks up my lawn. The dogs race to greet him, circling and sniffing at the paper sack full of tacos in his hand.

I think it's pretty obvious what I'm doing—I'm carrying an armload of extension cords and my plastic glow-in-the-dark Santa out to the middle of the lawn—but I explain anyway. "I'm decorating for the big day."

"You're not naked as I commanded," he grumbles.

"That was a command? You're going to have to work on your assertiveness when issuing commands, big boy."

"I'll take that under advisement, little girl. Now, seriously, go get naked."

"Are you going to be the one who explains to the cops why I'm hanging Christmas decorations while naked?"

"Why are you so set on hanging Christmas decorations all of a sudden?"

I stop and smile up at the gray sky. "Don't you feel it?"

"Feel what?"

"It's finally cold! 'Tis the season!"

"I thought we had a plan to eat tacos and fuck all day."

"We can do that after."

Manic groans. "Fine. I'll help you hang decorations on one condition—you have to get naked and jump on the trampoline for me afterward."

"It's a bit nipply out here, don't you think?"

"Yeah. That's the point." He winks. "I want to see those cold hard nips bounce for me, baby. Don't worry. I'll warm you up after."

"Deal." I hold out my hand to shake on it. But he sets a taco in my palm, which works as well as a handshake in my book.

"Eat," he commands, his voice full of assertiveness. "You'll need your strength for later."

I watch him pull his own taco out of its foil and take a big bite. Following his command, I do the same, watching him eat as he wearily eyes my boxes of Christmas paraphernalia.

"Who has this many Christmas decorations?" Manic asks from his perch atop my ladder, looping a strand of lights over the hooks affixed to the eaves of my house.

"Me and Clark Griswold."

"Okay, different question. *Why* do you have so many Christmas decorations?"

"For my neighbors, Mr. and Mrs. Yappy Crappy."

Manic looks down at me as I hand him the reindeer and sleigh to attach to the corner of the roof. "Mr. and Mrs. Yappy Crappy?"

I nod as I try to detangle a strand of lights. "Their real names are John and Carol Cartwright, but they are yappy-crappy people, and if the name fits, it sticks! Anyway, they hate me."

"Who could possibly hate you?"

"I know, right?" I huff and give up on the lights, tossing them aside. Manic comes down off the ladder and tries his hand at detangling. "John's practically never home, a hopeless workaholic, but Carol—she's always complaining about my house or my noise or my dogs. She called them vicious!" I gesture to my big love bugs lounging on the grass around us, calm and contented as can be. "It's breed discrimination, I tell you. Her yappy little fluff muffin is far more likely to bite than my gentle giants. Just because my babies have big mouths, everyone assumes they're maneaters. Anyway, I really want to wish John and Carol a very Merry Christmas, so I bought a lot of stuff on clearance last January, and I'm going full Griswold this year."

Manic shakes his head at me, mumbling something that sounds a lot like, "God, I love you."

I don't know if I heard him right, and I'm not going to ask for clarity. Because that word, the big L word is loaded for bear, and, heck, lots of words sound like "love." There's glove and dove. Lots of words rhyme with "you" too. He probably said, "God, I shove glue," or maybe—

"So you plan to blast them with Christmas lights visible from space and attack them with squirrels?" he asks as he gets one of the big knots loose from the lights.

I grin from ear to ear: *He knows the reference!* "*Christmas Vacation* is my all-time favorite movie. Clark Griswold is my hero."

"Oh yeah?"

"Yeah. He's this caring, creative guy whose family once thought he was a hero but now they treat him like a zero. All he wants is to give them a happy Christmas. but he gets shafted by his company, his neighbors are assholes, there's a squirrel in his Christmas tree, and Randy Quaid emptied the sewer line of his RV into the gutter in front of his house. And that's pretty much how I feel these days, too."

Manic stops untangling the light strand. "Even the Randy Quaid part?"

"Especially the Randy Quaid part! Look at all the shit people are dumping on my street." I wave my arm at the obnoxiously large McMansion that fills the lot next door. "That big beige monstrosity wasn't always there. It used to be a little blue house where this old Tejano man named Manny lived. He was a widower, and he'd sit alone on his porch most nights, so I'd join him sometimes, and he'd tell me stories about fighting in the Second World War. We were buds. But he died, and the house sold, and the yappy-crappy couple built that shit show." I wave my arm toward the empty lot on the other side of my house where a nice elderly couple used to live. "Same thing's happening over there."

"So fight back," Manic encourages. "Be the thing that doesn't change. Keep these lights up year-round."

"Oh, I should! My house could be like that bar that's been decorated for Christmas since the seventies."

"Fuck yeah, I love that place. Also, there's less labor involved in leaving all this up year-round. More time for sex."

Wait... Did he just... Is he making plans with me? For the future? I blush at the thought, finding myself, yet again, at a loss for words. I'm not even sure what to think about Manic's casual mention of making time for sex after Christmas. That's weeks away. Will he still want to see me then?

I turn my attention back to the box of Christmas décor and pull out a new strand of lights to untangle. Manic does the same, and we both whistle a little while we work.

We compromise and I keep my bottoms on while I bounce on the trampoline. It's still daylight, and I'm pretty sure it's legal to be topless in Austin, but not bottomless. Suck it, Carol Yappy Crappy! Call the cops! Let's see what they say about me freeing the nip.

I like the sensation of the cold air on my skin as I jump and jump, a little higher each time, doing the splits in midair, but Manic doesn't care about my sweet moves; his eyes are fixated on the bouncing boobs.

After about the fiftieth jump, I let myself flop onto my butt and slowly dribble to a stop. Manic comes over and grabs my ankles, pulling me to the edge of the trampoline and taking a cold hard nip into his piping hot mouth. I wrap my legs around his waist, and he carries me into the house and straight to my bedroom. But he goes past my bed and into my bathroom.

He starts up the hot water in the shower as he strips me out of the underwear I wore to bounce around, then strips his own clothes. By the time the heat is steaming up the room, he's helping me into the shower.

He washes my hair with the dye-safe shampoo, then rubs body-wash all over me with the loofah and moves me like a doll under the water to rinse every inch.

When it comes to his turn, I clean his hair with the dye-safe stuff. Even with it, our color is quickly fading, and a little trail of violet blue trickles from the tips of his hair down his back to the cleft of his ass, which I carefully, lovingly soap and scrub.

As I do, I think out loud. "I've come up with a name for you. Well, there are two possibilities for names, and you can pick which one you want."

Manic turns and rinses his back under the stream of water, staring down at me, that wet mohawk so sexy the way it lays across his head, loose tendrils escaping into his eyes.

I have to clear my throat to say, "Azul or Azure. They both mean blue, like your eyes and your hair. Both have a 'z' in them, which is totally punk rock. Azure is a bit softer, easier to say. While Azul is intense, like the name of a god, you know?" In my best impersonation of Gozer from *Ghostbusters*, I say, "There is no Manic, only Azul."

He laughs, and, *God*, I will never tire of hearing that sound.

"Which one do you prefer?"

He shrugs, which is disappointing. I want him to love his new name. That's the whole point of it. It needs to be a name that fits him and makes him happy to hear it. He seems indifferent.

But then he gets a wicked look in his eyes and comes close to me, his lips hovering right against mine. "I know how we can choose."

"How?"

"I'll eat your sweet pussy until you scream a name. Whichever name you scream is the winner."

I don't answer, but I'm betting my full-body shiver is answer enough.

Manic kisses my jaw, my neck, trailing a whole hot path of kisses down my body. I brace myself against the wall of the shower, setting one foot on the tub ledge, as he lowers to his knees in front of me. I like how he's all about oral. Too many guys aren't into it, or only do it to "return the favor." Not this guy. Pretty sure if he could survive on a diet of poontang, it's all he'd ever eat.

He pushes me back so the hot water cascades over my breasts like a waterfall. He opens his mouth, letting the water fill it, then he kisses my clit and forces the water between his teeth in a hot jet. I gasp and my knees tremble, and he helps hold me up as he goes to town. I watch, completely fascinated by the sight of him. He really is a beautiful man with that fine ass and strong back, the sleeves of his tattoos and the slash of his violet blue hair.

He's like Hades, personified. And God, that's hot.

I'm surprised I can still feel anything in my nether region after hours of sex this morning, but I feel every-fucking-thing. Spreading myself even wider, I shift so the water hits my back instead of my front. He opens his eyes to stare up at me, teasing with his tongue as he presses his fingers into my holes. Yes, *holes*, plural. I gasp, loving all the sensations of the hot water and cool air, his mouth so hungry, his fingers, grabbing and taking what he wants.

This is really working for me. In a matter of minutes, I'm huffing and shaking as he brings me to the brink of ecstasy. I half expect him to edge me away from it, but he doesn't. He takes me right over the cliff and into the deep blue waters of an amazing orgasm.

"Oh God!" I shout as I come on his tongue.

He keeps going until the aftershocks subside, then he chuckles against my pussy. "That settles it. My name is God."

He bites my thigh, then comes back onto his feet, kissing my mouth so I can taste the flavor of my excitement on his tongue. I stroke his chest, tracing wet fingers over his tattoos, thorny vines that loop down from his shoulders. "Actually, I've been thinking about it—"

"You were thinking while I was eating you out?"

"I think you're a Nix."

"Nix?"

"Yes. Nix is a name with both Greek and German origins. Nyx was the Greek Goddess of Chaos, and the name means 'night.' But in Nordic and Germanic tradition, Nix were water spirits who would lure women into the rivers and lakes with music."

"How do you know all that?"

"I have about a dozen baby name books."

Manic frowns, and I regret bringing up babies right now. Quickly he returns to the topic of Nix. "I don't play music."

I wink at him and stroke my finger down his front. "You have other lures."

"If you're naming me after a water monster, why not Kraken?"

"The kraken is just a giant squid. A nix is a shape-shifting merman, which is way sexier."

"I feel more like a kraken than a merman."

"Whatever, squid boy, you're a nix."

"Kraken."

"Nix."

"Kraken." He reaches down and cups my pussy with his palm, pressing his hand against my swollen clit.

"Oh fuck, Nix, yes, more of that," I holler and reach for the shower walls.

He shifts down to his knees again. "Fine, I'll be Nix. Now shut off your brain while I feed on you some more."

17

"My concern is you're not listening to what he's saying. You're hearing what you want to hear."

I scowl at Erica, my therapist. She's helped me a lot, and usually I love her, but right now she's harshing my mellow. There is a man in my bed for the first time in almost a year, and unlike the boys who've come and gone before, I really like this guy. So I told Erica everything, and this is her response? "What do you mean?"

"Nix told you to be careful of him, right? He's concerned he might hurt you. Don't ignore his words. He's expressing his fears. Arguing that his fears are unfounded doesn't make that true, and it won't assuage his concerns. Listen to him, talk about these things, set boundaries for yourself and for him, then stick to them."

"Boundaries?"

"Be mindful of the unhealthy habits you've exhibited in past relationships."

Here's where the list starts: co-dependency, treating men like fixer-upper projects, trust issues getting in the way of real communication… I'm a mess when it comes to men, and no one knows that more than Erica…and probably Ari.

"I don't want to deter you from exploring a relationship with Nix, but you need to be honest with yourself and with him about your expectations and desires."

This session is exhausting. Are we done yet? Erica doesn't have any clocks on the wall, and my phone is on silent in my bag, so I have no clue how much more therapy-ing is left. Might as well get my money's worth. "How do I avoid my unhealthy habits?"

"Recognize them and stop the behavior. Find ways to care about Nix without sacrificing your own feelings and needs."

"I haven't sacrificed—" Even before I finish, I know what she's going to say.

"You want a child. He's made it clear he does not. Ask yourself how you imagine that situation resolving."

"Are you saying I shouldn't fall in love with him unless he agrees to give me a baby?"

"No, not at all. He has every right to make the decision of fatherhood for himself. Ultimately, though, if his decision and yours are incompatible, you'll have to decide what sacrifices you're willing to make for him, for a baby, for yourself."

My exhaustion volcano erupts, and I'm drowned by a lahar of mud and debris that roils and rolls down the mountain of despair. How has Erica managed to crack me open and press the one button I don't want anyone pushing right now? I guess that's why my insurance company pays her the big bucks. She's good, too good. And I'm tired, too tired.

Erica's phone starts to flash, indicating it's time for me to copay and go. We settle up, and she gives me a friendly nod as she waves me out the door, where I have to navigate my issues on my own for another week. At home with the pooches, my thoughts are too loud. Too many. I need something else, something noisy. I need to dance.

The thump of the breakbeat throbs through me even before I enter the dance club. Tonight's DJ is a local chick, and I love when she spins. Right as I'm stamped in through the door, she fades from Fatboy Slim to The Chemical Brothers's "Hey Boy Hey Girl," and it's the best entrance music ever. I clomp my big dancing boots through the bright red lights of the hallway to where it opens up to the main room, a towering space full of people crowding the dance floor and filling every inch on the balcony above.

It's like walking into a gorgeous orgy, bodies moving in a hypnotic trance so in sync with the music and each other it's like we're one organism, writhing beautifully. I step into the crowd and let the organism take over my body, too, tilting my head back and moving my hands up to twist and curl my wrists to one beat as my hips sway with another.

God, it feels good. It feels like nothing and everything all at once. My brain stops working; only my body can function here, taken over with movement and sensation as one song transitions to the next. Sweat coats my skin and trickles down my back as Underworld's "Between Stars" begins. It's my current favorite, and I start to jump with the rhythm, my body totally out of my control now; it's part of the sound, part of the universe all around me, floating and dancing between the stars of the cosmos.

Some dude wraps an arm around my waist and brings me crashing back to earth. I wiggle away from Mr. Grabby Hands and go to a different part of the floor, where I work to get my rhythm back. It's the part of the song that always gives me chills, when the beat drops and they build it back again. Ready for the rhythm to kick in, I hop like an impatient bunny.

Some other guy clutches my waist, grinding his half-hard cock against my ass. I karate chop his arm so he lets me go and spin on my heels. "If you want to keep your dick attached to your body, you will keep your hands to yourself, got it?"

I might be small, but I'm fierce. Mr. Ass Grinder seems to understand the seriousness of the situation because he moves away, grumbling about "bitches." Whatever, asshole. I try to get into the rhythm again, but my mood is ruined. *Fucking men!*

My head has found me here on the dance floor, and it's groping at me, too, assaulting me with unwanted thoughts.

"Are you sure you're not using Nix as a surrogate for the child you want? You renamed him. You remade his appearance..." The memory of Erica's question from our session is a discordant sound that jars me out of the

euphoria of this space. Have I turned Nix—Manic…Nix!—into a fixer-upper project?

"Bipolar disorder is manageable with medication and other therapies, but some people struggle quite a bit with it. If he's concerned about hurting you, you need to learn more about his particular situation. Does he get violent when he has episodes?" The memory of her questions echo on the same loop as the music now. She has a point. I don't know much about his disorder. I haven't asked.

"Sheryl, you have a large capacity for love, and you tend to be a caretaker in most of your relationships, but you have to be mindful you don't give too much of yourself to someone who isn't giving anything back." Caretaker—since when is that a bad thing? People need care, and I give it. You're welcome, fuckers!

I wobble on jelly legs to a wall and find my phone to text Nix: "Are you working?"

"Home," he replies within seconds.

"I'm coming over. I have questions."

18

"Do you even like the name Nix?" As far as greetings go, it's a weird one, but I need to know.

"Why are you so sweaty?" he asks as he shuts the door behind me and follows me into his living room. I'm pacing around aimlessly, energized like a live wire. This is the first time I've seen his living room with the lights on. He has more sci-fi collectibles here, an ungodly amount. Wow. He's such a darling dork.

"I was dancing the demons away," I answer.

"Did it work?"

"Nah. So, your name. Do you like it, or did I just come in, style your hair, and rename you like you're a baby for me to mother?"

His eyes widen, clearly not liking that description of our relationship any more than I do.

"If you had your choice of any name for me to call you, what would it be?"

"Honestly, I prefer Manic."

"Really? Why?"

"Because," he sort of huffs and collapses backward onto the couch, "I earned it."

I stop pacing and scowl at him. "Earned it? It's a nickname that mocks your disorder."

"Yeah, *my* disorder. The disorder that tried to kill me and almost succeeded. But I fought back. I fight it every day. And I'm still here. That survival, *my* survival, has been hard won. So let people call me Manic. I don't give a fuck what they think it means. I *know* what it means."

Well. Shit. I collapse onto the couch, too, then burst into tears.

"Why are you crying?"

"I'm sorry. I'm so sorry."

"For what?"

"For treating you like a fixer-upper. You're already fixed. You're a DIY miracle! And I'm an ass."

"Come here," he says, and when I don't move, he drags me onto his lap. I curl against him, crying into the crick of his neck, feeling such relief to let the emotions out of me, even as I die of embarrassment for leaking them all over his shirt.

"You're not an ass." He strokes my back.

"Why were you going to let me call you some random merman name?"

"Because it seemed to make you happy. I like to make you happy."

"Oh my God, don't do that. Don't let me do things to you that you don't want. I need you to stand up for yourself, or I'll walk all over you, and you'll hate me for it and call me 'too much' and leave. Okay, Manic?" Now that I know he takes pride in his name, I never want to stop saying it. "Promise me."

"Okay, Sonny Cher. I promise."

I sigh with relief.

"Though I wouldn't mind you walking all over me. I still have my bed of nails."

I pull away enough to see his eyes, and he waggles his brows suggestively. "You're so weird. I really love that about you."

He blinks at my casual use of the L word. I blink at it too. What am I saying? What do I mean? Quickly, I change the subject. "Do you like your hair?"

Manic nuzzles and kisses my neck, licking some of the sweat off my skin. "Yes, very much. I've stopped wearing my cowboy hat at work."

"Really? You wore the hat to hide your hair?"

"My eyes," he mumbles, preoccupied with tasting my throat.

"I don't understand."

He pulls away enough to explain. "The cowboy hat is for tips. Tourists love to take a walk on the wild side and buy drinks from a punk-rock cowboy in a dive bar. But in the beginning, I wore it because then I didn't have to make eye contact with customers. People can't see my eyes under the brim, and I could nod at a customer so they'd know I was listening to them without having to look at them. But I like to show my Sher hair off. I only put the hat on if I'm having a down day."

"Was today a hat or no-hat shift?"

"No hat."

"So it's been a good day."

He nods against me.

"Awesome, because I have more questions."

"But you taste delicious. Can we save questions for after I lick every inch of you?"

"Have you ever been violent?"

His sexy, relaxed demeanor changes in an instant. His posture goes rigid and so do the lines of his face. "What do you mean?"

"You said you're afraid you'll hurt me. Do you mean during an episode? I want to understand—"

"I don't mean physically. Even at my worst, I would never hurt you like that."

"Then how would you hurt me?"

"I'm an asshole sometimes. I can be careless and cruel. I get into these moods where I say shitty things I don't mean. Or things I do mean, but I don't bother with tact. People always think they can handle it. They rarely can. Glen, the guy who owns the bar, is the only person who's stuck with me for any real length of time. I'd like you to stick around, too, but I'm terrified I'll fuck up, and you'll leave like everyone else."

"Oh, neat. We share the same fear of abandonment."

"I won't abandon you," he says.

"You say that now, but—"

"I won't abandon you." He repeats his words, this time with assertiveness in his voice. "As to your original question about violence— I have been violent during manic episodes, but it's been years since I got that bad, and the violence was always directed inward."

He lifts his left hand from my knee, flexing his tattooed fingers into a slight fist, then turns it over so I'm looking at the inside of his forearm. His tattoos are so beautiful—hyper realistic thorny vines that twist and tangle down his arms, connecting a whole variety of other tattoos into a pair of full sleeves.

"You can't see the scars as well since I added the tattoos."

I look more closely, trying to make out the patterns beneath the mask of his body art. He clenches his fist, so his veins and tendons pop out more, and right along with them I see the scars now. Half a dozen jagged lines across his wrist and forearm. I touch one, tracing my finger the full length. It breaks my heart to imagine there was a moment in his life when he was hurting so much he cut himself.

In an emotionless tone, he says. "This is what landed me in the hospital in Ohio and earned me a bipolar diagnosis. This was the lowest I've ever been, and every day I work to keep from getting there ever again."

He turns his hand over. "The knuckles came about a year later."

I look more closely at the knuckles of this hand—the hand that says OFF!—and there are scars here too, jagged and mangled. "What happened?"

"I punched a brick wall, repeatedly. I was changing medications and had an episode. Since then, I've found treatment that actually works for me, for the most part."

"What meds do you take?"

"Epilepsy medication, basically. In a bipolar brain, the meds work as mood stabilizers." He turns the question back on me. "What meds are you on?"

"Speed, basically."

"Is that where you get your energy?"

"No, oddly enough, the amphetamines calm me down. But if I ever have to take a piss test, my meds show up as speed, which is annoying."

"I tried amphetamines for a while. I've tried everything. Couldn't ejaculate on SSRIs, which sucked. Lithium built up a toxicity in my kidneys, also sucked. The anti-seizure meds seem to work though."

Manic grins a little, and I kiss him. It feels nice, this sharing and caring thing we're doing. It seems like the most intimate thing we've done together. I think I should feel vulnerable to have him know so much, but all I feel is…good.

Against my lips, Manic asks, "Have I answered all your questions?"

"The important ones."

"Can I lick you all over now?"

"Yes please."

19

MONDAY, DECEMBER 13, 2010

"So anyway, I think I'm in love with him," I announce to the family as we set the table in preparation for Family Dinner Night.

"Huh?" Several people pipe up. "Who?"

"Oh my God, Manic?" Ari squeals, her eyes big with excitement.

I nod and set down a bowl of fruit salad as she yanks me into her arms, hugging the oxygen out of me.

Ari hops a couple of times. "I knew it!"

"Wait. You're in love with Manic now?" Jake asks. "Didn't he stand you up last week?"

"That was ages ago and totally not his fault."

Nicole sounds all accusatory when she states, "I thought you were missile locked and aiming for insemination. When did falling in love enter the picture?"

"I was...am...was." I shrug.

"Make sense...like...now!" Nicole gestures with wide arms, indicating I should fill in the gaps of this conversation. As if I have anything to put in the gaps. This conversation is a ship with a rusty hull, nothing but gaps, and it's sinking fast.

"So...like...I slept with Manic, a bunch of times, and he's been spending the night at my house a lot, and I really like it when he does because he's super great and surprisingly sweet, and I think he's maybe possibly my boyfriend now." I consider for a moment. "No, he's *definitely* my boyfriend now, and I invited him to dinner tonight, so be nice and don't ruin this for me."

He *is* coming this time. I confirmed with him an hour ago.

Everyone stares at me for what feels like ages, but it's probably only a few seconds. Finally, I'm saved by the bell when the buzzer at the front gate goes off.

Not waiting for the actual residents of the house to answer, I scamper over to the security monitor, where I see him on his motorcycle, leaning toward the keypad. I smile at him, even though he can't see me, and buzz him through the gate.

Turning toward the door, I find everyone watching me, looking a bit stunned. With a shrug at them, I run out to greet Manic as he pulls to a stop and sets his Harley on its kickstand. When he's done all that, I pretty much tackle him with affection.

Manic chuckles a little as he returns my kiss and hug. Then, realizing I've climbed onto him and his bike, I climb back down and take his hand, pulling him off the motorcycle and toward the big house.

The next person to practically climb him like a tree is Tommy, who leaps off the floor when he sees his new friend and comes to exchange the elaborate handshake they invented while sitting on my trampoline. The adults greet Manic with slightly less enthusiasm. It's all very friendly, and very strange, like no one knows how to act around him.

It bothers me. I hate awkwardness that I haven't directly caused. So I directly cause some awkwardness: "What's the problem? Why are you all acting like you have sticks up your A-S-Ses? Am I not allowed to bring a date to Family Dinner Night? Am I always supposed to be the sad, lonely spinster?"

"No, babe, it's not that," Nicole says for them all as she does the weirdest thing—sort of hugging me—as she continues, "It's just you never have. In all the years we've had the family dinners, you never introduced us to any of your boyfriends."

I smirk and shrug. "Because I never had any boyfriends."

Oh shit. We keep throwing around the B-word with Manic present. I glance over to see his eyes are wide, bugged out so big they look like they could fall right out of his head. *Okay*, so, maybe I should have tested the B-word waters before I dove in. No one better let my L-word revelation fly too.

But before I can freak out too much, Manic slides his arm around my waist and squeezes. I guess he approves of the B-word usage. And I guess this means I have a boyfriend now.

Ha. Weird.

"Let me take that off your hands," Ari says, and I realize Manic has slipped off a backpack holding a couple bags of chips in it—his contribution to the potluck. Just then, the buzzer on the oven beeps, and it's time for dinner. Everyone leaps into action, all of us going through the motions of a potluck, dishing up food onto our plates, making our drinks, and reuniting around Jakole's dining table.

This time, for the first time ever, we have an even number of adults at the table and fill all the seats. Tommy and Mia enjoy their time at the kiddo card table, and I feel like an actual grown-up at the big kid table.

When we're all seated and have started eating, it's Greg who pipes up, sounding like a big brother when he asks, "So, Manic, what are your intentions with Sheryl?"

Everyone sort of blinks, then laughs and comments.

"Good to know we can still leave it to Greg to make things awkward."

"Are you practicing for when Mia is dating, and you're interviewing her suitors?"

"What? I don't want to see her get hurt." Greg turns to me. "Sher, I care about you. We all do. If you're bringing a guy around then that means he's special to you, and I want to know you're special to him too."

Aww. It makes me feel all warm and fuzzy inside to think that Greg cares enough to grill my boyfriend like a protective dad.

"Sher is very special to me," Manic answers as he turns to me and adds, "My intention is to keep her smiling, best I can."

Aww. I turn to Manic, even more surprised by his declaration than I was by Greg's question. The fork load of my first bite of food hangs out there, long forgotten and getting cold.

Manic turns his full attention to me and adds, "I like when she smiles."

I'm glad I didn't take that bite of food because there's no way I could swallow it, not with this lump in my throat. Seriously, when did Manic get so…sweet? Cuz, that was *so sweet!*

I smile so wide my face hurts. Manic winks at me, and I wink back.

As we eat and chat, everyone acts super freaking cool with him, like he's another member of the family. And when the twins start to caterwaul for titties, Nicole nurses them, and then we pass them around for cuddles.

I don't expect Manic to hold them, figuring he'll pass little Biggie—aka Baby Greg, who I started calling BG, and then it naturally morphed into Biggie—from me straight to Alex. But he doesn't. He adjusts himself in his seat a little better as he nestles the tiny bundle in his arms and stares down at the baby.

My heart melts and drips all over the floor, and my mind skips like a broken record, remembering all those mantras I've been repeating to myself as of late. *Just because a man is good with kids doesn't mean he wants to be a father.*

But…oh my God…he *so* good with kids. Biggie stares at Manic as he makes funny faces and lets the little guy awkwardly clench his fist around one of the carabiners dangling from his ears.

"Getting ideas for your next sideshow act, Manic?" Ari asks. "Swing the twins from your earlobes?"

Laughter rumbles through Manic, but he doesn't change his expression even once as the little tike curls his tiny fist around the blue and silver hoop and tugs Manic's ear a little.

Oof, my ovaries just plain explode.

When he passes the baby away, and we're both empty-handed, Manic reaches for me under the table, his hand squeezing my knee. I reach down and cover his fingers.

As Lou Reed sings on the stereo about what a perfect day it is, Manic turns his hand over to lace our fingers together, and it's simply the most romantic moment of my whole entire life.

Any uncertainty is behind me now. Baby or no baby, I'm definitely, totally, completely, hopelessly in love with this man.

20

MONDAY, DECEMBER 13, 2010

"You're singing."

"Sher." Manic's voice is stern, brooking no argument.

"Manic," I argue.

"Fuck," he huffs as he relents.

Clearly I'm better at the stubborn stare than he is. Noted. With a wink, I smile as he comes to his feet. "You can do it, big boy."

"Lead the way, little girl," he grumbles as I tug him onto the stage, and the DJ cues up the song I requested.

When we're ready, mics in hand, the opening chords of Sonny & Cher's "I Got You Babe" start up. Manic groans and rolls his eyes at me, but he sings. It's awful but a hilarious version of awful. He never lifts his voice to any sort of octave, just a low gravelly drone through the lyrics. I do all the work of Cher, making our rendition totally awesome. The crowd loves it.

Back in our seats, as everyone's attention focuses on the next act, I throw my arms around Manic. "That was so fun!"

He grumbles some more. "I hate that song."

I pull away. Blink at him. "You do?"

"I do."

"Then why do you always call me Sonny Sher?"

"I call you that because your name is Sher and you're *sunny*, like the sun. Not Sonny, like Bono. Though in hindsight I see how you could have made that mistake." He sort of grins for the first time since I dragged him to Karaoke Night after Family Dinner Night.

"Huh." A giggle bubbles out of me, and his grin grows into a full smile.

He leans a little closer so I can hear him over the dude screeching for someone to pour some sugar on him. "The first time I ever laid eyes on you, your hair was dyed bright yellow—not blond, yellow—and you were wearing a yellow unitard to match. You were very sunny that day and have been pretty much every day since."

"The banana chase!"

"What?"

"I was dressed like a banana, and all my skate mates wore monkey ears and tails and chased me around town while some guy played "Yakety Sax" over and over again on an old boombox. It was a promo event for roller derby."

"That explains why your first words to me were, 'Hey handsome, want to eat my banana?' "

I giggle. "What'd you say?"

"No."

I laugh fully now. "Sounds like something you'd say."

"I've changed my mind, Sher." He nuzzles his nose against my neck and licks me there. "I desperately want to eat your banana."

"That sounds—"

He kisses me, right there in the middle of my sentence, right there in the middle of Karaoke Night. He kisses me with a whole lot of energy and passion, fizzing my mind and sending zings of excitement all through my body. I wrap my arms around him and climb into his lap so we can properly make out.

"Get a room," a couple of people joke, and it's a solid suggestion. Manic moves to stand, and I wrap my legs around his waist so he can carry me up the ramp and out the door. Outside, the cold is bracing, but everywhere we touch feels hot.

He'd parked Sally on the curb out front, so it's not far to walk before he sets me on his seat and hands me the helmet. He mounts the bike, and I wrap my arms around him again, from behind this time.

When he cranks that throaty engine, everything vibrates. God, I'm so horny for him. He drives us through the empty streets to my house, a few blocks over on the east side, and parks in my drive, right beside my green monster.

It fits so right. *He* fits so right. It's all just…so right.

We're back at it, making out as he tries not to trip over my stepping stones and garden gnomes on the way up the lawn. On the porch, he spins me around and presses my front to the door as he starts to pull my skirt up in the back. His fingers probe everywhere, and his breath is hot on my neck as he whispers, "Want to give the yappy-crappy neighbors a show?"

I can't answer. And I can't get the key in the lock. Everything is too distracting. His hands, his mouth, the cold breeze on my bare booty as he slides my underwear down to my thighs. Inside, the dogs are barking like mad.

I drop the keys, and his laugh rumbles through me, tickling everywhere. He goes down to his knees behind me, and I feel his mouth on my ass, his tongue stroking the seam, then probing between my thighs to taste how wet my pussy is for him.

With a groan, he comes to his feet. Keys in hand, he pushes one into the lock, turning the knob and getting us inside. My dogs are way too curious, and I have to push their nosy noses away as Manic lifts me up out of their reach and carries me to my bedroom, kicking the door shut behind us.

He tosses me on the bed, and I bounce face down onto the covers as he falls on top. His hands move in a frenzy, pushing all my clothes out of the way as his mouth goes again to my behind.

His fingers press into my pussy as he licks and bites at me, then, with his fingers coated in my wetness, he presses one into my backside. I gasp, still not quite used to that sensation. He groans and comes up to crush me fully under his weight, his breath hot at my ear again as he whispers, "Your ass is so perfect, baby. I want to fuck you here so badly."

"So do it?"

"Let's get you ready first."

"Ready?"

"To take me."

With that, I hear him unzip his jeans, and suddenly I'm full of him, overwhelmed as he shoves his cock deep into my pussy. He pulls me backward, until I'm on my hands and knees as he takes me hard and fast from behind.

"Play with your clit, baby. Come for me."

I do as ordered, gasping and groaning as he adds a second finger to my ass then fucks me fast and furious, that Prince Albert hitting me in just the right spot. He curls his fingers in a come-hither tease, and, whoa, the new sensation has me squealing. Wrapping my hair around his empty fist, he yanks, pulling me up until I'm on my knees and flush against his chest as he nails me from behind.

Fuck. Me. This is so good. This is so… "Fuck!" I come so *hard*, and he groans and huffs, filling me with his cum. I like how it feels, warm and wet when it drips down my thighs as he keeps moving inside me.

I've never liked it so messy and dirty and rough before. He's so far beyond the usual lazy stoner fucks I've generally known. He's intense and attentive and—

I yelp as he pulls his cock and fingers out of me. Then I feel cold when he steps away from me, going into the bathroom. He comes back out with a warm washcloth and a towel, encouraging me to roll onto my back so he can clean me up.

He's so gentle right now, and it's so different from how he was when he was railing me only moments ago. It's like I just fucked Mr. Hyde, and now Dr. Jekyll is handling the aftercare. I like it. No, I love it: the two faces of him, the sweet and the sour parts of what make up the Manic mosaic.

When he gently slides the warm washcloth up my inner thigh and strokes it over my pussy, I spread my legs to give him better access, and then I just say it, "I love you."

Manic freezes, his hand with that warm cloth stopping midstroke as he stares at me with unblinking eyes. Did I Medusa him and turn him to stone?

No. There, he blinked. He's freaking out, which makes me freak out too.

Quickly, I backpedal. "I mean, maybe it's not the big L kind of love. Maybe it's, like, a lot of little L kinds of love, you know?"

Manic's frozen posture thaws. He settles onto his side beside me, tossing the washcloth away and turning all his attention to me. He strokes his fingers through my hair, then down my cheek, resting his palm there as he stares me right in the eyes.

He looks pensive, like he's thinking really hard about something. When he comes to some conclusion in his head he finally says, "I love you, too, Sher. And it's the big L kind of love."

Now I want to take my backpedal back, because that's what I meant, too, and if he's saying it now, then I'm saying it too. Except, when I open my mouth, a different thought comes flying out. "But what about Ari?"

He frowns. "What about Ari?"

"I thought you were in love with her."

"What? Why?"

"Because you're always flirting with her at the bar."

"It's part of the job. I always flirt with you too."

"No. You tease me, like I'm your kid sister."

"Wow, I'm worse at flirting than I thought." He grabs both sides of my face, holding me still so I have to stare up at him. "Look, the truth is this—Ari is hot, and if she'd ever been up for it, I would have fucked her, no question about it. But the way I feel about you is different. You're like a demon possessing me."

That doesn't sound like a good thing.

"You possess me—mind, body and soul." *Better.* "When you're not around, you're all I can think about. And when you are around, you're all I care about. You make me feel things I didn't know I could feel. It's scary and amazing. I fucking love being possessed by you. I love everything about you. I love *you*."

Okay. Wow. I'm stunned. I'm scared. I panic under Manic's weight, looking up, down, anywhere else—finally closing my eyes to avoid his piercing gaze.

I need a moment, need to think. Need to mull this over. Because I know from vast experience, the only time men ever say sweet words is when they lie. Men only *love* you when they want something from you. But what could Manic want that I haven't already given him?

Fuck. I'm freaking out.

And why am I freaking out? I started this whole thing. I said it first!

Opening my eyes, I stare intently into his, trying to navigate the deep blue ocean of his gaze and find the truth. But when I look, the truth is all I see. There's no lie detected here, no mask he hides behind. He's made himself vulnerable to me, flayed himself open with all his insecurities, showing more and more as my tense silence stretches and yawns between us.

Oh God, it's true. I trust him. And it's terrifying. I burst into tears.

"What's the matter?" Manic asks with a gentle voice, his hand stroking away the tears from my cheeks. It's so sweet. He's being so ridiculously *sweet*.

I cry harder but manage a few words in a squeaky tear-stained voice. "I believe you, and I'm not used to being able to believe people when they use that word. It's freaking me out."

He grins a little. "It's freaking me out too. I should take the word back."

Like I did. Hesitantly, I ask, "Do you want to?"

He wipes more tears off my cheeks and brings his fingers to his mouth, tasting the salt of my tears. Then, in a quiet voice he says simply, "No."

"Okay, good, because I regret taking my L word back a minute ago. I love you, Manic, in the big and little ways."

Softly, slowly, he smiles as he presses his forehead against mine. Then he kisses me, and that is soft and slow too. This time, when we come together, it's different from every time before. This must be what "making love" is. And I love it, because when we come, we come together in every way imaginable, and it's like nothing I've ever known in all my life.

"Weird," I say afterward.

"What's weird?" he asks.

"The sex is different when you're in love, I guess."

"How do you mean?"

"It's like that Foreigner song. This totally felt like the first time."

Manic buries his face in my hair and laughs. "God, I love you, Sher."

21

Ultraviolet Void doesn't fit my mood anymore. Manic has been filling all my voids lately, so I turn to Passion Pink to express my current state of being.

Manic still likes the void for himself, so we spend the morning dying each other's hair before I need to go to my shift at the shelter. The animals like my new shade and the sweet smell of the hair product as they nuzzle me between checkups and shots.

When my day is done, Manic's shift is only starting, and I have my weekly headshrinker appointment. I hurry home to shuck my scrubs, put on a bright, sunny dress—I can't get enough of him thinking I'm sunny—and hug the dogs before heading back out. The sun sets early this time of year, and it feels later than it is. My yard shines with a few thousand lights and a glowing Santa as I start my journey, pumping my legs hard to get my blood flowing for my trek under the freeway to the west side of town. I reach Manic's bar just as he's throwing someone out.

"Oh my goodness, was someone besides me causing drama?"

Manic curls his finger in a sexy come-hither gesture. I skate into his arms, and he grimaces. "Jesus, you're as cold as a cherry popsicle."

He rubs all over me to warm me up. "Do you like the taste of cherry popsicles?"

"Very much," he says, then he devours me with a kiss that fills me with heat from my lips all the way to the tips of my toes, totally melting my popsicle.

A little stunned and wobbly, I need Manic's help to steady me as he pulls me inside and leads me to a seat. He's about to fix me something to drink when I stop him.

"Nothing for me, I'm just here for a quick visit before I head to my shrink's office."

"Oh."

He looks uncomfortable at the subject, so I ask, "Don't you see a therapist?"

He nods and sort of grimaces. "Yeah. Tom, I hate him."

"You hate your therapist?"

He shrugs. "I hate him with love. He's too good at his job. Always calling me on my bullshit."

"What bullshit? You're a straight shooter. Me, on the other hand—I try to hide behind a lot of words. Erica always sees through it. I guess I hate her with love too."

He chuckles. "My bullshit doesn't come in the form of words, it's actions—like drinking alcohol. I shouldn't. But I do. Tom has managed to get me to recognize when I'm feeling down or paranoid and limit myself on those days. But if he had his way, I'd be a teetotaler."

Interesting. All those times he didn't drink with me, maybe it wasn't personal. Who knew? I want to ask for more details, but he speaks first and what he says stuns me.

"He called me on my bullshit when I got the vasectomy too."

We haven't talked about that big ole elephant in the room since our naked swim almost a month ago. I've wanted to understand it better, but I'm like a bull in a China shop when I start probing for details, and I wanted to be more mindful about that when it comes to Manic.

And now, as he extends the red carpet for questions, all I can muster is, "Why?"

Manic frowns as he considers for a moment, but he never takes his gaze from mine, staring deep into my eyes as he answers, "He said I should have discussed it with him before having the procedure done. That my reasoning for it wasn't sound. He considers my vasectomy another form of cutting, an act of self-harm."

Holy shit. I'm stunned. What a thing to say. What an insight to share. I contemplate skipping my appointment with Erica so I can sit here and listen as he dredges these revelations from his depths.

"Was it?" I ask.

He purses his lips like he's thinking it over. But when he finally opens his mouth to answer, someone from the other end of the bar hollers for his attention, holding up an empty pint glass. And with that, whatever truth spell was cast over us bursts like a bubble. I want to kick that customer square in the butt with my skate, but Manic grins at me and shoos me out the door. "I guess you better head to your appointment."

"Uh."

"Can I come over tonight after my shift?"

"Uh…" Seriously, he's left me speechless. Finally, I form the right words. "Yeah. Of course."

"I'll see you then." Manic leans across the bar and plants a soft kiss on the tip of my nose, of all places. He turns away, grabs his cowboy hat from the gargoyle head by the liquor bottles, and crosses to the customer who needs a refill.

"What about children?" Erica asks me.

"What *about* children?" I counter, Manic's vasectomy revelations still fresh and at the front of my mind. It's irrational—to be angry with Erica. But I don't want to be here talking *about* Manic when I could be back at the bar talking *to* Manic about all this.

Erica crosses one leg over the other and leans toward me, and in her gentle voice she says, "For as long as I've seen you, you've always indicated that children are important to you, more important than a romantic relationship. But in your last two visits, you've primarily talked about Nix—"

"Manic," I interrupt, wishing to nix the whole Nix thing.

She's clearly confused, so I explain it all for what will hopefully be the last time. Nodding, she starts again. "Since you've begun talking about Manic, you've stopped talking about your desire to have children. Last week we discussed honoring the boundaries, limits, and needs Manic has expressed to you. And it seems like you've been mindful of that. Now I would like to discuss *your* boundaries, limits, and needs. For example, have you told him of your need for children?"

"I don't know if it's a need so much as a want. Was a want... Is a want..." I huff. My mouth is betraying me...as usual. Making me sound as defensive and discombobulated as I feel.

"What's changed?" Erica probes.

Manic. I don't say that out loud. I don't say anything out loud. Erica doesn't either. She watches me, making me squirm, forcing me to listen to the thoughts that whisper and echo and scream in my head. When I can't take the silence anymore, I fill it: "I have this fantasy, sort of a Goldilocks fantasy. Not, like, some smutty three bears kind of thing, but more this idea that, for once, I'm *just right*. Not too much or too little. Just...right." I blather on. "And kids, they love me. I'm just right for them, so maybe I wanted a kid so they'd love me. Because a kid, well, they kind of have to love you, at least for a while. Then they hate you for a while, and that's normal, but as long as you do a decent job of raising them, they won't hate you forever. And I plan to do a decent job—more than decent. I'd do a damn fine job raising a kid. I wouldn't be like my parents at all. I would be present and accounted for and making chocolate chip pancakes and shit. I'd be a good mom.

"Then Manic came along. Well, I mean, he didn't just *come along*. I've known him for ages, and I always knew I could count on him. Even when I didn't know his real name or where he lived or what he looked like naked, I knew deep in my soul that he was a solid person, a solid friend. But then..."

I drift off, not sure how to express the magnitude of what I'm feeling. On Thanksgiving, everything changed for me. The twins were born. I'd declared my intention to be a mom, and I thought that was all I wanted, all I needed. But then came Manic, and it was like meeting him again, but for the first time. And every day we spend together I get to meet more of him and love more of him. And it feels like bubbles in my chest that fizz and pop and excite me, and that feels good. Maybe this is what I need. Forget about all the rest, I just need—

"But then?" Erica brings my train of thought back from its derailment.

"But then we had sex…like, a bunch of times, and we started to cuddle and talk and stuff, and then the word 'love' came up, and when it did, this epiphany bomb went off in my brain. It was like, 'This is all I've ever wanted. Just to be loved.' "

I blink at the sound of my own voice as it says those words, a bit stunned by the revelation. And even more stunned when I keep talking. "And Manic—he's a full-grown adult with an adult brain who can make choices for himself, not some kid trapped in a relationship with their parent for better or worse. He could leave at any time, but he doesn't. And I love that. I need that. I need him to choose not to leave."

I glance over at Erica, who's been silent for a while, and I see her smiling at me. Her phone is flashing, indicating our time is up, but she doesn't seem to be in a hurry to shoo me out the door. Instead, she says, "I'm pleased to hear you're putting a lot of thought into this."

I'm so overwhelmed with questions now, desperate for advice. But we've already gone over our time for the week. Erica stands, and I'm expected to follow as she eases me toward the door.

She must see the lost look in my eyes, because—in lieu of the usual farewell pleasantries—she says, "Sheryl, talk to Manic about your wishes as you explore this relationship with him. Talk, listen, and learn about each other. Establish your boundaries as you recognize his. And *enjoy yourself.* New relationships can be fun and exciting. Let yourself feel that."

"Was it?"

Manic stares at me, then asks, "What?"

"Was your vasectomy a form of self-harm?" I pick up our conversation where we left off.

Manic freezes for a moment like he's rewinding his evening so he's back with me, on the same page. "I…uh…can I come in?"

I realize we're still standing in my doorway, the dogs circling around us excitedly.

"Sorry." I back up to let him in the house.

Manic seems unsure of each step he takes as he slips off his motorcycle jacket and lays it over the back of my couch. When he turns to me, it's like he's schooled his expression, shuttered the windows in his eyes. He's unreadable.

I open my mouth to ask more questions, but he swoops in for a kiss, silencing me very effectively. His lips are cold from the ride over here, but his mouth is hot. It's a jolting combination of sensations, and it fritzes my brain.

Oh, this is bad. He's using his mouth magic against me. With a huff I pull away and collapse onto the couch. My dogs join me. For the last hour and a half it's been me and the pooches here in the dark, sitting with our thoughts, snuggled together while we waited for Manic's shift to end. Seeming to sense when they're needed, they pile around me now, my sweet sentinels guarding my heart.

"Sheryl, I'm tired. Can we talk about this tomorrow?"

"Your kiss didn't feel tired."

With a groan, Manic collapses onto the couch beside my pit bull pity party, and a few of the dogs, recognizing his need for love and kisses, turn on me to administer to him. Traitors. He rolls his head on the back of my couch to face me and grins a little. "Different kind of tired."

"So you want to fuck instead of talk?"

With another groan, he reaches over to find me among the dogs, pulling me out from under them to set me on his lap. "How about if I keep my cock warm in your pussy while we talk?"

I guffaw, letting out an obnoxious laugh, but I mean… *What?*

He raises a brow at me. "It's a kink. Cock warming. Look it up."

I keep laughing.

"Are you kink shaming me?"

I bite my lip, a little annoyed that he's so thoroughly changed the subject, and even more annoyed that I think it's *cute*. Also, it's distracting how I can feel his hard length pressing against me through his jeans.

I stand, and his eyes widen with what looks like horror, as if he's lost without my weight on his lap, which only encourages me as I slip my underwear off and climb back on top. Unzipping his jeans, I pull him from his briefs and slip down onto him.

Oh God! His clothes and skin are still cold from his ride over here, but his cock is *so* hot and big and fills me up. We both groan at the new sensations, and then… That's it. He doesn't move to fuck me; he just fills me and stills. Pulling me against his chest, he encourages me to rest my head on his shoulder as we stay like this, my pussy warming his cock. Honestly, it feels weird but also amazing, like a new, more intimate way to kiss or hold hands.

"Yes, with Tom's help I've come to recognize that my vasectomy was a clinical form of self-harm," he says after we've been together like this for a while. This cock-warming thing is so distracting. I wasn't expecting him to actually talk. I'm even more surprised when he keeps going. "I had the vasectomy when I was angry about my diagnosis. I was pissed off at my mother for passing her crazy genes down to me. I didn't want to pass it down, too, so I had the doctors cut me."

"I'm sorry," I say and wiggle a little to adjust on his lap. He lets out a sexy groan from the sensation my movement gives him, and I repeat myself, but for a different reason. "Sorry."

After a moment, he continues. "Regardless of why I had it done, it's done. And I never thought about it again…until you."

That last part grabs my attention. I look up and find him staring down at me. He pulls a lock of my hair away from my shoulder and twirls it around his finger. The look in his eyes gives me pause; there's a twinge of terror there, like allowing himself to think about all this is overwhelming him. So I tell him what I've been thinking since I watched him jump around on the trampoline with Tommy. "You're so great with kids. They adore you."

"When I'm having a good day. But what about when I'm not?"

"I've spent a day with you when you were down—"

He shakes his head. "That was barely a blip. It's been a long time since I was truly down. The medication helps keep me steady, but if I ever change meds or hit a low they can't help, what would that do for a kid? I know what it does—I lived with my mom for sixteen years. It was a fucking nightmare. I don't want to be someone's nightmare."

The way he looks at me when he says that, I wonder if we're actually talking about kids now, or if he means me. He frowns. In the dim light of my living room, his expression throws shadows that exaggerate every emotion in his face, turning his frown deeper, more intense. I want to change that expression, have his intensity pulled elsewhere, so I roll my hips. It's a tiny little movement, but it has a big impact.

With a groan, his expression changes, from lost to lust in an instant. His lips part on a groan when I move again, and I lean up to kiss him softly, my mouth open to his, both of us sighing and gasping.

Slowly, and so sweetly, we make love. Every tiny movement rolls through us in powerful waves until we come in a breathtaking climax that has us gasping and groping and desperate, like we're the air and the soul and the life of each other. Between this and our foray into Tantric sex, I've never known anything as intense as what I feel with Manic. I've never known anyone as intense as him, and I'm hooked, addicted to him.

As we stay linked together, his cock still warm inside me, I rest my cheek against his chest, and he strokes every little strand of hair off my face as he whispers, "I love you, Sheryl. And if it's within my power, I will give you anything you want."

"But what do *you* want?" I ask, my voice is breathy, sounding so light for such a heavy question.

"You."

22

"All we ever do is lie around naked at my house," I say as I snuggle a little closer to Manic on the bed, reveling in his warmth as the dogs grumble from my movement.

He hugs me against him. "I know. It's fucking great."

"Let's do something different today."

He frowns.

"Or I'll start to think all you want from me is orgasms."

He tries to hide his smile, twisting his lips into a smirk as he asks, "What would you like to do instead of having orgasms?"

Well, when he puts it like that…

No! Today we will do something that requires clothing. After Manic's revelations on Thursday night, I've been thinking a lot about our relationship, and it occurred to me that our closeness seems to come when we're naked. But we need to get close in other ways too. So I sit up and bounce a little. "Let's go to the park."

Whether or not Manic is excited by my suggestion or just nodding as he watches the bouncing boobs, I don't know, but the dogs are definitely excited. The word "park" to them is like the sound of their food container when I open it to scoop out their kibble: a fan favorite.

The pooches leap off the bed, huffing and whining as they spin in circles. Majority and dogs rule in this house, so it's decided.

Trying to fit one big man and four big pit bulls into my Subaru is entertaining. Despite his name, Mr. Wigglebottom is the elder among the dogs and a pretty chill dude, settling down in the middle of the back while Dallas, Darryl, and Sodapop joust for position at the windows, sticking their fat heads out to feel the wind in their jowls as we head to the dog park. Their excitement only ratchets higher when I pull into the small lot and they see the other dogs.

From the backseat it's a Hallelujah chorus of doggy glee, with the boys all bouncing and barking, anxious to be out of the car and into the park so they can frolic with their friends. I struggle to keep hold of their leashes as they drag me toward the gate, but Manic grabs on and helps me get them inside the first fence. There we unclasp their leashes and then open the second gate into doggie paradise.

My four love bugs go bounding into the park, so excited to visit with their friends, read the urine signals, and sniff some butts. It's adorable.

"Gotta love the purity of it," Manic says with a grin as we watch the animals. Is he talking about the purity of sniffing butts, because that's a kink we haven't— "Kids and dogs, they're so much better at experiencing joy than us jaded adults."

Oh. Yeah. Definitely more pure than where my mind was headed. Before I can put a lot of thought into his casual mention of kids, he unfolds the lawn chairs we brought and beckons me to sit with him as the dogs explore. Dallas and Darryl are my social butterflies, always down to party. They join in a game of frisbee with Jeff the Labrador and Kevin, one of Jeff's humans. Across the park, Sodapop frolics in the shade of a wide oak with his girlfriend, a Standard Poodle named Fanny Fancypants.

Mr. Wigglebottom isn't as social as the others, never has been, and when he settles onto his rump with an old-man groan, he's at Manic's side. My guy rubs the big dog's head, and Mr. Wigglebottom looks up at him with such love in his eyes it gives my heart a little flutter.

Wiggles was my first baby, my first foster fail. He was a rescue, brought to the shelter by animal control. They responded to a call of neglect and found him at the end of a chain, emaciated, dehydrated, and forced to lie in the sun at the height of summer. The shelter was full, and I'd already been approved for foster status, so they were happy to send him home with me.

An expert in dog neglect I was not, but showering him with love and attention seemed to work, so I did that a lot. After a few months, my sad, lonely boy was transformed into an absolute lover and my staunchest protector.

These days, Mr. Wigglebottom is a wise old man who judges everyone I bring home—both human and canine. He, more than me, decided we would fail at fostering Dallas, Darryl, and Sodapop, making room for them in our little pack. And, astutely, he never liked that heartbreaker Stephen Lowe. I should have taken my elder dog's aloofness as relationship advice, but I wasn't paying attention then. I'm paying attention now.

Manic says something to Mr. Wigglebottom, and the big dog turns and licks my man's cheek. The smile that spreads over Manic's face is the most beautiful sight I've ever seen in my whole damn life. Wiggles's smile is pretty epic, too, and his message to me is loud and clear: Manic is worthy to join our pack.

"I love you," I say to both of them because I feel those words too much to keep them inside.

Manic's smile grows even wider, even more beautiful, as he leans over to kiss me. It's a sweet kiss, simple and perfect. It's a lazy Sunday afternoon at the dog park kind of kiss. And I needed it more than I realized. To know what I feel for Manic isn't just a naked-at-night sort of thing, but a dog park in the daylight sort of thing, too, is amazing and perfect, and I want to jump around and do cartwheels.

Fortunately for me, Kevin has packed up Jeff's frisbee and is making noise about having to head home, so I have a socially accept-able way to jump for joy, pulling my frisbee out and resuming the fun and games with the boys. Manic plays, too, throwing a ball that Mr. Wigglebottom lumbers after and fetches for him.

And God, the joy I feel in this moment is like the alien in John Hurt's stomach in that movie, bursting right out of me.

When the dogs are exhausted, so are we, and it's time for some much-needed naps all around. It feels like only moments after my head hits the pillow and Manic's arm drapes across my middle that I'm awake again, sighing at the sensation of his soft fingers as he strokes my cheek.

"What time is it?" I ask with a stretch.

"Almost sundown."

I flutter my eyes open, half expecting him to kiss me and strip my clothes off for some naked shenanigans.

Instead, he asks, "Have you ever been to the Trail of Lights?"

Is he kidding with this question? Who does he think he's talking to here? "I absolutely love the Trail of Lights! I go every year with the whole gang as a celebration of my birthday, but we haven't been this year yet, probably because everyone's so busy with the babies—"

"I've never been," he says to get my train of thought back on track.

That doesn't surprise me. Something as wholesome and family friendly as the city's massive Christmas light display is hardly Manic's scene.

But he brought it up. "Wanna go tonight?"

His smile is so sweet as he nods. "Yeah."

The city doesn't allow fur babies at the annual Christmas event, so we take Manic's motorcycle over to Zilker Park and fit it between a tree and an SUV, then walk over to the line of people waiting to get inside.

The place is overrun with children of all ages. Tiny tots in strollers kick their little feet while older kids bounce around with all their excited energy. Part of me feels like we should have invited Jakole and their brood to join us, but it's clear Manic is treating this as a date, so the smarter part of me abstains from turning this into a group activity. I'm humming "Just the Two of Us" again as he stands behind me with his arms wrapped around my waist and his chin on my shoulder. I never would have guessed that Manic was the cuddlesome kind, but he totally is. I love it, and I love the heat he's sharing with me, too, because when the sun set, it took its warmth with it.

I nestle a little deeper into his toasty embrace as we silently listen to the chitchat of the crowd. Behind us, an inquisitive kid tries to understand how Santa can be both here and at the mall on the same night. "Santa has a busy schedule," his dad answers. "It's a good thing he has all those elves to help him stay organized."

Manic chuckles, and I close my eyes as I feel that sensation rumble through me. Quietly, he whispers, "You'd be so much better at that."

"At what, lying?"

"Spinning a tale."

"To-may-to, to-mah-to."

"How would you have answered that question?"

I consider for a moment, then dip into Manic's sci-fi roots for a good explanation. "I'd say that Captain Kirk once gifted Santa with a sleigh-sized transporter to help him and the reindeer bring gifts and good cheer to little boys and girls all over the world in a fraction of the time."

Manic squeezes me tighter, and another laugh rumbles through him as he kisses my cheek. "You'll be an amazing mom."

I blink at his word choice, a little stunned. He said, "you'll," as in you *will*—suggesting it *will* happen. He did not say, "you'd," as in you *would*—suggesting it *might* happen. That difference feels hugely significant, but before I can ponder it, the line finally starts to move. Within a few minutes, we have our tickets and we're inside the park.

We hold hands as we walk through the first tunnel of lights. Quickly moving families and groups scurry all around us, but we take our time, letting the magic of so much color and twinkling brightness wash over us. On the other side, we stop at Candy Cane Lane for funnel cake and hot chocolate, then wander some more. Everywhere you look, there are trees wrapped top to bottom in single-color strands. They sparkle like massive gems of red and green and pink and yellow and blue. There are shapes too—a globe, a grinch, a guitar—all lit up with lights.

At the North Pole section of the trail, Manic suggests we join the line for the Ferris wheel, and I wholeheartedly agree. The view from the top is breathtaking; all the light and color of the park and the big city skyline make me fall a little more in love. I'm in love with this man at my side, this city I call home, this life I get to live. It feels amazing, and when Manic tilts my chin up to whisper, "I love you," against my lips before he kisses me at the top of the Ferris wheel ride, it feels even better than amazing. It feels perfect.

He pulls away, pressing his forehead to mine and smiling that wicked smile of his.

I tell him, "You give good date."

"I give good date?"

"The best. This is the best date I've ever been on," I declare as the Ferris wheel brings us back down to Earth. "I think we should head over to the big tree, then hustle home for some naked shenanigans."

"Or, we could skip the tree and go right to the naked shenanigans."

"Gasp!" I say. "You did *not* suggest that we skip standing under the big tree and taking an epic selfie of us in our first couples photo, did you?"

"Certainly not. Let's go." He clasps my hand in his and takes off in a run, tugging me with him as we make our way to the climax of the trail. The Zilker Holiday Tree is a one-hundred fifty-five foot tall Christmas tree made entirely of Christmas lights draped from one of the city's fifteen historic moon towers.

Standing near the center, I look up and spin until I'm dizzy with all the colors and motion and gloriousness of everything. Manic just watches me, so I tug him in for a hug and ask, "Do you feel it?"

"Feel what?"

"Joy."

He takes a moment to consider, then says slowly, "Yeah, I do."

That makes me smile so wide it hurts, but he kisses the pain away. When we come apart this time, I grab my phone and open the camera. "Time to vogue, big boy. Strike a pose."

Over the years, I've come to the conclusion that Manic hates posing for photos. He never smiles or says cheese. He generally seems to barely tolerate having his image snapped. But tonight he poses, and his expression is sweet. He grins a little in one, kisses my cheek in another, rests his head against mine for a few, and when he starts to get bored—beyond ready for us to head home for nakedness—I scroll back through the images. Manic wraps his arms around my waist and sets his chin on my shoulder again as he looks at the photos with me. When I find my favorite, I get agreement from him, then warn him, "This is going to mean we're Facebook official. Are you ready for that level of relationship?"

"I'm ready, but I'm not on Facebook."

"What?"

He shrugs. "I tried Myspace for about half a minute. Not my thing. All those weird background colors and dumb songs playing on every-one's profiles. It was a sensory overload nightmare."

"Facebook is different. But... Whatever." I shrug and post the photo, then change my relationship status. "There, it's official. We're dating."

"It's been official for a while."

"Now it's *official* official."

"Sweet, let's go fuck...officially." He turns around and leans down, then gestures to his back. "Hop on, little girl, I'm gonna take you for a ride."

I do as ordered, and he hustles us back to his motorcycle. I rest my head on his shoulder, letting all the bliss of this day and night sink into me, all the way into the marrow of my bones. Full-body bliss.

23

"Happy Birthday Week!" everyone says at once, and I nearly jump out of my skin. Not from the surprise birthday wishes—I knew those were coming—but from the volume. It's the loudest I've heard anyone speak at Jakole's house since the twins were born.

I look around, surprised everyone's exclamation wasn't the starter pistol to a screaming contest between the babies. It's quiet. Well, as quiet as it can be when six adults and two toddlers burst into an awkward rendition of the birthday song.

Gaw, they're the sweetest as they wish me an early birthday with all this pomp and circumstance and balloons. It gives me the biggest smile to know that—even with all the new babies and whatnot—my friends haven't forgotten tonight is *my* night.

It's become something of a tradition in this family that they throw me a big birthday bash on the Family Dinner Night prior to Christmas. This is because they all fly off to bumfuck or Tennessee or wherever on my actual birthday.

All my life, I've been the receiver of combo gifts—combination birthday and Christmas presents—and my parties are awkwardly scheduled around other people's travel plans and holiday work events.

It's the curse of having a Christmas birthday. I've never known the joy of celebrating my big day on the actual date because it's Jesus's birthday, too, and he gets all the attention.

To be honest, I'm a little resentful of Jesus's iron grip on *my* day. But when I look around at the faces of the people I love—the people who love me—I could cry. A good cry. Tears of joy, but tears all the same. It means the world to me that they've made this a new tradition. When Jakole first started these Family Dinner Nights, I was excited to even be invited. Now this. It gives me all the warm fuzzies a birthday-week girl could wish for.

Blowing kisses to everyone, I shimmy out of my jacket and set it on the coat tree so I can dive into the melee for a hearty helping of love.

They all have warm hugs and cheek kisses for me, and when I've circled the whole room and come to my place at the dining table, staring at a pile of gift bags and wrapped boxes waiting for me, I nearly cry again.

Smiling over at Manic, I'm surprised by the look on his face. He looks…scared? Is that fear? Eyes wide, brow furrowed deeply, his lips pressed into a tight expression. It's a new sight. But if I had to guess, he's afraid of something.

"What's the matter?" I ask him in a hushed voice.

He leans into me, and whispers in my ear, "I didn't know I was supposed to bring a present."

Oh.

Whoops. I forgot to warn him this was a very special birthday edition of Family Dinner Night. "Worry not, just put your dick in a box and give it to me later, and you'll make me the happiest early-birthday girl ever."

He chuckles and steals a kiss. "That sounds creepy, like Bobbitt creepy."

"Trust me, I prefer your dick attached to you." With that, I turn my attention back to everyone else as we start dishing up dinner. Loudly, I proclaim, "It feels great to talk at a normal volume again, but where are the wee little crybabies?"

"Upstairs with a sitter, so we can get noisy down here tonight." Nicole glances at Tommy, whose daddy is setting him up with a plate of chicken strips, and says a little more quietly, "And I've been pumping all day so the twins will have milk in the morning, and momma can drink tonight."

With that, Nicole and Ari clink glasses of wine and offer some to Manic and me. I accept a glass of red, and in the end, it's just the three of us drinking—Violet's preggers, Jake and Greg are both five years sober, and Alex and Manic are driving.

We eat and talk and it's so nice, the comfortable cadence of us, the easy conversation, the laughter and sharing. When it's time for dessert, we all take giant slabs of cake, with frosting that turns our lips hot pink to match my hair, something Ari apparently planned.

When Mia comes over and demands I open my presents, I help her up onto my lap so she can open them for me. Not wanting to be left out, Tommy climbs up into Manic's lap before he can say anything about it, and it's so precious to see the tiny little future rocker on the lap of my tough and gorgeous tattooed man.

I tamp down the tulle layers of Mia's powder pink princess dress as she reaches for the nearest present.

"Uh. Not that one. NC-17," Ari says.

I quickly take the gift bag out of Mia's hands, and set a big box in front of her instead. This one is from Jakole, and Nicole nods that it's safe for children's eyes. It's heavy though, so I help Mia with unwrapping it.

"New skates," I shout when I see the box, and Mia wiggles with excitement too—total future derby skater, no doubt. Popping the lid, I pull out a hot pink street skate with glittery gold wheels and toe stop. "Oh my God, I love them!"

Nicole smiles and sips her wine, and we all turn our attention to Tommy so he can open the next gift from Manic's lap. They are so cute together, and—*ugh*—my heart squeezes.

Tommy tears into the wrapping paper of Greg and Violet's gift like it offends him, and when he gets to the box inside, he pops the top and frowns down into it, saying with no small amount of disgust in his tone, "It's just hair."

I peek around Mia—who's obsessively spinning one of the wheels on my new skates—to look inside the box in front of Tommy. It's a wig.

"Oh my God! Is it a Fifi Mahony?"

Greg and Violet nod. My smile grows wider as I take the precious cargo out of Tommy's reach and hold it up to inspect the style. It's so me: hot pink with a shelf of bangs and a bouffant and pony tails on both sides.

Squealing, I twist my hair up onto my head and slip the wig over it, turning to Tommy to ask dramatically, "How do I look, darling?"

With a giggle, Tommy informs me, "Like a pink bat!"

"Sweet, that's exactly the look I was going for!" I tickle him and hug Mia and thank her parents profusely for bringing me this lovely gift from New Orleans.

"Legit, did y'all color coordinate my presents?"

"Yes," Violet and Nicole say in unison. Violet adds, "But we had no idea you'd coordinate with your pink hair too. We must be psychically connected."

"Though it's not like you're subtle," Nicole adds. "You frequently quote that Julia Roberts line from *Steel Magnolias.*"

Everyone in the room says in a saccharine, Southern accent: "Pink is my signature color," and they laugh.

"Well it is!" I sip my wine and take a closer look at the skates. They're gorgeous. I can't wait to wear them.

Since they're brand new, Nicole grants me permission to put them on and skate a few circles on her fancy floors. Pretty sure I look amazing in my pink bat hair and pink skates, taking the kids for a couple of rides around the room.

When it's their bedtime, Jake and Greg take Tommy and Mia upstairs, and that's when I get to open my grown-up present from Ari and Alex. It's a new butt plug, this one silicone and— "Seriously, you got me pink, too?"

Ari grins and waggles her brow.

As I handle the butt plug, Manic takes a look inside the bag I set aside and pulls something else out. Suddenly, the plug in my hand starts to wiggle. I yelp and nearly jump out of my skin. Manic laughs, and I look over at him to see he's holding a remote control. He pushes it again, and the vibration in the butt plug changes a little, starts to pulsate. Oh wow. "It's a remote-controlled butt vibrator?"

"Yup," Ari confirms.

Manic amps up the vibration more, until I'm laughing from the weird stimulation to my hand. With a wink, he says, "This'll be fun."

Indeed.

Now that the kids are down and the dads are back downstairs, we settle around the living room. I sit beside Manic on one of the couches, and he pulls me up onto his lap, settling me against his chest and stroking my legs in teasing touches that make me squirm.

The others talk a little about their impending travel plans to visit Ari, Greg, and Jake's families on both sides of the Appalachian mountains. The last couple of years, Ari and Alex have flown Alex's mom out there with them so they have all their family together on Christmas. It's so sweet, it hurts.

These conversations are always a bit bittersweet. I have no one to visit during the holidays. Even if I wanted to see my mom again, I wouldn't know where to find her. The people in this house—they're it for me. And every year, on my birthday, they leave me to visit their real families.

More than once, Ari and Alex have offered to fly me out to Tennessee with them, but I always say no. Then, when I'm sitting home alone on my birthday, I always regret saying no.

"What about you two? Any big plans for the holiday-slash-birthday weekend?" Ari asks.

I open my mouth to say no, but Manic speaks first. "I'm going to throw Sher a birthday party at the bar."

I turn to frown at him, confused. "You are?"

He gives me the sweetest, softest smile and says, "I am."

24

SATURDAY, DECEMBER 25, 2010

I wake to his mouth on me, his tongue teasing, the piercing tickling my clit until I'm a boneless writhing mess under him. When I've come down from that orgasm, he kisses his way up my body and slides his rock hard cock inside, making love slow and sweet until we're both coming undone. He flutters soft kisses all over my face as he whispers to me in his sexy groggy morning voice, "Happy birthday."

I grin as we get out of bed and into the shower together, where he takes more time washing me than washing himself. So I help, lathering up his dick with soap until he's hard again. We kiss as I jerk him off, and he fingers me until we both come again.

"Join me when you can, birthday girl," Manic says once he's dressed. He kisses me one more time, then gives the dogs pets and lots of love as he leaves.

Now, alone, I sigh, and it sounds a bit melancholy. Today I turn the big three-five. I'm geriatric now. Looking in the mirror, I search for lines, gray hairs, and sag. I don't see it, not yet, but it's lurking. That's life, ain't it? I'm at the top of my roller-coaster ride, and it's all downhill from here. Okay, sure, I'm not actually "over the hill" until I turn forty, and these days, forty is the new thirty, but I feel ancient this morning.

Ugh. Time to turn this frown upside down, dammit! I slip into some jumping gear and head out to the trampoline, put some tunes on my iPod and jump around, managing to execute all of my sweet moves despite my age. Still got it!

Inside, I shower again and decide today calls for not just pink, but *hot* pink. I slip into a pair of patent leather hot pink hot pants, a pink glitter tube top, and my new pink skates, then top it off with my new pink wig.

It's a brisk skate to Dirty Sixth. I come rolling through the door of Manic's bar, shivering as I find the place isn't as deserted as I expected. A lot of familiar faces turn to me and shout, "Happy Birthday!"

It's a little startling but also touching. When I turn my attention to Manic, I notice the bar is decorated. Which is unusual. This place is not known for its decorations. No twinkle lights at Christmas or cobwebs for Halloween. The decor here is always the same: ghoulish and grown-up, demonic gargoyles with glowing red eyes and massive paintings of 1950s pinup models.

Except today, there is a big pink banner taped to the wall behind the bar that reads "Happy Birthday," and silver tinsel hangs from the gargoyle's necks, catching me a little by surprise.

Okay. Wow. What is happening right now? Manic said he planned to throw me a birthday party, but I figured it would be low key. I wasn't expecting party guests or decorations or this big warm-fuzzy sensation in my chest as I smile at all the people.

Tank and a few other familiar bartenders are here, nursing Bloody Marys on this fine Christmas afternoon. A lot of the familiar regulars are here too. Well. Shit. I'm glad I dressed up. I match the decorations, as if we planned it.

I skate to where Manic swings the bar top up so he can come through and catch me in his arms, placing a big kiss on me as I try to climb him like a tree. He helps, clasping his big hands on my ass to hold me against him so I can wrap all around him.

When we come apart, he whispers against my lips, "Happy birth-day, sexy girl."

"I love you a ridiculous amount, sweet boy."

The smile he gives me is the warmest, most beautiful sight. He presses his forehead against mine and whispers again, "I will never tire of hearing you say those words."

"What words?" I play dumb.

With a devilish grin, he says, "I love you."

God, I feel like I could cry. Oh, there it goes. I'm crying…a lot…on his neck, burying my face as I sob. He wraps his arms a little tighter around me and carries me into the bathroom, latching the door behind us so we're alone.

"What's the matter?" His eyes search my face for more information, wiping my tears for me.

"Nothing." I sniff as I try to find my voice and tell him, "I'm happy."

"You are? Because the sounds you're making are different from happy noises."

"I'm happy and a little sad and a lot excited and some scared and totally overwhelmed."

"Ah."

"I love you, Manic. Like, I mean it. I really, really do. And that feels amazing and strange and scary."

Now his eyes soften, and he cups my face in his palms. "I love you, too, Sher. And it's scary from where I'm standing, also, because you have me thinking and feeling all these new things, and I've been putting a lot of thought into what you said about—"

Someone pounds on the door, shouting, "I've gotta take a piss."

"Use the ladies room," Manic shouts back, turning his focus back to me.

But the reality of this moment sinks in. Literally, Manic has set me on the sink of the men's room at his bar. This is not the place for a relationship heart-to-heart.

We both laugh a little nervously, and Manic helps me off the sink and onto my skates. Washing our hands, we leave and are greeted with a few chuckles from the bar patrons, who assume he just gave me a bathroom birthday boff.

Whatever.

Manic directs me to an empty seat with a little gold Reserved sign in front of it.

"Y'all have reserved seating?"

"No. I stole that from the wine bar next door."

I laugh, and he kisses the tip of my nose—a little habit of his I'm coming to truly adore. He takes his place behind the bar and pours me a fancy and tasty reddish-pink drink. It's probably the pinkest thing ever poured in this dive, and I love it. I sip it with my pinky out, like a fucking lady. Manic gets busy, refilling a few beers, then he vanishes into the room behind the bar.

He's gone for a long moment before he returns carrying a cake with pink icing and one big glowing candle. Everyone is in a festive mood, singing the birthday song like it's a Christmas carol as Manic sets the cake in front of me. The confection is so cute and...awkward. About two layers high, a little lopsided, and hand iced. None of that store-bought symmetry—this is clearly homemade.

Did… did Manic bake me a cake?

Stunned, I stare at him for a moment as he sings my birthday song with everyone else. But I need to concentrate, work on my birthday wish. Birthday wishes are serious business. This is no time to get distracted.

Focusing, I stare at the dancing flame atop the candle, appreciating that there aren't thirty-five of them. As the flame dances and wiggles in the breeze, I look to its center, seeking to know the thing I wish for most. And I find it there.

With my wish in hand, I repeat it to myself three times so it will come true: "I want it all. I want life, liberty, and love. I want a family—in any form that comes to me—be it my friends, my dogs, and my strange, sweet man. Of course, I want more too. It's human nature to always want more, but I know now my happiness is here with him and with whatever else he's comfortable sharing with me."

Then I blow out the candle and inhale its power in the warm smell of smoke that curls between me and Manic. He smirks at me, like he's curious what took me so long. I don't tell him. My wishes are my own ritual, no need to explain.

With the knife he usually uses to cut lemon and lime wedges, Manic slices the cake and lays a massive hunk of it on a paper plate that he hands to me with a plastic fork. He then shares what's left with the regulars who want some, and when he's placed the last piece on a plate for himself, I grin and take a bite.

It's amazing. The pink icing is buttercream and the cake? It's lemon! He baked me a lemon cake.

I remember that conversation we had while swimming naked at Hippie Hollow, when Manic first told me of his bipolar disorder.

Between moans of orgasmic delight, I repeat what I said that day. "I really like lemon cake."

With a smile and a wink, he repeats himself too. "So do I."

25

After cake, Manic cuts his shift short. Tank takes over bartending, and I get hugs and love from everyone as we leave. There's not a single mention of Christmas, which feels weird and awesome. For the first time in my entire life, my birthday is all mine.

But it's not just my birthday today. It's also my first Christmas with Manic when we're, like, a couple and shit, so I've got a new outfit for the occasion, and I'm dying to put it on.

While Manic plays with the dogs, I disappear into the bathroom and strip out of my daytime pink. It's time to amp things up to night-time pink. Starting with the pink plug Ari gifted me. It takes a lot of patience, relaxation breathing, and lube to situate that thing, and I have to wiggle a little until it feels tolerably comfortable.

Next, I dig out the new panties and bra I hid at the back of my bathroom cabinet—in case Manic got snoopy. They're so pretty, and I look super hot in them.

The bra is a bow with straps and underwire, but the only thing covering my tits are two strips of fabric that I tie together in the center so he can unwrap me like the gift I am. The matching undies are a barely-there pair, with the fabric rucked at the middle so they fit perfectly, making my booty look super fuckable.

I know what I want to give Manic for Christmas, and it's what I want him to give me too: butt stuff!

When I open the bathroom door and lean against the frame, Manic stops what he's doing. In the middle of wrestling with Sodapop, in the middle of breathing, he stops it all and stares.

"Santa tells me you've been a very good boy, this year," I say in my sexiest voice. "Are you ready to open your present?"

Manic stares some more, and when he finally manages to speak, he mumbles something that sounds like, "How did I get this lucky?"

"You haven't gotten lucky yet, but you're about to."

That shakes him out of his sentimental state, and he hurries to get the dogs out of the bedroom and shut the door, leaving them whining and scratching to get in.

He turns and stares me up and down and back up again. "God damn, woman. You take my breath away."

I'm not sure if it's the words or the reverent way he says them that takes my breath away too. But there it goes. Goodbye breath.

I've never felt so adored, so desired and loved. Manic freezes me with his gaze as he comes toward me. His eyes are feral and hungry, like a wild beast stalking his prey.

He strips off his shirt as he comes closer. I stare, loving the way his ragged breaths move through his chest, breathing life into all those colorful tattoos.

When he's in front of me, he stares, too, fixated with the way the ribbon shows the full curve of my breasts. After a long moment, he reaches for me, stroking his fingers along the underside of each breast. Then he clasps them in his fists and squeezes.

It's almost too hard, almost. But instead of pain, all I feel is toe-curling pleasure. I moan. As if he's punishing me for enjoying his roughness, he lets go. But his fingers don't go far, teasing and tickling the peaks of my nipples through the fabric.

He flicks one, then the other, and I yelp a little and moan a lot. He grins with half his mouth, watching me with hooded eyes, enjoying this game.

When he's teased me enough for now, his fingers play with the bow at my center. Slowly, oh so fucking slowly, he tugs on the ends until it comes unraveled, and I come unraveled too, pretty much melting at the throaty groan he makes when my breasts are exposed to him.

He stares for a moment, his rough fingers so gentle as he worships my soft skin and the hard peaks at the center, twirling the little barbells that pierce through my nipples. That gets a moan from me, and my head nearly falls back. But I don't want to miss the show as his mouth joins his fingers in worship, licking, sucking, and teasing me with wet, hot heat.

Now it's his teeth that tease and tug my piercings, nibble and suck my nipples. I shiver like I'm having convulsions, barely able to stand what he's doing to me…literally.

Manic clasps his hands on my ass and picks me up. I scratch my fingernails through his hair and wrap my legs around his waist as he presses my back to the wall, so he can take all the time he needs to indulge his oral fixation with nibbles and sucks and a teasing tongue.

Down below, his fingers explore, too, squeezing and delving toward my center. That's when he finds the plug. The sound he makes in the back of his throat is pure, animal sex. "Such a good girl," he whispers against my flesh, darting his tongue out to tickle my nipple as his eyes stare up at me, demanding my full attention. Those deep blue pools look dark and dangerous like he means to drown me in them tonight. And, oh boy, I cannot *wait* to be drowned by him.

"Where's the remote?" he asks around my nipple.

I nod over to the bedside table where the remote sits beside a bottle of lube.

He glances over, then back to me and raises a brow, silently asking what I'm hinting at here.

Not one to beat around the bush, I'm out with it: "My ass is your Christmas present, big boy."

Now his other brow rises to meet up with the first. He considers for a moment, but only a moment before he growls—like seriously growls, and holy fuck he's such a sexy beast—and he spins to turn me away from the wall and carry me over to the bed. He crashes us down onto the mattress, and crushes me beneath his glorious weight. His kiss this time is hard, merciless, complete. There's a beginning, middle, and end to it. This kiss is a whole story, and he tells it so well.

Manic works his mouth down my throat to my shoulder and then down to my breasts again, and he spends time with them, teasing, worshipping, and making me desperate for more, more, more of him. I'm soaked, and he hasn't even touched my clit yet.

Suddenly, there's a zap of movement coming from inside me… inside my ass. I yelp, and Manic chuckles as he adjusts the speed on the plug with the remote from the bed table. He doesn't rev it too high, though, just keeps it vibrating at a low level, a constant internal buzz for me to adjust to as he traces his tongue in a line down the center of my body. The sensation is almost ticklish, and I giggle with the distraction, yelping again when his mouth reaches my panties.

He traces the top hem with his tongue, and I wiggle impatiently. But he's determined to take his time, even if the anticipation kills me. He has me right on the edge of sanity as he teases me with nothing but his hot breath blowing heavy over the soaked fabric. That sensation, coupled with the constant vibration, is doing strange things to my nervous system, making me boneless and too heavy to move. I lay there like a bug on my back, gasping and helpless, mewling desperately for him to satisfy me.

Then he lowers his mouth and presses a soft kiss right over my clit, and I think I could come from just that if he did it again. Instead, he slips my underwear down my hips and thighs, and I go to widen my legs, but he stops me, holding them together so all he can reach is my clit.

"Oh God," I sort of moan and yelp at the same time when he kisses it again, but this time there is nothing between us. And this time, after the soft kiss, he sticks out his tongue and licks me like a lollipop right up the center. And, *oh*, his tongue piercing is perfect for this position; everything is so concentrated, so tight. That buzz works through me from behind as his tongue starts to work me from the front, and I'm gasping and writhing and arching and trying to move, despite myself and despite all his weight on my legs, bound together by his arms.

I scratch my fingernails through his hair, pulling and pushing, like I need more of him and less of him at the same time. Like it's all too much and exactly right, like I don't know if I'm coming or going.

Oh! I'm definitely coming. The first wave hits me from deep down somewhere, my ass I guess, and I buck as I come hard and loud, begging and screaming his name.

The dogs on the other side of my door are upset, but I hardly notice as Manic keeps me coming, tasting and sucking my clit as the waves of ecstasy take me under, drown me.

When I can't take anymore, I yank his hair to pull him away, demanding mercy. He lays his head on my thigh, catching his breath and grinning up at me with shiny lips and tousled hair.

Is there any sight on this green earth more beautiful than that?

As if to answer my question, Manic stands and shucks off his jeans and shoes and socks. I'm faced with a fully naked, fully erect, gorgeous, tattooed, pierced god standing between my scissoring thighs, and my question is answered. Yes, this sight is more beautiful, and so sexy.

I try to sit up so I can suck his cock, but Manic pushes me down onto my back again, then surprises the hell out of me when he flips me over onto my stomach. "It will be a miracle if I last even a minute in your sweet little ass. I definitely don't need your mouth this time."

Oh.

His hands slide up my thighs, his fingers seeking that plug. He teases me with it, pressing it deeper then tugging it out a bit.

He sits on my thighs as he plays this push and pull game a few more times, and I groan and yelp and mewl and whine. He grabs the lube and coats everything: his cock, my ass, everything. I angle so I can see him over my shoulder, getting even more wet as I watch the way his muscles bunch when he jerks his length a couple times. Then, holding eye contact with me, he presses between my clenched thighs, miraculously managing to reach the entrance to my pussy from this position, and pushes inside.

It feels so wet and smooth and warm and full, and that butt plug is still vibing as he presses as deep as he can from this position. My hands fist the sheets, and Manic groans as he rocks his hips in and out so slowly, too slowly. God, I need him to fuck me hard right now, but he's intentionally making love like it's punishment—a kink.

Then, he bumps up the speed on the vibrator. I yelp and buck like I'm trying to get him off me, but I am *so* not trying to do that. In fact,

I'm in heaven when he lies on me, pressing me into the mattress with all his weight, his cock pushing so much deeper as his hips start to move faster and harder.

Yes. That. Is. What. I. Need. Right…there.

He grabs a fistful of my hair and pulls my head back to whisper hot, sweet nothings in my ear. "I need to feel your pussy clench around my cock before I take your ass. Give it to me, baby. Then I'll give you what you really want."

Those words, coupled with his deep strokes and that full vibration inside me has me so excited and scared and horny and spent. Every sensation and emotion under the sun courses through me. And when he growls his demand again—"Come on, baby, give it to me"—I do. I so fucking do.

I come so hard I scream, and my fingers clench fistfuls of the sheets as I shake and tremble. Manic ups the vibe, making the orgasm almost overwhelming, and I keep coming. There's a flush of wetness between my thighs like I've actually squirted, a first for me.

He must feel it, too, because he praises me with all the best words. "Your pussy is so perfect, baby, and now, I need your tight little ass too."

Oh. Okay. Here we go. Manic keeps pumping into my pussy in slow, deep strokes as he sits up and starts to move the plug. Pushing it a little deeper, pulling it a little shallower. He pulls it so far that the largest part passes through my opening. I groan and gasp, then moan when he pushes it back inside. He pulls it out again, drizzles more lube on it, and pushes it right back in, getting me used to the sensation of keeping my muscles open, stretched, ready.

After so much teasing, and a whole lot more lube, he pulls the plug all the way out, then slips a finger in. It feels weird and amazing and I want more. A second finger is better, but it's not what I really want. "Baby, I need your cock."

Like my wish is his command, he pulls his fingers out, strokes himself a couple more times, then pushes his broad tip against my small opening. It's so much pressure, and leading the way is his piercing, poking and prodding as he demands entrance. I'm about to whimper and ask him to stop when his pressure works, and he presses inside.

Oh. Okay. Ouch.

Even after the plug and all that prep, I'm not ready for the over-whelming sensation of his cock inside my ass.

I gasp and whimper. Manic pets my hair, stroking it out of my eyes and leaning forward to kiss the side of my face, being so tender as he presses deeper, moving oh so slowly as he takes more of what I'm giving him.

After a moment, he stops moving and lets me adjust. Kissing me all over as he whispers, "You're such a good girl. Your ass takes my cock so well, baby."

This is better than I imagined. Manic's praise has my toes curling, despite the discomfort.

Tears wet the corners of my eyes. But it's not the pain that has me crying, it's the weight of, like, everything. It's as if his cock up my ass is a therapist, helping me see through all the nonsense I fill my head with, all the distractions. Right now, there is only one thing I can focus on, one sensation, one man with his massive, pierced dick pressed so deep inside me.

After a long moment, he moves, and finally it doesn't hurt or burn or feel like I'm going to split in half. This time, it feels fucking amazing. I see stars and sense the solar system all around me. It's cosmic and alien and transcendent. Manic feels it too—I can tell. He's hugging me like he'll never let me go, his love filling me so completely as he takes my ass in increasingly longer and deeper strokes.

The orgasm that builds here is so different from the orgasms I get from my pussy and my clit. And when I come, it's cosmic. It's a big bang blowing me apart. It's a whole universe of orgasmic pressure bursting forth from oblivion to creation. I scream and writhe and beg for more and less at the same time because this orgasm, it's so…much.

Manic's strokes increase as he's about to burst apart too. He kisses my forehead as he does, his hot breath blowing across the plains of my face as he shouts, "Oh fuck, baby, yes! Fuck," and his cock bucks hard as he fills me with his cum.

When we come back down to Earth, Manic gently pulls out and

shifts to my side, tugging my limp, spent body into his arms, and we embrace for a while as our heart rates slow and we catch our breaths.

Sticking with my cosmic theme, I ask him, "How does it feel to boldly go where no man has gone before?"

Manic grins and kisses the tip of my nose. "I thought I'd already trekked uncharted territory with you when I got you to fall in love with me."

Now I grin, too, as I consider his words and come to the realization: he's right. I've never done any of what we did today. Not the butt stuff or the birthday party on my actual birthday or skating into the arms of the man I love. This is all new for me, and it's awesome, and for some reason that revelation makes me want to cry again.

Instead, I change the subject. "You totally sodomized me on Christmas day. You naughty boy."

"Yeah, I did. Fucking my girl's sweet little ass ranks as one of the best Christmas presents ever."

"Ranks?" I am aghast.

"Yeah, it ranks number one." He tickles my side.

I play with his nipple rings as I say with a sigh, "Well, thank you for the best birthday of my whole entire life."

"I know what it's like to have to share your birthday with everyone else's holiday."

"Wait. What? When's your birthday?" How do I not already know this? I am aghast again.

"April Fool's Day."

I laugh. "No way."

I don't actually believe him until he untangles from my arms and goes to his pants on the floor, coming back with his driver's license in hand to show me the proof.

"Why didn't you ever tell me?"

He scoffs. "And have you come rolling in calling me James and making a scene at my expense while I'm trying to do my job on the dumbest 'holiday' of the year?"

"Oh, right." It's his way of saying I'm too much, and it's fair, I am too much. "Sorry."

He tosses his ID aside as he crawls back into bed with me, tugging the sheet up over us so we're a cozy little couples burrito as he asks, "Sorry for what?"

"For being so weird."

He frowns, like truly, deeply, madly frowns and stares long and hard at me, tracing his finger down my cheek to stroke my hair off my face. Then his expression transforms into the softest smile. "Maybe to others you're weird, but to me you're perfect."

I scoff. "Perfectly weird."

He clasps my chin in his fingers and places an achingly soft kiss on my lips. "Weirdly perfect."

26

FRIDAY, DECEMBER 31, 2010

This wasn't the plan.

I asked Manic if he was working tonight, and he said he always worked New Year's Eve. I assumed that meant I'd be spending the night alone. When Nicole called to ask if I could watch the kiddos while she went to Jake's New Year's show, naturally I said, "Fuck yes."

So when Manic calls and tells me he managed to trade shifts with someone and wants to ring in the new year with me, I'm surprised.

"Cool," I tell him, then caution, "but I have babies."

"What?"

"I mean… I'm babysitting. But you're welcome to come over and help… If you want."

"Jake and Nicole's house?"

"Yup."

"I'll be there in half an hour."

"Did you hear that?" I ask Kiah and Biggie and Tommy.

"Manic's coming over!" Tommy hollers a little too loudly in this bathroom, and Biggie crinkles his little nose like he's going to start wailing. Big Brother T-Man is quick to the rescue with a bunch of silly faces to get his brother's attention. *It's adorable.* While Tommy keeps

Biggie wide-eyed and curious, I wash Kiah's head with baby-safe shampoo.

When the gate buzzes, I send Tommy downstairs to tend to it, with strict instructions not to open to anyone but Manic. It's not long before I hear their voices coming up the stairs and down the hall toward me. I glance to the door, and my heart squeezes as I see Tommy's hand in Manic's, pulling him into the room.

Manic takes a look around my little bathing operation and bursts into laughter. "What are you doing?"

"Bathing them."

"Looks like you're the wettest one in here."

It's true. The twins are testing their little legs and practicing kicking this week. I'm wearing more bathwater than what's left in the little tub in the sink.

"Did Jake and Nicole actually ask you to bathe the twins while they were out?"

"Well. Uh. No."

He chuckles.

"But I wanted to. I like the smell of baby shampoo."

He grins a little, just one corner of his mouth, but I still see it, and it fills my head. He peels out of his long sleeves, so he's in only a T-shirt and comes toward me. "How can I help?"

I pull Kiah out of the water and hold him up so he's drip drying. "We need to dry this little tike, then it's bedtime for the wee ones."

"Not me!" Tommy hollers.

"Nope, not you. You have very special permission to stay awake until midnight and watch the fireworks." He's explained this to me at least a dozen times.

My arms are getting tired so I lower Kiah to dry him on the stack of towels Manic laid on the counter for me, but before we make it, the little guy pees…all over me.

Now I'm bathed, too, and in one of Nicole's favorite T-shirts and some hot pink booty shorts I found in the back of her closet. I join all the boys in the twin's bedroom. It's so pretty in here, everything painted in shades of blue in a pattern that looks like Van Gogh's *Starry Night*. Manic and Tommy are standing over the twin's side-by-side cribs, doing an equipment check of the baby monitor so we can be sure we'll get an alert if the babies stir or cry or move at all. Apparently it's motion sensitive.

When that's all set, we go downstairs, pop some popcorn, and watch all the New Year's Eve festivities on television. Clearly it's pile-on-Manic day, because Tommy claims his lap, while I curl up against his side, and he drapes an arm over my shoulders to bring me in even closer.

On TV, everyone in New York is waiting for the ball to drop over Times Square, and they show clips of the celebrations that already happened in Europe. As much as Tommy wants to stay awake with us grown-ups, his little eyelids are heavy by ten o'clock, and he's completely passed out by ten-thirty. Manic settles him onto the couch beside us and drapes a blanket over him as we cuddle quietly and sigh contentedly. I've been doing that a lot lately, sighing contentedly, like a dog when they roll over in the middle of a long nap.

When the clock strikes midnight in New York City, the Times Square ball drops on TV, and Manic kisses me like he's practicing for an hour from now—our first kiss of 2011—when it will be the new year here too.

It's only now that it occurs to me I've never rung in the new year *with* a boyfriend. I've kissed dogs and friends and random strangers aplenty, but I've never crossed over that annual threshold as a couple.

It's exciting and a little scary. I was doing the math yesterday, and Manic is now officially the longest relationship I've had. And it feels so good, not like most of my relationships that begin to fray and weather after a couple days or weeks. I think this thing with Manic could last, like for months…maybe even a year.

I imagine ringing in 2012 with him and shiver a little. Long-term is such an exciting concept to me. But I'm getting ahead of myself, already skipping to *next* New Year when this one is still fifteen minutes away.

"What's your New Year's resolution?" I ask at a normal volume, but it's been a while since either of us spoke, and my words startle Manic.

"I don't have one," he eventually answers.

"What?" I'm appalled. "You have to have a New Year's resolution. It's important."

"Says who?"

"Says me. Duh." I level with him. "Listen, if I'm going to be in your life long-term, you're going to have to start taking this more seriously."

"Take what more seriously?"

"Resolutions and birthday wishes and important shit like that."

"Why are those things important?"

"Because!" I whisper shout so I don't wake Tommy. "They give us hopes and dreams and goals. Without them, all we do is exist. But with them, we *live*."

He smiles, like *really* smiles. Even his eyes are smiling. And with a squeeze of his arm around me, he takes my breath away with only a few words, "I love the way your mind works."

Sigh.

Then he asks, "What's your resolution?"

Oh no, he didn't just try to deflect. "I asked you first."

Manic gives the question some thought, considers it a few moments more, then answers: "I want to get better. I want to *be* better…for you."

Well that's vague. "Better how? You're perfect."

He smirks. "Perfectly weird."

"Weirdly perfect." I give back, remembering our exchange from Christmas. It's stuck with me, tugs at me, like a fishing lure caught in my heart.

Manic's grin fades a little as he continues, "I mean my condition. I want to understand what impact it could have on my loved ones…my family."

That word. It loops in my brain like a skipping record. Family—I don't think I've ever heard that word pass his lips. It doesn't sound like English when he says it, completely foreign on his tongue.

He stops talking, waiting for a reaction from me. But how do I react when I don't understand what he's trying to say? "Elaborate."

He does. "I went to the library a few weeks ago. Nicole helped me find a lot of books. I'm surprised she didn't tell you."

"Oh no, she would never do that. Nicole takes librarian-client privilege very seriously. This one time Matthew McConaughey came into her library and checked out a bunch of books, and she wouldn't tell me what those books were, no matter how much I begged and pleaded and tried to pry it out of her. I'm still dying to know, honestly, but—" Shit, I'm rambling. "Sorry. I interrupted you."

Manic smiles wider now. "She sent me home with a stack of books about living with bipolar disorder… And parenting with it."

I blink. Once. Twice. A bunch of times. Did he say—

"I've been doing a lot of reading and thinking about my vasectomy lately, considering my reasoning for it then…and now. I've always been a real stubborn bastard, but not when it came to that. I gave up so easily, let one bad experience color my entire perception of my disorder."

"To be fair, I'd imagine being committed for a week is an extremely bad experience."

"Yeah, it sucked. But it's behind me now. I'm not that guy anymore. I know how to manage it better, I'm working on better communication, and with therapy and my medication I think…"

He stops, and I hold my breath with anticipation, desperate to hear his next words. It feels like a few minutes tick by, and I'm turning blue from lack of oxygen, so I prod, "You think?"

He looks over at Tommy, so cute as he sleeps on the couch beside us, and then he looks at me. "I think about getting you pregnant and raising a kid with you. I mean, I have been since you first came at me asking for my sperm. And I guess my thoughts on that keep… evolving."

"Evolving?"

"You've helped me understand I'm not broken. I'm different, yes. Of course, I'm different, but I'm not broken. And if I have a kid who inherits this condition, he won't be broken either."

"She," I interject.

He grins and nods. "She won't be broken. She'll be different, but there's nothing wrong with being different."

I dare not get too excited, but oh my God, I'm so excited! Encouraging his line of thought, I say, "Especially if she's raised by parents who understand how to treat it and live with it, thrive with it."

"I think you'd be a good mom to that child."

My heart skips a beat. Seriously, Manic's resolution revelation is going to be the death of me. "I think you'd be a good dad to that child too."

He takes a deep breath, lets it out with a slow sigh, then turns to me and says, "I'm not talking about making any decisions right this minute. This resolution has a whole year to work. But I think I want to get to a place where, maybe, in the future I can consider having my vasectomy reversed."

Wow. He added a lot of caveats in there, but still… Wow.

"So," he lightens his voice, "what's your resolution?"

Well it was going to be "read more nonfiction books," but Manic has my mind stuck on repeat with nothing but, "Wow," over and over.

Is he seriously considering starting a family…with me? The one thing I've wanted all my life but never dared to dream would happen.

After dating me for a month, most men flee, but Manic is talking about not only staying but also, like, cementing this thing we have with a good ole sex ritual to make a new life.

Fuck. Me. This is so awesome. "My resolution is all that, but the girl version."

Manic opens his mouth like he has more to say, but the television commentators announce it's two minutes to midnight in the central time zone.

We both come to attention and turn to Tommy. He's sleeping so peacefully, but he will be devastated if we let him miss this.

I get up and go over to his end of the couch, scratching his back as I gently wake him. "Tommy, it's nearly midnight."

He blinks bright green eyes like his mom's at me and sits up a little. His long black braids—just like his dad's—are adorably disheveled. I look at him and see his parents so clearly, the love between them that formed this wonderful new life, and my heart about bursts.

I tell him, "We're going to go outside to watch the fireworks. You coming?"

He nods as he rubs his eyes and starts to shuffle his feet tiredly toward the back door, but Manic lifts him up in his arms and carries him out to the backyard with us.

One of the things that sold Jakole on this property is the view. To the east, the river winds between the north and south sides of downtown. And within a moment of our arrival at the Sixkiller's firepit, the first explosion pops. A brilliant burst of red lights up the sky and flashes in reflections on the buildings and the water. It's beautiful, awesome.

I hold the baby monitor close to my ear to make sure the explosion hasn't upset the kiddos, but they sleep like their daddy, dead to the world, and I relax with Manic, who holds Tommy between us as we watch the fireworks.

"Happy New Year!" Tommy shouts and wiggles.

Manic sets him down so he can jump and cheer at the fireworks, then wraps his arms around me, whispering, "Happy New Year," as we kiss. It's the sweetest kiss I've ever known. It's a kiss so delicate it could break like glass. It's so unlike us and our kisses. Like he's thinking the same thing, Manic breaks our glass kiss with a growl as he clutches my cheeks in his palms and devours that kiss with another—

"Ew, y'all are kissing." Tommy follows his words with adorable little gagging sounds.

Manic and I bust out in laughter together, then come apart and grin at the disgusted child. With one arm still wrapped around me, Manic rustles a hand over Tommy's hair, mussing it all up, then spins the kid around so we're all watching as flashes of fire and light burst in the sky and rain down over the city.

It feels like the start of something, and it feels good.

EPILOGUE
FRIDAY APRIL 1, 2011

"I should probably be a boring lay for this," Manic says as I crawl back up his body after sucking his cock for a while.

"Boring? Why?" I ask as I sit on his stomach, ignoring the demand of his hard dick poking at my ass, opting instead to tug on his nipple rings.

"What if I get you pregnant, and the little one asks how he was made—"

"She."

"—and we have to tell her, 'Well, sweetheart, your mom stuck a fox tail up her ass, and I bent her over my knee to spank all that naughty wanton lust out of her, then I nailed her against the wall as we howled like wolves at the moon until I unloaded hot cum into her pussy. But some of it dribbled out, so I pushed it back in, then made her lick my fingers clean. And that's how you were made.' "

"That sounds perfect. I packed the tail, so I'll go get it."

Before I can move off him, he shifts his hips to align us down under and presses all the way up inside me.

I let out a hiccupping gasp at the sudden invasion and he rumbles with a laugh as he moves deeper still, and it's so perfect and complete and…slow. His movements aren't the mad, ravenous fucking I'm used to; they're kind of…sweet. "This feels like making love. Are you seriously trying to make a good story for the kiddo?"

"Baby girl, now that I have the all clear from the doctor to fuck again, I will be fucking you constantly, every goddamn second. We're going to fuck so often, it will feel strange when my cock *isn't* ramming into your hot little pussy. You're not going to know when one fuck ends and the next begins. I'm going to fuck you in so many ways we'll have no idea which one did the trick, so we'll have a whole variety of stories to tell him."

"Her."

"I figure, if I stick a nice romantic fuck into the mix, it gives us storytelling options."

"Well, what are you waiting for? Let's make this story happen. Fill me with your white hot love goo. I want all your babies inside me."

"You say the sexiest things, little girl."

"Get to work, big boy."

He rams hard and deep into me, and I squeal at what a big boy he is. He pulls me tight, hugging me against his chest. When he rolls over, I'm caged by his whole body, and he puts all his weight on me, making it impossible to move and difficult to breathe. He stares deep into my eyes as he moves his cock inside me, slow and smooth.

It's amazing and it's maddening. He has me squirming and wiggling for more as he builds the tension between us. And trapped beneath him like this, there's nothing I can do but take everything he gives me when he decides to give it to me.

I'm lost to his control, begging and crying for more until finally, *finally* the orgasm starts to build in my belly and stretch out to my limbs, tingling through my whole body until I begin to come.

It's then that he kisses me, taking my ecstasy right out of my breath, and letting it fuel his own. We come together as we come apart.

The orgasm we share doesn't stop; it bounces between us, back and forth, on and on. It's intense. I can't help it when I start crying. He hugs me and tells me he needs me and loves me, and he'll never let me go, and his words feel almost as amazing as the sex.

"Damn, talk about a good story to tell the kid." I giggle as Manic pulls back enough to let me breathe on my own.

"You think that did the trick? Are you knocked up now?"

I grin at him. "Oh, totally, I'm pretty sure your baby batter just put a bun in my oven."

He wipes the tears off my cheeks. "Well, let's keep trying, just in case."

"Not right now. We've got places to be."

"Where?"

"There's a very special birthday edition of Family Dinner Night tonight."

He grumbles, "There is?"

"Don't sound too excited about it, birthday boy."

"But I want to stay balls deep in you all day."

"Socialize now, balls deep later."

Outside our hotel room, New Orleans is bright and beautiful, especially at night. The lights and colors of neon signs illuminate the darkness as we wander along Bourbon Street, heading toward the drag bar where Greg told us they'd be. Manic drapes his arm around my shoulders as we meander, people watching and sipping drinks along the way.

When we reach our destination and step inside, it's incredible—super fancy and full of people. The last time I was here was right after Hurricane Katrina. It was a difficult time for this city. I'm glad to see this wonderful refuge has weathered the storm.

We watch Miss Bea Haven do a stunning performance of Diana Ross's "I'm Coming Out." Manic whistles, and I howl as she takes a bow. Between acts on the stage, we move toward the bar where Miss Bea Haven's partner, Jezebel Jewel, holds court and a lot of sexy, scantily clad young men serve drinks.

"Darling." Jezebel flutters over to me for air kisses. "It's been too long."

"Are you always this busy?" I ask, still glancing around at the crowd.

"Oh, honey, no. This is a slow night."

We laugh together, then Jezebel turns her assessing gaze to Manic. "And who do we have here?"

"Miss Jezebel Jewel, please meet my boyfriend, Manic."

"So this is the famous Manic we've been hearing about." This voice comes from behind us, and I turn to see Miss Bea Haven towering over us at six-foot-six in those stiletto heels.

I exchange kisses with her, too, then introduce Manic. Bea and Jezebel are arm in arm now, and they give Manic a pair of hard stares, looking him up and down.

"Well, he's attractive and strange," Bea says.

"Just the way we like 'em," Jezebel adds. "But Sher, baby, tell us—does he treat you right?"

"Oh hell yeah." I drape an arm around Manic's neck, and he hugs me against him. "And when I ask really nicely, he treats me wrong, too, exactly the way I like it."

Everyone laughs, even Manic, who seems surprisingly relaxed despite the crowd and all the new people. We didn't pack his social-anxiety-support cowboy hat for this trip. He's doing all this with just his blue mohawk to fall in front of his eyes from time to time. Very impressive.

Bea and Jezebel wink at me "Girl, hold onto this one then. Come on, everyone's out in the courtyard, ready for your birthday party, Mr. Manic."

"Mr. Manic?" he asks me as Bea and Jezebel hand us cocktails we didn't order, and we all head toward the wall of French doors.

"If you ever want to go into drag, that can be your stage name."

"Hmm." He gives it some thought as we reach the courtyard. It's a lot less crowded out here, much more quiet, and the place is lit up with festoon lights strung between the buildings.

I see our crew, camped out at a couple of tables in the back corner and near the set of stairs that lead up to where Bea and Jezebel—aka Paul and Andre when they're not in drag—live.

Everyone's here. It's a big weekend for us all, as Jake's band will be playing a massive concert at the Superdome, and we get to watch from some swanky private suite. Plus Greg and Violet just welcomed their son, Max, to the world, so we get to meet him.

It's a bit of a combo birthday for Manic, but this is his first with the family, and I'm so touched they've made him a birthday banner and cake.

We run the gamut of hugs, kisses, and back pats with Ari and Alex and Jakole, then we come to the new mom and dad. Violet is queen of the courtyard, lounging in a gorgeous hot pink kaftan and matching head wrap, sitting in what looks to be the comfiest chair out here. Greg stays close to her as he paces with a little bounce in his step, his baby boy in a kangaroo pouch on his chest.

In my usual Auntie Sheryl way, I swoop in and instantly fall in love with the baby. He's asleep, so I don't get to see his eyes or play with him, but I fall in love with his long curly eyelashes none-the-less.

"How are you able to get him to sleep with all this noise?"

"When you're born in New Orleans, you learn early how to sleep through pretty much anything," Violet says with a broad smile as she reaches up and takes Greg's hand in hers, squeezing.

"Where's Mia?" I ask them, then turn to Jakole and add, "And where's your brood of spawn?"

Jake answers for everyone. "Mia and Tommy are upstairs playing some game on Uncle Paul's new Xbox, and the twins are at the hotel with the au pair."

"Wow, rockstar, you have an au pair? How fancy!" I jab at him.

Jake doesn't seem to mind the occasional joke about how stinking rich and successful he is. I mean he's playing the Superdome tomorrow night. He can stand to get ribbed every now and again.

Manic sits on one of the picnic tables reserved for our group, and it's Alex who says first, "Happy birthday, motherfucker."

"He's not a mother fucker, yet, but he soon will be if I have anything to say about it," I announce.

Jake laughs. "Oh right. How's the vasectomy reversal healing?"

"Real fucking well." Manic slaps my ass, then tugs me onto his lap.

Jake nods. "Good deal. I for one will *not* be getting my vasectomy reversed. Three is enough."

"Eight," I say, and everyone looks at me like I'm speaking another language. "Eight is enough," I clarify.

"Eight?" Manic sounds horrified. "You want *eight* kids?"

"No, that's the name of that old TV show, *Eight is Enough*. For three, you should say *Three's Company*."

Everyone stares at me, then Jake bursts into laughter. "I'll take that under advisement."

"Jesus, you scared me." Manic presses a palm to his chest over his racing heart.

"We can have eight, though, if you want."

He stiffens.

"April Fools!"

He grumbles.

"I'll be happy with just a couple, or one, or three. Honestly, I'm very flexible about this."

"You're very flexible about a lot of things." Manic waggles his brow, and it's easy to know what he's talking about.

"TMI," everyone else says at the same time.

Manic wraps his arms around me. I nestle a little deeper into his embrace.

"So, what's it like to have a birthday on April Fools' Day? Lots of lame jokes?" Nicole asks.

Manic rolls his eyes and nods. "I never tell my patrons about my birthday. I'd quit my job if I had to endure a day of bad jokes every fucking year. Learned that lesson with the circus. Anytime I performed on my birthday, the emcee liked to make a big deal about it. It drove me nuts. Except this one time. We all went out after the show, using my birthday as an excuse to get shitfaced. And somehow, through some friend of a friend of a friend, we found ourselves in a German sex dungeon. That was a weird birthday."

Everyone laughs. Ari smirks. "Weirdest birthday I ever had was when I celebrated my twenty-ninth birthday at Greg's grandpa's funeral."

Greg chuckles, still bobbing the baby. "Ah, yes, the event that inspired us to open our marriage and changed, well, pretty much everything."

Everyone nods, recognizing the truth of it. This wonderful little family of ours wouldn't exist if Ari and Greg had stayed together. I, for one, am so glad they got a divorce. But that seems like a rude thing to say, so instead I go with: "My weirdest birthday was this last one, when Manic took my anal virginity."

Greg lets out of burst of laughter that almost wakes the baby. Ari chokes on her drink. Someone else mutters, "TMI" again.

"Jake got me preggers with the twins on his birthday," Nicole shares.

"Hoping to do the same with this ovulating little vixen tonight," Manic says, and Jake gives him a high five.

"Wouldn't that be weird if it happened that way?" I ask Manic.

"Perfectly weird."

"Weirdly perfect." With a naughty grin he kisses me, and it's a really good kiss. It's a curl-around-in-his-arms-and-straddle-him kiss. It's the kind of kiss that could totally get me pregnant if life science worked that way.

"They're so sickeningly cute," Violet says.

"We should sing the song and cut the cake so they can go hump each other in private," Jake adds.

"Hump? Who says hump anymore?" Nicole asks.

"Me, I say hump," Jake replies. "And I'm going to hump you so hard when we get back to the hotel, Quana."

"Promises, promises."

I giggle and glance around at everyone, *my* family, as we sing Manic the birthday song, and then they hack the cake up into pieces and pass them around.

It's lemon cake, and it's delicious.

The End

Thank you for reading the Lost in Austin series. If you're a fan of my writing, check out my firefighter series, for cat dad, single dad, and dog dads fun.

HEARTS *on fire*

CHAPTER 1 - CHLOE

"Hey, guy, what part of 'stop peeing on my porch' is unclear?"

The asshole blinks at me like he doesn't understand. Which, of course, he doesn't; he's a cat. I mean, he's a cute cat—a beautiful brown tabby with gorgeous green eyes, a missing leg, and a bobbed tail that wiggles adorably when he pisses on my porch. Nonetheless, he's pissing on my porch, which pisses me off.

"Are you marking your territory? Cuz, this is *my* territory now, buddy."

He—I don't know for certain he is a 'he,' but any animal that pees all over a stranger's porch must be male—cocks his head to the side, gives me a long-suffering stare, crosses to a different corner of the porch, and pees there too.

Dick.

Too tired to care, I roll my eyes at the pissy visitor and drop my ass with a harrumph to the top step of the porch stairs. Overheated, I fan my face while I guzzle a bottle of water.

The yard is a rocky landscape with feathery plumes of savannah grass, spiky rosettes of yucca, and long, lavender fingers of purple sage waving in the breeze, and I marvel yet again at how different this terrain is from the other side of Austin. My house on the east side of town has a lush green yard made of thick clay soil, covered with ivy, and shaded by towering pecan and sycamore trees. Here, only thirty miles west, the topsoil barely covers the limestone bedrock, and nothing but mesquite, persimmon, and scrubby clumps of live oak take root.

At least the heat here is drier. After a morning spent tearing down the rotted ceiling of my living room, I'm coated in a layer of sweat and century-old plaster dust, and I'm thankful for the shade and breeze the wraparound porch provides.

I hold the still-chilled bottle of water against my temple and finally start to feel refreshed but jump about a foot in the air with the tickle of whiskers against my arm. The cat jumps, too, his back arches, and his stumpy tail poofs out about three times its original size.

"Whoa there, buddy. Warn a girl before you rub up on her."

The cat blinks at me and deflates from his defensive stance, meowing like we're having a nice chat.

"We're friends now, are we? You're a fickle little pisser, aren't you?"

He meows again, and I hold out my hand for his inspection before I try to pet him. He gives my fingers a sniff and crinkles his nose at my stink.

"I know, right? Whose genius idea was it to renovate this house in August?" It's got to be one hundred and five degrees today, *in the shade*. And inside the house—even with all the windows open and a box fan spinning at top speed—the heat index is surely pushing triple-digit teens.

The porch pisser shares a bit of his cat wisdom with me and flops down onto the dusty old floorboards, glancing over his shoulder, expecting attention. I give it.

With a few pets, he transforms from standoffish to a lusty love monster. Like a demon possessed, he flops to-and-fro, scoots hither and thither, and meows madly, demanding affection.

"Wow, dude, you're kind of intense."

The cat gets back on his feet, his dark-striped coat now dusty and covered with bits of leaves and cobwebs. He meows loudly and head-butts my arm in response.

"What's your name?" He's not wearing a tag, but—despite his dirt bath—he looks clean, cared for, and well-fed. Plus, he's way too friendly to be a stray. Someone, somewhere loves this guy. "You lost?"

This close, I have a better view of his back end. With his stubby tail and missing left hind leg, it's clear he suffered a terrible injury, but he walks almost as well as a four-legged cat. "What happened, buddy? You get hurt?"

He meows, and I'm starting to like this guy. He is my type, after all: a beautiful, scarred boy who pisses all over everything.

"Well, it was nice meeting you, but I have to get back to work." I give the cat a couple more heavy pets as I rise to my feet, wipe the dust off my ass, and head toward the door.

The cat meows and tangles himself around my legs a few times. I take a last deep breath of the fresh air before putting my respirator and goggles back on. With a goodbye wave, I close the door in the cat's face and return my focus to the renovation project.

The Krause house is old, as in one-of-the-first-German-settlements-during-the-early-days-of-Texas-statehood old, and once upon a time it was the only house up on this dusty hill. But over the years, the land was subdivided and developed into a comfortable country neighborhood. Now, this old house is just one of a dozen acreages dotting Lazy River Road.

The neighborhood is a strange blend of suburban sprawl meets rural backwoods. Some properties are ringed by ranch-rail fences with electronic gates and concrete driveways that curve around scrawny oaks and manicured agave toward big brick McMansions. Less prosperous neighbors line their land with barbed wire, and gravel drives angle past evergreen thickets of Ashe juniper shrubs toward double-wides set on cinder block.

Rich or poor, though, none of the houses fit in here. The signs and symptoms of humanity look out of place in this rugged land.

Despite its age, the Krause house is no exception. The bright white Folk Victorian farmhouse hardly blends with its rocky surroundings. Inside, the misfit nature of the house continues. Turning my aspiring-architect eye to the details, I glance around the empty rooms of my family's legacy, always so fascinated by the blend of styles.

Over the years, each generation of Krause updated and expanded the house. Only the wide plank floors remain from the original dogtrot farmhouse. The breezeway was enclosed after the Civil War. Near the turn of the twentieth century, the porch was outfitted with all sorts of gingerbread detail. In the living room, the far wall was outfitted at some point with ornate Craftsman-style woodwork and built-in curios flanking the fireplace. There's crown molding around the ceilings, too, which were raised several feet when electricity was installed. The back of the house was extended when plumbing came in. And it was weather tightened when air-conditioning was added.

And it's that air conditioner that is the bane of my existence. While I would love to spend time imagining what architectural detail I'll add to the blend of family history, it seems my generation has been left to clean up the mess my family left behind. In this case, an antique air conditioner that flooded the living room ceiling.

Removing rotten drywall and ancient plaster off the ceiling of a twelve-foot-tall room when all you have is a pry bar and an eight-foot ladder is challenging. Within an hour, I'm coated with a second layer of dust, itching all over, and about to succumb to heat exhaustion.

Out on the porch for another water break, I find the cat still there. He meows loudly and weaves between my ankles until I give up trying to walk and plop down on the doormat. I tear the respirator and goggles off my face and take a deep breath of the fresh air. The cat climbs up my arm, pawing at me—not asking for attention but demanding it.

"Jeez, dude, chill." I take a deep drink of water before I start to pet the needy guy. If there was any doubt, it's clear the cat isn't a stray. He's spoiled rotten.

I glance up and down Lazy River Road, a narrow two-lane with more bends than its namesake, but everything is spread out, and the only place I can see from my porch is Inez's house next door.

Getting an idea, I chug the rest of my water then pull my phone out and snap a few photos of the cat sprawled like a Playgirl centerfold across my porch. I compose a quick message—"Who's cat is this?"— and attach a couple of the images, then text them to Inez.

Inez Rodriguez—devoted widow to Emmanuel, mother of three,

and grandmother of twelve—brought over with a tin of her homemade pecan pralines the first morning I moved in.

She'd managed to tell me her life story and the full history of her Tejano family back to the days before the Alamo, then programmed her number into my phone within the first fifteen minutes of knowing her. She's the best next-door neighbor I've ever had, and already, three days later, I've found my first occasion to reach out.

I startle when Inez says, "¡Hola! ¡Buenas tardes!"

The little woman steps through a gap between her climbing roses— our properties are among the few around here without fences—and waves. She's beautiful, with straight silvery hair cut in a bob at her chin, bright curious eyes, and deep laugh lines bracketing her smile, evidence of a life filled with happiness.

I push to stand, dusting off my hands and backside. Compared to her colorful, embroidered blouse and cornflower capri pants, I feel woefully underdressed and rather gross in my shorts and tank top, coated in sweat and dirt.

I respond, "¡Hola, Inez!" as she crosses the yard to meet me in the shade of the porch.

"I see you've met Bodhi," she says as the cat goes to her, and she gives him a scratch under the chin. She's a tiny woman and barely has to stoop to reach him.

A quick glance at the barren state of my porch reminds me of what a terrible hostess I am. Such a gorgeous wraparound, well adorned with whimsical, gingerbread trim, and not a chair in sight. I can't offer my neighbor a seat.

Inez doesn't seem to mind, contentedly crouched as she babies the cat. "He must have slipped his noose again."

"His noose?"

Inez grins at me. "His collars. He's always losing them."

"Is Bodhi your cat?"

"Oh no, he's Drew's baby."

"Who's Drew?"

"This little devil's daddy."

Daddy?

"He lives in Ricky's house." Inez points in the general direction of her own house.

I scan through my memory of that first data-dump conversation I had with Inez. Ricky is the youngest of her three sons. He lived in the house next door to Inez until a few years ago, when he moved to San Antonio.

Okay. I nod with more certainty now and deposit two new names into my memory bank—Bodhi the cat and his daddy, Drew.

"Nothing but trouble."

"Trouble?"

My mind flashes to all the crime documentaries I've seen about small-town Texas trouble—meth-lab chemists, racist Klansmen, weird family disputes that stretch as far back as Sam Houston's Lone Star Presidency—so I laugh when she shakes her head and her expression goes grave. "Too good-looking, just like this handsome man. He's irresistible, and he knows it. Nothing but trouble."

Her serious expression cracks wide with a smile, and she waggles her brows suggestively as she flicks the stump of Bodhi's missing tail. He purrs and meows for more, and my heart melts. Totally irresistible. Nothing but trouble, indeed.

"What happened to him?" I ask about Bodhi's missing leg and tail.

"Fire," Inez answers and shifts on her feet like she's uncomfortable. Is it the topic or lack of seating causing her discomfort? I change the subject from one to the other. "Inez, would you like to sit down? I can grab the stool from the kitchen and make us some tea."

"Oh no, *cariño*, don't trouble yourself. If I sit, I might not get up again. I was heading down to visit Al at the hardware co-op and saw your message. Thought I'd stop by for a quick visit. Thanks for keeping an eye on this boy while his daddy's away," she says as she turns and leaves, waving when she reaches the end of my drive.

"Okay, well, bye then," I say to myself and glance down at Bodhi. He's lying on his back, his three legs splayed, shameless and purring loudly. "Where's your daddy?"

Bodhi answers me, but I don't understand.

"You know, I don't remember volunteering for this cat-sitting job."

I frown at him. "You turn up and pee on my porch, and now I'm responsible for you? Not cool."

He ignores me, intensely focused on grooming his genitals. The layer of dust coating my skin itches. It's time for me to clean myself as well. I leave Bodhi to his bath and go inside for my own.

CHAPTER 2 - CHLOE

Pinned beneath the unbearable weight of the car, I can't move. The pain in my arm is excruciating. My nostrils fill with the acrid stench of smoke. Strobes of red and blue lights glitter in the broken glass. Dizziness and panic twist together in my belly, turning sour like sickness.

Except… *Wait.* This isn't real. It's the nightmare. My brain's playing her stupid games again. In the hazy place between wakefulness and sleep, I try to remember the coping exercises my therapist, Erica, taught me.

"Wiggle your toes and fingers," she says in my mind, her soothing voice centering me as I do what she instructs to push myself through the sleep paralysis. "Take a deep breath in and out."

But something's different this time. Something's…purring, and the weight bearing down on my chest moves; it steps on my left tit.

"Ouch!" I yelp and bolt upright. A cat tumbles onto the sheets beside me.

I roll off my mattress and almost kick over the lamp on the floor as I try to turn it on. When there's light, I find Bodhi in my bed.

"What in the hell? How did you get in here?"

Still groggy and confused, I rub my sore boob as I glance around the room, finally noticing the opening in my window. I'd stuffed a piece of rigid insulated foam into the gap beside my window-unit air conditioner a few days ago when I'd installed it. Now the foam is on the floor, leaving my bedroom open to the outside world.

"Wow, so you're a porch-pissing home invader! Inez is right— you're nothing but trouble."

Bodhi blinks at me. I glance out the opening in the window; it's at least a three-foot drop to the ground from the windowsill.

"Pretty spry for a tripod, I have to admit." I look back at the cat, who's settling comfortably in my sheets. "Oh no you don't. This isn't your house. You need to leave!"

He angles those beautiful green eyes at me as he snuggles deeper into my sheets, looking small and vulnerable in my bed. I glance again out the window at the dark night. What's out there roaming the Texas Hill Country at this hour? Coyotes? Mountain lions? I imagine all manner of monster poised outside my window, waiting to gobble up this poor, little three-legged tabby cat.

"Okay. Fine," I huff. "You can stay tonight. But that's it. You got me?"

I stuff the foam block back into the window beside the air conditioner and click off the light. Returning to bed, I nestle beneath the sheets while Bodhi curls into a ball beside me, purring loudly. The vibration relaxes me.

"I don't take kindly to men manipulating me to get into my bed," I tell him as I pet him.

He headbutts my chest softly, then tucks his head beneath my chin, and I'm putty in his paws.

It's too early. The orange light of the rising sun cuts through the darkness of my bedroom and serves as another reminder I need window coverings in here.

I stir slowly, feeling such peace this morning. It's the cat. Bodhi is curled up against me, so soft and sweet. He purrs in response and does a big stretch, then blinks his beautiful eyes open.

"Good morning, handsome. I'll bet your daddy misses you." Bodhi gives me one of those cute little chirpy meows and rolls over to go back to sleep. "Oh no you don't. Time for you to go home, buddy."

Bodhi is either too tired or enjoys the affection too much to protest as I pick him up and carry him out of my bedroom, up the long hallway, and out to the porch.

Setting him down by the steps, I hustle back into the house before he can dart past me and shut the door in his face. Bodhi stares up at me through the glass portion of the door, looking betrayed.

I explain through the glass, "You don't live here. Go away now, okay?"

The strangeness of this situation warrants an eye roll. "What the hell am I doing? I'm talking to a cat. And now I'm talking to myself about talking to a cat. I need coffee."

In the kitchen, I dig into a box of breakfast bars as I brew some coffee. When I'm fed and awake, I don my work clothes and protective gear, grab the pry bar, climb the ladder—which is still set beneath the massive mess of rotted wood and drywall drooping from the living room ceiling—and get back to demolition work.

A couple hours of toil later, I stand under the hole in the ceiling, wiping the sweat from my brow and trying to catch my breath through the respirator. My muscles are screaming from my work, yet I can barely see the progress I've made. I need a sledgehammer, bigger arms, and a crew of people to help.

Really, what I need is a break and a trip to the hardware co-op. Setting my goggles and respirator by the door, I consider a shower. I'm coated in sweat and drywall dust like I've been tarred and feathered, but I'm sure it's nothing Al at the hardware co-op hasn't seen before. I opt out of the shower and go to the bedroom for my purse.

"What the hell?" That's all I can articulate when I find Bodhi curled on my bed, the block of foam discarded on the floor again. I don't mind the cat so much, but every time he knocks that block of foam out of the window, he invites all sorts of country critters inside. There are scorpions and tarantulas in this part of Texas, and I do not appreciate having to worry about creepy-crawlies in my bed.

"Stop it. This is not okay."

Bodhi doesn't listen. He stretches across the rumpled sheets. I fit the foam back in place, grab the cat and my purse, and head out the front door.

Outside, I deposit Bodhi onto one of the big limestone boulders beside the driveway, then hop in my car and go. As I back out, the cat narrows his eyes at me, plotting. I narrow my eyes, too, plotting back.

At the hardware co-op, I sling an eight-pound sledgehammer over my shoulder and head to the home decor section for some bedroom curtains. In Lawn and Garden, I find a roll of chicken wire to use for keeping uninvited cats out of my bedroom. As I make my way to the register, I pass the pet aisle and stop. There at the end, shining beneath the overhead fluorescent lights, is an engraver machine and beside it a whole assortment of collars and tags.

I consider Bodhi, collarless and wandering the great outdoors. What if he tries to break into someone else's house, and they think he's a stray and take him to the pound? I'm pretty sure the animal shelter out here in the county is a kill shelter, unlike the no-kill Austin shelter. If Bodhi got busted and euthanized because I was too selfish to share my bed, the guilt would crush me.

Which is absurd; he's someone else's cat. I shouldn't be sharing my bed with other people's cats. At least if I get him a collar, no one will mistake him for a stray.

Browsing the collection of collars and tags, I find the perfect set. The collar is bright orange with a jingle bell, and the tag is a matching orange bow tie. It's dapper and daring, and the orange will complement his green eyes. Bodhi will be an icon of country cat fashion.

At home, I dump my new work tools on the living room floor then move to my bedroom where, sure enough, the cat is back.

"Hey, you little porch-pissing home invader, I got you a present."

Bodhi responds to the gentle tone of my voice, trotting to the corner of my bed to meow sweetly at me. I scratch his ears, giving him all my love right before I snap the collar around his neck.

To say he dislikes it is an understatement. The moment the collar closes, Bodhi freaks out. He hisses and claws at the thing. He tears circles across the hardwood floor, trying to outrun it. But where he goes, it goes, and the bell jingles delightfully along with him.

When he calms a bit, he stares daggers at me from the corner, his back arched and stubby tail puffed. He's telegraphing his emotions: We're not friends anymore. I've betrayed him.

But, hey, I didn't ask for him to pee on my porch. I didn't invite him to break into my bedroom repeatedly, letting all the cold air out of the only habitable room in the whole house.

I'm mad too, I remind myself, as I shove the foam back into the open window and nail the chicken wire to the sill so it can't be pushed aside again. When that's done, I open the bedroom door and Bodhi races out. He comes to a screeching halt at the front door, irritably waiting for me to let him outside.

When I do, he rockets across the porch in a few leaping bounds, moving impressively fast for a cat with a missing leg. He jumps to the ground, darting toward the road through the dry prairie grass, cactus, and cockleburs.

That's when I see the truck. It's a big, black pickup I've seen before, always driving too fast on Lazy River Road. I panic as Bodhi aims right for the tires. *Oh God, please don't let me kill that stupid cat over a collar!* But the truck passes without incident, and Bodhi runs after it like a dog chasing cars.

I close my eyes with relief, breathe easier, and shut the door. Excitement over, I don gloves, goggles, and respirator mask and get back to work. With my new sledgehammer, I perform a good under swing and bring it up to smash against the ceiling. Everything in the house rattles, big chunks of drywall crash to the floor, and dust rains supreme.

CHAPTER 3 - DREW

I pull into my drive, nursing fantasies of my bed and the hours of sleep I desperately need, when Bodhi jumps through the window of my truck and starts cussing up a storm. Little man is big mad about something, and he's making a dainty jingling sound as he paces across my lap and the seat beside me, telling me about his day. He stops his caterwauling long enough for me to get a good look at the orange collar around his neck.

The fuck is this shit? My cat's collar is not orange. It's never been orange, and it will never be orange. It's black, and it doesn't have a jingle bell on it or a cutesy little bow tie tag that sure as shit doesn't say "BS" on it.

"BS? Who the fuck tagged you BS?"

Bodhi bitches some more. I pick him up and carry him over to Inez's house. This seems like something she'd do. And if she didn't, she'll know who did.

Little man squirms in my arms, and that stupid bell tinkles, doing more to emasculate Bodhi than getting him neutered did. Inez looks like she's struggling to keep a straight face as I near her. I narrow my eyes at the little old granny, and she bursts into laughter.

"Bodhito, look how handsome you are in a bow tie."

"Did you do this?"

"Oh no." She laughs again. "Must have been Chloe. Bodhi's taken a shine to her."

"Chloe?" *Who the fuck is Chloe?*

At the sound of this Chloe person's name, Bodhi squirms again, jingling like a Christmas elf. I don't dare let him go, though, not with some crazy cat tagger lurking around.

"Chloe Krause, Hazel's granddaughter."

"Hazel had a granddaughter?"

"Yes. She's a sweet little thing. She's moved in to renovate the old house."

What the fuck? That was going to be my house. Hazel's son, Denny, all but promised to sell it to me when I'd found the guy packing up his mother's belongings shortly after her hospitalization last spring.

I try not to scowl at Inez, the unwitting bearer of this bad news. With a curt nod, I cross through her yard to the Krause property.

I liked Hazel Krause and her house on the hill. I'd help her sometimes when she needed a hand. She always feed me afterward, and we'd sit and watch the sun set over the Hill Country from her porch. Then Hazel got sick last year, and while she spent her last months in hospice, her house sat empty, falling into disrepair as it languished.

I had my sights set on fixing the old place up. It would've been hard work, but that was the appeal, a project. I'd imagined long days of labor followed by lazy evenings watching the sun set from a rocking chair. Disappointment tastes rotten on my tongue, and I try to swallow it away as I take the three creaky steps up onto the porch and aim for the front door.

I go to knock but freeze when I hear music playing inside. It's loud. It's good. It's Rage Against the Machine's "Sleep Now in the Fire," a personal favorite. I smile to myself, charmed by this Chloe woman's taste in music.

In sync with the powerful kick of the drums, a tremendous banging comes from inside the house. Each time this extra wallop hits, the whole building trembles like it's taking a beating with a wrecking ball.

What the fuck?

I frown at Bodhi, still clutched in my arm. He frowns back at me. Curious, I cup my eyes and peer through the window in the door. Off to the left, in the center of the living room, a woman balances on a ladder, swinging a sledgehammer at the ceiling. With each stroke, the house rains dust and bits of shattered ceiling all around her.

Is she trying to bring down the whole house with herself in the middle of it?

The instant the song quiets a bit, I pound on the door. My interruption startles her and throws off her rhythm. The sledgehammer swings wide, and the change in momentum nearly pulls her off the ladder.

Shit! I almost burst through the door like I plan to catch her if she falls. But she manages to steady herself and descend the ladder with the sledgehammer slung over her shoulder like a badass looking for trouble.

Hot.

She approaches, swings the door open, and… She's tiny. Barely above five feet tall, she stares up at me in a pair of too large safety goggles that give her a bug-eyed look. The P100 half-mask respirator is smart lung protection considering the dust she's stirring up, but it's adjusted so high on her nose her goggles fog up every time she exhales.

Cute.

Her protective gear ends with nothing more than a pair of leather gloves and bulky steel-toe boots. Her legs and arms are exposed in a tank top and tiny shorts, every inch of her coated with a dusty sheen of sweat.

Hot again.

With a harrumph, she sets the sledgehammer on the floor beside the door and pulls the respirator down below her chin. It leaves angry red marks and outlines where the grime on her cheeks meets the edges. She pushes the foggy goggles up onto her head, tangling them in her dark, dusty hair.

Her big brown eyes captivate my attention. I'm stunned stupid, standing there like an idiot staring at her. She furrows her brow. "Can I help you?"

Oh. Right. I look down at Bodhi in my arms, the orange bow-tie tag reminding me why I came here. I point at it. "What is this?"

"A cat," she answers, looking at me like I'm the asshole here.

"Very fucking funny. I know it's a cat. It's *my* cat, and he's wearing *your* tag. You put a tag on *my* fucking cat. Who do you think you are claiming things that aren't yours?"

"Claiming?"

"Yeah, claiming. That's what a tag is. Like you landed on the moon and stuck your fucking flag in the ground. You think you can just move in here and start staking your flag everywhere?"

"I'm not *claiming* your stupid cat. I collared him as a favor to you. He was wandering around without one, and I didn't want someone thinking he's a stray."

"Everyone out here knows Bodhi, so no one would mistake him for a stray except you. *And* you didn't just tag him, you fucking renamed him. BS? You renamed my cat BS?"

"I didn't—"

"Look, lady, this is my fucking cat, okay? Don't go collaring him. Don't go renaming him. Just leave him be."

There's a spark in her eyes, like I've poured gasoline on her, lit a match, and flicked it—ignition. She erupts.

"Leave him be? How about you and your porch-pissing home

invader leave *me* be? Take *your* fucking cat and your shitty attitude and get the fuck off *my* property."

"Gladly." I reach for the snap release on the collar, and it falls off Bodhi's neck, landing unceremoniously with a clatter and jingle. Marching down the steps of her porch and across the yard to the road, I hold my head high like I've won some great battle. But the sinking feeling in my gut tells me I'm the loser here.

Grab a copy of **Hearts on Fire** to keep reading
about Drew and Chloe and the cats.

The plan was to fix up the farmhouse, sell it, and leave. Then I met Drew...and his cat Bodhi.

I'm a stranger in this place. When a car accident nearly killed me, Mom took me away from my father and this small Texas town. Now, I'm back, and while everyone seems to remember the little girl I used to be, no one knows the woman I've become. That's okay. I'm not here to reconnect or fix what's broken between my father and me. I'm just here to fix the house I inherited, sell it, and go.

Then I meet Bodhi, the three-legged cat who keeps peeing on my porch. And along comes Bodhi's dad, Drew, the protective firefighter with rough hands, a smooth smile, and such a dirty mouth.

Drew has a reputation for rescuing strays. Is that what I am, another stray for him to rescue? Or this time, maybe I'll be the rescuer.

Hearts on Fire is a sexy, full-length, small town romance featuring a cat dad firefighter and a feisty heroine. It is Book One of the Hearts of Texas series.

THANK YOU

Thank you for reading *All the Rest*. If you enjoyed Sheryl's story, please spread the word!

xoxo,
Christina

And don't forget to subscribe to my newsletter
subscribepage.io/Td7TPB
or join my reader's group
facebook.com/groups/christinaswildberries
for the latest news and new releases.

ACKNOWLEDGMENTS

To my readers, thank you! You give me a reason to keep writing. In fact, you're the reason this book even exists. Sheryl was just a side character in the original three books, but you wanted her to get a happily-ever-after. I'm so glad I listened and wrote her and Manic's story. They were a fun pair to write. Hope I've done them justice.

Thank you to my incredibly supportive family. Errek, you are so great about sharing my time with all these fictional men. I love you. Mom, Dad, and Karen, you all inspire me so much. I count my lucky stars to be part of this amazing family.

Nikki and Heather, thanks for forming the "Shit or Get Off the Pot" club with me. I don't think I would be here, publishing my seventh book, had it not been for the kick in the pants from you two! xxx

Christina Consolino, thank you for always being there as a friend and an editor. I couldn't do this without you.

Kim Wilson, thank you for these gorgeous covers. I can't wait to meet you in Toronto!

Meghan Scott, I could not do any of this without your incredible medical input on every single book I've ever written.

To my beta and sensitivity readers, thank you for all your help in getting my facts and tone right. Lizzie Stanley, Kevin McKinney, and Chris Castleberry, your feedback for this book was invaluable.

And finally, I'd like to thank Austin, Texas, circa 2005. It's weird, I know, to thank a specific time and place, but this series is 100% inspired by that moment in our history.

Austin's not the same anymore. And that's okay. Change is okay. But this series is absolutely an homage to the way it used to be when the Frost tower was the tallest building in the skyline, the rebirth of roller derby was brand new, and Emo's was still at the corner of Sixth and Red River.

Austin, you're a hot mess sometimes, but I still love you. Thanks for the memories: past, present, and future.

ABOUT THE AUTHOR

Christina Berry is an award-winning author of sex-positive contemporary romance. Her debut novel, *Up for Air*, won "Sexiest Consent" in the 2021 Good Sex Awards, and her first two Lost in Austin series books won the Readers' Favorite Gold Medal in Romance - Sizzle in 2021 and 2022.

A citizen of the Cherokee Nation, Christina is originally from Oklahoma, and currently resides in Austin, Texas. When not writing, she's usually helping her husband with their never-ending home remodeling adventure or marathon watching true crime television.

www.christinaberry.com

facebook.com/christinaberryauthor
instagram.com/authorchristinaberry